A SURFEIT OF MIRACLES

AN ELA OF SALISBURY MEDIEVAL MYSTERY

J. G. LEWIS

*For my dear friend Margaret Lukoff, lover of history and art and—
as a trained physician—capable of healing with or without
miracles.*

ACKNOWLEDGMENTS

Many thanks, once again, to Rebecca Hazell, Betsy van der Hoek, and Judith Tilden for their close readings and helpful observations.

CHAPTER 1

Salisbury, January 1231

"How do you think they moved the stones here?" Ela Longespée, Countess of Salisbury, rode toward the great circle of standing stones that dominated a chalk plain a few miles north of her castle. Ela rode her gray horse, Freya, and enjoyed a steady canter over the fields toward the ancient monument. "They're not made of local stone."

"We know exactly how they got here," replied Sir William Talbot, her ally and confidant, his silver-streaked hair tossing in the wintry gusts that swept across the open country. They were out for a rare pleasure ride in the wake of the Epiphany festivities. "They were brought here from Ireland by Uther Pendragon, with the magical assistance of the wizard Merlin. Geoffrey of Monmouth wrote of it in some detail. I read his history aloud to your boys not a year ago, so it's fresh in my mind."

Ela laughed. "You don't really believe these great stones were moved by a wizard's magic, do you?"

"Why wouldn't I?" Bill looked perplexed. "It's recorded history, written by a respected historian."

"Geoffrey of Monmouth lived less than a hundred years ago. This circle is far more ancient than that. He's just repeating the stories that hover around these stones like a murder of crows." Crows did indeed hover nearby in the branches of a gnarled, ancient tree with a trunk the size of a castle turret.

"In that case, should I believe nothing else he mentions? He claims that the people of Rome once occupied this land. There's evidence: the remains of their straight roads cut across the countryside. In London, when someone digs a foundation for a new house, sometimes they come across an old floor of the Romans' multicolored mosaic tiles."

"I don't dispute all of the history written down by Geoffrey of Monmouth, but you must admit that much of it is too distant to be verifiable. Even if the men of England's past had all the means we have today—our great siege engines and mighty warships, for example—they would have struggled to move such great stones across the countryside."

"Monmouth reported that the stones were originally from Africa. He said that they were moved from there to Ireland, where they stood for many centuries before King Vortigern ordered them brought here so he could erect them as a memorial to his fallen warriors."

"I think it just as likely that they were brought here by a race of giants who carried them on their shoulders," said Ela with a sigh. "No one knows who raised them here, but I suspect they'll still be standing here long after we're all gone and forgotten."

"God forbid." Bill Talbot crossed himself.

Ela laughed. "You expect to live forever?"

"You will not be forgotten, my lady."

"Oh, yes I shall." She smiled indulgently at him. "And likely sooner than even I expect."

They rode up a short rise and across the ditch that led

into the circle. Ela liked to ride into the center of the stones and contemplate all the men and women who'd occupied this part of the world before her. The presence of such ancient history made her day-to-day worries seem small and ephemeral.

"What's that?" Bill Talbot pointed to the center of the circle. Ela couldn't see what he was talking about, her view being blocked by the giant stones. As they rode forward, Ela saw something on the ground—a heap of red and white rags.

"I think it's a man." Bill Talbot spurred his horse to a trot. "And there's no good reason for a man to be lying in the grass on an icy January morning."

Ela's heart quickened as they drew close. The man lay sprawled face down. He wore a tunic of wool, undyed except for the spreading red patch on his back.

They dismounted and tucked up their reins before approaching the body. Ela could see a knife sticking up from the center of the red stain on the man's back. She crossed herself. "He's been stabbed. Is he dead?"

Bill knelt next to the body and felt for signs of life. "There's no breath left in him. Shall I turn him over?"

"No," said Ela quickly. "We must call for the coroner. He hates when the body is moved. It hinders his examination." She glanced around the stone circle for any sign of the man's assailant. She saw no movement. The frost had melted away so the sheep-bitten grass bore no footprints. "Has rigor mortis set in yet?"

"He's cold but not stiff," said Bill. "But I'm not sure if that's because he's freshly dead or if rigor mortis has worn off. The wound is no longer pulsing with blood."

"I wish we'd brought more guards with us so they could ride for the coroner and jurors. Then we could stay here to search the scene," said Ela.

"He's not going anywhere."

"I suppose you're right." She glanced around the landscape looking for smoke from a nearby cottage or any other sign of close habitation. "It seems there's no one living close enough to either guard him or disturb him. We'll ride to the castle and back as fast as possible."

They mounted their horses and covered the countryside back to Salisbury castle at a brisk clip. Ela used to ride alone sometimes, back when her husband was alive. Now, as the widowed Countess of Salisbury and High Sheriff of Wiltshire, she was far too visible a target to risk venturing out without an armed escort. She usually took at least two guards with her, but Bill Talbot had proven his willingness and ability to defend her life, so she considered a quiet ride with him to be a reasonably safe adventure.

Ela told the guards at the gate to send out word to raise a jury at once. They then rode directly to the home of Giles Haughton, the coroner, who lived in a neat house within the castle's outer wall. Inside, Sir Giles was eating a meal of fresh bread and cheese and a cup of ale.

"A dead body inside the circle of stones?" He rose at once from the table, patting his mouth with a linen napkin. "Could it be a result of ritual sacrifice?"

Ela stared at him in disbelief. "You speak as if pagan druids still stalk the fields of Salisbury. Have you heard of such a thing?"

"Well…" Haughton donned his cloak and his wife helped him put on his gloves. "One does hear stories. But for all I know, they're just that."

"Stories of druids sacrificing humans in the stone circle?" Ela knew Giles Haughton was a sensible man and not given to flights of fancy.

"Well, no, but of those who gather there during the winter and summer solstice, when the light falls among the stones in a particular way."

"God forbid we should have pagans worshipping their heathen idols here in Salisbury," said Ela, as they hurried outside to their horses. "Why has no one told me of such a thing?"

"I suppose because no one has been found dead there until now."

∼

Ela and Haughton hastened back to the stones with guards in tow, hoping to get there before any of the jurors might arrive and disturb the site. The ride was long enough that it was mid-afternoon before they returned, and their shadows lengthened as they rode. When they approached the stones on horseback, Ela tried to spot the body where it lay among them. "It's right in the middle," she said, peering between the megaliths.

But as they grew closer and the gaps between the stones widened, she realized that the body had vanished.

"He was right here! He lay face down, with a dagger sticking out of his back and his tunic drenched with blood," she insisted. Bill Talbot had returned to the hall to see to her sons' education, but she wished he was here right now to back her up.

She jumped down from her horse, not wanting to trample the ground. Surely some evidence of a bleeding body still lay in the grass? She scanned the circle for any sign of where the body might have been dragged.

Giles Haughton, now dismounted, scanned the landscape in all directions. They could see jurors approaching behind them, some by horse and cart and some mounted, from the castle. Sheep grazed among the stones, but there was no sign of any other person nearby. "It's a shame there's no snow.

The ground is frozen too hard to show footprints," exclaimed Haughton.

At least he didn't accuse her of imagining the whole thing.

"He was dead as these stones," said Ela. "Bill listened for a pulse. Someone must have dragged the body away."

"These stones are a good distance from the castle. Almost eight miles. Several hours must have passed since you were last here."

"That's true, but surely we'd see some sign if a man had dragged a dead body across Salisbury Plain?"

They tried—in vain—to find any trace of blood or signs of disturbance of the grass. The sheep, who favored the shelter of the stones from the winter winds, had cropped the grass so close that their footsteps didn't bend or crush it. When the jurors arrived, Ela described what she'd seen. The looks of incredulity on their faces almost made her doubt her memory.

"He wore a tunic of plain white wool. Dark brown hose and plain leather shoes. The clothes of a working man, not a noble." She tried to conjure the image for them.

"What color was his hair?"

"Brown," said Ela.

"Light or dark?" asked Hal Pryce the young thatcher. "Long or short?"

"Somewhere between light and dark, I think." She hadn't paid close attention to his hair, though it was certainly brown. "And I didn't see his hair from the front but I'd say it fell to midway down his neck." She wished she'd paid closer attention to such details. She'd expected to examine the body at leisure, not find it gone on her return.

"Was he a heavyset man? Or a scrawny one?" asked Hugh Clifford, the wine seller, looking from Ela to the empty grass.

"A lighter build, I'd say. Not a fat man or one with a thick build. But not very thin and frail either." She realized again that her memory was vague. She could see the body in her mind's eye, but with the man's tunic spread about his torso and his hose bunched along his legs, she couldn't get a true sense of his physique.

"And you saw no one else about?" asked Clifford.

"Not a soul. Either as we rode toward the stones or once we were up here among them."

"Perhaps whoever stabbed him hid behind the stones, keeping themselves from view as they saw you approach."

"That's entirely possible. Sir William Talbot examined the body quickly and said it wasn't stiff with rigor mortis, so he may have just been killed. But the wound wasn't pumping fresh blood, either."

"So whoever killed him had time to return home for a cart to remove the body," said Hal Pryce.

"Despite the short grass, I think we'd see the marks of cartwheels," said Haughton. "The metal edges tend to dig into the ground even when it's frozen."

"So likely he just hauled the body away by hand."

"Or threw it over a horse or donkey," suggested Haughton. "We should search the area for hoofprints that weren't made by the Countess or Sir William. Let's each set out in different directions and search among the stones."

By this time, five jurors had arrived. They fanned out and walked among the inner and outer circles of stones. None found fresh hoofprints that couldn't be attributed to Ela and Bill's horses, or their own. And there was no sign of anyone hiding behind the stones. There was also no trace of the body or the weapon or even a drop of blood.

"You must speak to Sir William," said Ela to Haughton, eager to convince him that the body wasn't a figment of her imagination. "He may remember some salient detail that I've failed to mention. In the meantime, I suppose we must wait to see if someone is reported missing. Until that happens I struggle to imagine how we can identify the victim."

"He may not even be local," said Haughton. "If he was on his way from Southampton to Bristol, and was waylaid here, we may never know who has missed him."

"He wore no cloak," said Ela. "And had no bags and baggage with him. Not that we saw, anyway. He was dressed more like a local shepherd than a traveler on a journey. The killer can't have gone far. If he took the body to hide evidence of his crime, he must have hidden it somewhere, or may have buried it in haste."

"A body is heavy and hard to maneuver," said Haughton. "Being long and limp and uncooperative. So it's likely close by. Let's fan out and search the area around the stones. Take special note of disturbed ground or areas under trees and hedges where the grass is thin or non-existent."

∽

THE JURORS and other assorted villagers and guards hunted high and low for the body. They scoured ditches and wells and the ridged furrows of fallow fields. They searched abandoned sheds and ruined cottages and the barns and hay sheds of nearby farmers.

Ela's sons, Richard and Stephen, joined in the search with vigor and returned frustrated and empty-handed for the midday meal.

"How can a dead man just disappear?" asked fifteen-year-old Stephen.

"He can't," replied Richard, his seventeen-year-old brother, reaching for a bread roll. "He's out there somewhere. We'll find him."

"Perhaps he had help?" suggested Stephen. "Maybe there's more than one killer?"

"You mean like a gang of thieves?" asked Richard. "They'd have an easier time carrying the body, but surely someone would have noticed a group of strangers in the area. Unless there's a criminal gang living among us in plain sight."

"God forbid," said Ela. "As sheriff, I'm sure I'd know if such a band of miscreants existed."

A commotion at the door made them lift their gaze to it. Old Albert the porter hurried toward them in his shuffling gait. "My lady, the dead man has been found!"

"Thank Heaven. I was beginning to think he'd been spirited away," said Ela. "Where was the body discovered?"

Albert blinked and looked back to the men who stood in the doorway. Then he turned to Ela again with disbelief in his eyes. "He walked through the west gate and into Salisbury. He's standing in the castle courtyard right now."

CHAPTER 2

Ela sprang to her feet. "Call for the jurors at once and bring him here." Her appetite vanished as her eyes searched the knot of men in the doorway. Richard and Stephen stared. Bill Talbot also rose to his feet and Ela saw his hand go instinctively to where the hilt of his sword would be—if he was wearing it, which he wasn't.

"How can this be?" asked Bill. "He was as dead as I'm alive. I listened for his breath and felt for his pulse and he had neither."

Ela held her breath as the group of men at the door parted. Two guards ushered in a man of medium height, dressed in a plain wool tunic. His brown hair was disordered and his face pale as he approached.

"This can't be him," said Ela, surveying the man as he walked, unaided, toward her. He was about thirty, with an unshaven chin. His nose and ears were red from the cold. "The man we saw had been stabbed and had a knife sticking out of his back."

The guards gestured for this man to turn his back to face

her. He hesitated for a moment, then turned very slowly, as if reluctant to turn his back on his countess.

Ela heard herself gasp as she saw the spreading bloodstain—now dried and darkened—that covered the back of his tunic.

"Call Giles Haughton at once," she barked, rather more brusquely than she'd intended. The sight of this man—now alive and walking—shocked her deeply. How was this possible?

"He's risen from the dead," said her son Stephen, his voice hoarse. "Like Our Lord."

"Not like Our Lord," corrected Ela swiftly. "This is very much a mortal man and I wish to see him examined closely by the coroner. When Bill and I saw him he had the hilt of a dagger sticking out of his back with every appearance that the entire blade was plunged into his torso. I fail to see how he could survive such a wound and live to walk into my hall."

"I'm still bleeding, my lady," said the man quietly. "The pain is something awful."

Ela's gut flared with warning. She knew she should feel compassion for this badly wounded stranger. Instead, she felt…uneasy in his presence. She half wanted to stick her fingers into the jagged tear in the back of his tunic and feel for the bleeding wound to see if it was still there. Her instincts warned her that some trickery was afoot and she wanted Giles Haughton's expertise with wounds to help her uncover it.

"What's your name?" she asked the man, surprised it had taken her this long to pose the question.

"John Bird, my lady." He attempted a tiny half-bow, then winced as if the agony of the gesture overwhelmed him.

"How did you come to be at the gate of my castle?"

He blinked at her for a moment. "I don't remember all the details of what happened to me, my lady. I woke up inside the circle of stones with my whole body throbbing and a screaming pain in my back."

"Was there a dagger inside you?" Ela glanced at Bill.

"I think it fell out of me as I climbed to my feet."

"Where is it?"

"I don't know, my lady. Still there, I suppose."

"It wasn't there when the coroner and the jurors searched the site this afternoon. Where were you while that happened?"

"I don't know, my lady. All I remember is seeing this great castle hovering over the surrounding countryside and my feet bringing me slowly toward it, one painful step after another. I knew that help and succor would be found here."

He swayed and Bill Talbot reached out to steady him. Alarm stung Ela's fingers.

I don't trust him.

"Shall I fetch him a chair, Mama?" asked Stephen.

"Uh, yes, I suppose so." Everything about this man and this situation set off warning bells deep inside her. How could he have a knife sticking out of his back and no signs of life, then walk all the way to the castle—a distance of several miles? And how did he manage the journey without anyone seeing him?

Stephen put a chair behind John Bird and helped him lower himself into it, which he did with some groaning and moaning.

"We should tend his wound, Mama," said Richard.

"Indeed we must, but first it must be examined by the coroner."

"But what if he should bleed to death right here in the hall while the coroner is still on his way?" asked Stephen.

"He does look pale," agreed Richard.

Despite her misgivings about the strangeness of the situation, Ela had to assume he was the victim of a crime. As such,

A SURFEIT OF MIRACLES

he deserved help and medical treatment. "Send for the doctor," she said to Elsie, who hovered nearby. "He shall attend him...in the mortuary."

"The mortuary?" said John Bird, alarmed.

"There's a long table where it will be easy for the doctor to examine you," explained Ela. The armory, even closer, had a similar table—used for cleaning and polishing the swords and lances and halberds stored on its walls—but she felt wary enough not to want this strange man inside a room where freshly sharpened weapons glittered on every surface.

~

JOHN BIRD WAS BROUGHT to the mortuary and laid out on the long table. Giles Haughton arrived before the doctor and had the man remove his clothing above the waist so he could examine the wound on his back.

Face-down on the table, the man twitched and writhed. "I'm in pain! The table's so hard and cold."

The unheated mortuary was indeed frigid, a blessing when storing a corpse awaiting burial. It was not a space intended for the living.

"Hold still," commanded Sir Giles. "So I can examine your wound."

"Are you the doctor?" asked Bird.

"I'm the coroner."

"I'm not dead!"

"I can see that. If you were dead, you wouldn't be squawking so." Ela could see that Haughton found the man irritating. "The wound on your back is quite superficial. Barely more than a scratch. It's not even bleeding, so your protests of pain seem excessive."

"It's healing then, thanks be to God!" exclaimed the man.

"I swear on God's Holy Word that I saw a knife sticking

right up out of his back as if it lay plunged into his flesh right up to the hilt," said Ela. "And Sir William Talbot saw it, too."

"Perhaps the blade got caught up in his clothes," said Haughton. "Because nothing's been plunged in here more than the depth of a fingernail."

"The wound has certainly bled copiously," said Ela, looking at the man's blood-soaked tunic. "This stain suggests a wound fairly gushing with blood."

"Sometimes wounds bleed more than expected," said Haughton.

"Does the wound require stitches?" Ela had seen the doctor stitch up deep or long cuts using sinew and a sharp bone needle.

"I'll defer to the doctor because my expertise does not extend to the living, but I'd say not."

Doctor Goodwin arrived. A tall man with white hair and a long, serious face, he examined the wound and agreed with Haughton that it was superficial. He also seemed surprised by the quantity of blood that had leaked out of it onto the man's clothing.

"Do you have wounds or injuries elsewhere on your person?" asked the doctor.

"I don't think so," said the man, whose thrashing and wriggling had subsided. "Can I get up now?"

"I shall apply some ointment to help the wound heal without festering, so hold still."

The man braced himself and whimpered a bit during the application of the cold ointment, which the doctor brought in a small earthen jar.

"Since he's not near death and doesn't require treatment," said Ela. "We shall bring him back into the hall for further questioning with the jurors."

The man reached for his bloody tunic.

"I'm sure we can find a clean tunic for you," said Ela.

"This one will suffice," said the man quickly. He pulled it over his head before anyone could snatch it away. "Can I go now?"

"Not yet," said Ela. "We must investigate the crime that left you for dead in the middle of the stone circle."

"But since I'm neither dead nor dying, surely the crime is but a small matter."

John Bird looked around the dimly lit mortuary like a canary in a cage, looking for an exit.

"Hardly," said Ela. "And I find it surprising that you are so unconcerned about finding and prosecuting the one who did this to you. Why did you come to the castle if not to seek justice for how you were cruelly set upon?"

～

After the doctor took his leave, Haughton and Ela headed back to the hall. The guards brought John Bird along with them.

"I'm sure I'll be just fine," he protested. "There's no need to make a fuss." A twitchy and chattery sort of man, he seemed increasingly restless as he was brought into the hall where several jurors had gathered—for the second time that day—to hear his story.

"Nonsense," said Ela, taking a seat at the head of three tables assembled into a U-shape. "You've suffered injury and we must uncover the circumstances."

The jurors, who'd ridden out to the stone circle expecting a body and found it empty, now walked around John Bird exclaiming over the blood that soaked his tunic.

"What happened to the knife?" asked Stephen Hale, the cordwainer, once they were all settled in their seats, with John bird on a chair in the middle.

"I don't know, master. All I know is that I came to, in

terrible pain. I spotted the castle in the distance and decided to head for it."

"While we were all making our way from it," said Paul Dunstan, the miller. "Did you not see us coming from the castle or heading back to it?"

Bird fidgeted. "I did indeed. But not knowing who'd set upon me and for what reason, I hid in a hedgerow until you'd passed by."

That was at least a reasonable explanation for why they hadn't discovered him.

"Where do you live?" asked Ela. She didn't recognize the man, which didn't mean much as there were many villages in the surrounding area, and she typically only met the villagers in need of either alms or judicial punishment.

"I'm only passing through the area, on my way to visit my dear old mother in Paignton."

"Where's Paignton?"

"In Devon, my lady. By the sea."

"Is that where you live?" asked Ela.

"No, my lady. I live in Norfolk. A small village called Beeston."

Ela frowned. "Norfolk to Devon is a very long journey. Almost right across England. Where are your bundles or bags?"

"I suppose that's why he set upon me, my lady. To steal them." He had an annoying habit of rocking back and forth in his chair. He paused to feel around at his waist. "And my coin purse is gone, as well as my cloak to keep out the cold. However shall I manage now?"

"And did you see your assailant?"

"No, my lady. I don't know what happened at all. I had stopped to sleep in the shelter of the stones. When I woke up, all my goods and chattels were gone and I'd been stabbed in the back."

"Surely sleeping outside in January is ill-advised."

"If it weren't for my dear old mother being ill-to-death, I'd have waited for the warmer months, but word arrived that her condition was grave, so I had no choice but to set out at once."

"Why didn't you stay in an inn?"

He looked at her like she was touched in the head. "I'm sure I would have if I had coin to weigh down my purse. Alas, I'm not so blessed."

Ela didn't know what to make of this man and his bizarre penniless, cross-England journey in the dead of winter. It only added weight to her suspicions that he wasn't who he claimed to be.

"What do you do when you're at home in Beeston?"

"I make my living as a shepherd, my lady, guarding the flocks for a local yeoman farmer on the fens."

"And what was stolen from you that we might identify your attacker when such goods appear among us?"

"Well, my brown cloak, a handkerchief with a crust of bread and a piece of cheese, and my battered leather purse with a few pennies in it."

"I doubt those will surface, my lady," said juror Paul Dunstan. "If only the attacker had left some trace."

"He did leave the knife sticking up out of his victim's body," Ela reminded him. "Though it seems to have vanished into thin air in the meantime." She turned back to John Bird. "Did it not occur to you to bring the knife with you as evidence of the crime against you?"

He shook his head. "I suppose I was confused and in pain and didn't think of anything but finding help before I bled to death."

"Except that you were apparently in no danger of bleeding to death. It does seem odd that your attacker would abandon his knife inside you, both because it might serve to point the finger at him, and also because a good knife is often among a man's most prized possessions."

"Perhaps he came back for it?" suggested John Bird, fixing his beady gaze on Ela.

"I dare say he did," said Paul Dunstan, the miller. "And he must have been careful to stay hidden since all of us jurors were coming toward the hill looking for it. He must have concealed himself nearby, just as you did."

"I'm just glad to be alive," said Bird, still rocking in his chair. "And if you don't mind, I'd like to be going on my way."

Despite her reservations about his outlandish story, Ela couldn't think of any good pretext to keep him in custody. Since the jurors had no further questions John Bird was released.

Ela expected him to ask for alms or at least a cloak, but he didn't. She could have offered them from the castle stores, but since she still didn't entirely trust the man and his story, she held back. Mostly she was relieved to see the back of him, bloodied though it was.

Until it became clear that he and his back had no intention of leaving Salisbury.

CHAPTER 3

*E*la next heard news of John Bird from the lips of her priest, Father Thomas Dickinson, who conducted the Hours and Masses inside the castle keep. "He was raised from the dead, my lady! Have you ever heard of such a thing outside the pages of the Holy Bible?"

Father Thomas was a man of simple faith and quiet habits. Only a few years older than Ela, he'd conducted services at the castle for nearly ten years. She made her confessions to him and trusted him to keep her fears, doubts and personal indiscretions to himself—which was no small matter. She dutifully followed any penance he set, and generally respected him as one of God's holy representatives on earth.

But these words gave her pause.

"I don't believe he was ever anywhere near death, Father Thomas. Giles Haughton and Doctor Goodwin examined his wound and found it superficial. His life was not in danger at any time."

"I examined it myself and it's almost entirely disappeared,

my lady!" His eyes shone. "The deep stab wound is vanishing, healed by the miraculous touch of Our Lord."

"I suspect it's just healing naturally since he's a reasonably young and healthy man."

"But did you see his tunic? The amount of blood he shed suggests a deep and painful wound. For such a wound to heal so fast and completely—it must be one of God's holy miracles."

Ela felt her stomach twist slightly at Father Thomas's words. "Is this what people are saying in the village?"

"Yes, my lady! They're all as excited as I am to be in the presence of such a holy mystery." The priest's eyes shone. "I sent word to the Bishop as I suspect he may want to contact the pope. Imagine, a sacred miracle right here in Salisbury!"

Ela had a sinking feeling in the pit of her stomach. "I hardly think the pope will get involved, Father. I admit I'm not sure how that much blood soaked the back of his shirt when the wound was so slight. That itself is something of a mystery, I suppose."

"By the grace of God, he's been made whole again."

His earnest joy at this seemingly miraculous event would have touched her if she wasn't so sure they were not in the presence of God's work. "Why is he still in the town?" she asked. "He told me he was on an urgent journey to Devon."

"He paused to take sustenance, my lady. He's exhausted and recovering from his wound. The landlord has given him free accommodation at the Bull and Bear. Now that word has spread, half the town has gone there to visit him. I'd never even set foot in the place myself until today. I rushed there at once when I received word that a man had risen from the dead and now walks among us in Salisbury."

"He must be some kind of trickster," said Ela to Bill Talbot as they walked out through the castle gate and into the village inside the castle walls. "Perhaps he came here to prey on the people of Salisbury? Already he's gained free accommodation and food. It won't surprise me at all if he starts offering blessings in exchange for coin."

"But the man I saw—that we saw—was dead! I'd swear it on the Holy Bible. His flesh was cold as a stone. I listened for his breath and his pulse and there were none."

"Do you truly think that a man with a knife stuck in him up to the hilt and dead as the standing stones, has risen and is now supping ale in the Bull and Bear?"

"I don't know of any other explanation," said Bill rather apologetically.

Ela glanced around to see if anyone else was in earshot. "What if it's not the same man?"

"What do you mean?"

"What if our miracle man killed a man and left him—dead —in the standing stones? Then, after we came along, he managed to hide the body and—to avoid being arrested as a murderer—took on the identity of the man he'd just killed and came right to the castle to establish himself as the victim."

"Too risky! If he'd killed a man he'd likely have just slipped away out of the district, leaving us none the wiser."

"Unless he felt there was a way to turn events to his advantage."

They turned onto the street that held the Bull and Bear and saw a crowd gathered outside.

"Goodness," said Ela. "I doubt the Bull and Bear has seen custom like this in years." Since the new cathedral had been built down the road from the castle, many people had moved to the village springing up around it. The remaining businesses had suffered and often decamped to the new town as well.

"I suppose John Fitch has good reason to offer free room and board to a man who draws all of Salisbury to his door," said Bill.

Fitch, who ran the Bull and Bear along with his wife Martha, was only letting up to forty persons inside the premises at once, where the newly named miracle man sat by the fire. The ones outside waited impatiently, their eagerness quenched only by cups of ale that Fitch sold them at a penny apiece.

Ela approached the door, confident that Fitch would make room for his Countess. And indeed he did.

"Come this way, my lady! May I offer you a cup of our finest ale or perhaps a plate of my wife's homemade sausage or some roasted duck?"

She politely declined his hospitality and Bill Talbot led the way—with some difficulty due to the crush of patrons—toward the great fireplace inside the inn. John Bird sat in a high chair only an arm's reach from two trussed birds roasting on the spit. As she approached, Ela saw that a wooden bowl—the kind that might hold soup or porridge—lay at Bird's feet, its base covered with coins.

"My lady." John Bird looked up at Ela with some surprise. "Forgive me for not rising but I'm still recovering from my wound."

"I hear your recovery is nothing short of miraculous," said Ela drily. "And that God himself has had a hand in it."

"Does not God govern all things here on earth and in the Heavens above?" asked Bird, warming to the topic. "For sure he has brought me back from the dead and raised me to walk among men." A smile spread across his face, and she saw his eyes glance toward the bowl of coins on the stones of the hearth. "I can hardly argue that a miracle has been wrought in my own life."

"Have the people been giving you these coins?"

"Yes," he said, apparently unembarrassed. "They take pity on my plight in being left penniless and for dead. I suspect some of them also hope to buy God's grace by giving alms to one in such desperate need."

"Their generosity is to be commended," said Ela, her voice flat. If this man was some kind of swindler, his ruse was working to perfection. "Will you be leaving Salisbury today?"

"The dear proprietor has offered to lend me a bed for another night, my lady. Being still weak from my injury and the shock of this disorienting situation, I'd be a fool not to take him up on his kind offer of hospitality."

"Indeed. Well, I intend to deepen my investigation into the horrible crime committed against you, so please attend me at the castle first thing tomorrow morning."

Bird's face fell. "I'm sure I've already forgiven the miscreant that left me for dead."

"Well, I'm the sheriff and I haven't. I intend to see him punished for his crimes." Ela still had no idea what had happened, but she was growing keen to find out. "Tomorrow, you shall accompany the coroner and me as we revisit the scene of the crime and try to discover exactly what happened. Perhaps your memory of the shocking events will return?"

Or you'll get your story mixed up and reveal yourself to be a liar.

She wasn't entirely sure what she hoped for, but she didn't intend to let John Bird sit quietly in the Bull and Bear, tricking the people of Salisbury out of their hard-earned money.

"But coming to the castle in the morning will prevent me from starting bright and early on my journey to Devon. I believe I mentioned that my elderly mother is ailing and may have but days left to live."

Ela grew increasingly sure that his mother was neither ailing nor in Devon. "In that case, the sooner we can discover what misdeeds befell you, the sooner you can be on your way. You can hardly expect me to allow a murderer to roam unchecked around Salisbury."

His mouth twitched. "I suppose not, my lady."

"I shall expect you after the bells for Tierce."

～

THE NEXT MORNING, Giles Haughton arrived at the castle before Bird. "I'm afraid John Bird is delayed. I passed him as I walked through the village. He's surrounded by a throng of people exclaiming over him as one of God's miraculous works."

"I half hoped he'd sneak away before dawn and that we'd seen the last of him. Even if that would have cheated me of the satisfaction of getting to the bottom of this story, it would have spared the people of Salisbury from his mischief."

"What if he is indeed resurrected from the dead, my lady?" asked Haughton. Ela looked into his face and was relieved to see a familiar twinkle of mischief in his eye.

"Far be it from me to say that God cannot work his holy miracles on earth when he sees fit, but I'm quite sure that John Bird's continued health isn't one of them."

"But how did he manage to stab himself in the back, my lady? I admit that I am deeply perplexed by the situation."

"I don't think he was stabbed in the back. I do think he somehow contrived to give himself a flesh wound near his spine, enough to confound our investigation, but I don't believe for one instant that he ever had a knife protruding from that wound. I feel sure that the dead man Bill and I saw was an entirely different person."

"Then where is that body now?"

"I wish I knew. I hope this morning's expedition can lead us somewhat closer to it." Ela asked Elsie to bring her cloak and gloves. "Let's retrieve John Bird from his crowd of admirers and take him back to the circle of stones."

∼

A crowd of people spilled out of the market square and halfway down the next street, and Ela's guards had to clear the way for her to pass through the throng. She spied John Bird standing, dressed in a fine gray cloak and a new black hat, in their midst.

"Master Bird," said Ela, as her guards cleared a path to him. "Perhaps you forgot that I called you to my hall this morning."

"I am on my way to your hall right now, my lady," said Bird apologetically enough. "I'm afraid I've been waylaid by those curious about the miracles God has wrought in my life."

Ela looked around at the faces in the crowd. She recognized some of the people, but others were unfamiliar.

"People have been traveling to Salisbury from the surrounding towns," said Haughton. "Word has got out that a miracle has happened in our midst, and they want to lay eyes on the man who is raised from the dead."

"And I can hardly deny them, can I, my lady?" said Bird, clearly glad that Haughton seemed to have taken his side.

Ela wanted to point out that disobeying his countess could get him locked up in the dungeon, but given the enthusiastic crowd of admirers gazing at him, she thought this more likely to reflect poorly on her than on him.

Ela addressed the crowd. "The coroner and I intend to solve the mystery of who attacked this man. You are preventing us from doing our duty. Please disperse at once and go to your homes so that the streets of Salisbury are not clogged."

Hardly anyone even stirred.

"It's not every day that you see a miracle from God," murmured someone behind Ela. She spun around, but couldn't decide which of the middle-aged women behind her might have muttered the words.

"I can return to the marketplace later today," announced John Bird. "But I must attend to the countess at once."

Ela wasn't sure whether to be annoyed or gratified by his comment. A murmur rose from the crowd, and they parted—with some reluctance—to let Ela and Giles Haughton gather up John Bird and walk on with him toward the west gate, where their horses waited. The distance was too great to walk. Ela and Haughton rode, and Bird traveled in a horse-drawn cart flanked by guards.

"What's that jingling sound?" asked Ela of Bird, as he climbed up into the cart.

"I don't know what you mean, my lady." Bird gathered his cloak about himself as a gust of winter wind assailed them.

"It sounds like a purse of coins," said Haughton.

"Ah. 'Tis possible that it's my purse, then," said Bird, without looking at either of them.

"May I see your purse?" said Ela.

"Whatever for?" asked Bird, looking shocked.

"I'm curious about how much money you've managed to collect since being found robbed and indigent only two days ago."

"I'm grateful for the alms I've received," said Bird quietly, forging on.

Ela stopped. "Please show me your purse at once."

One of the guards grabbed Bird's arm. Reluctantly he parted his cloak and revealed a leather pouch on the belt at his waist.

"Hand it to me," said Ela. She rode up close to the cart.

He looked at her for a moment, possibly wondering if he could say no.

"Do you expect me to rob you?" she asked. Quite possibly he did. Some sheriffs didn't shrink from enriching themselves at the expense of their local citizenry.

"Of course not, my lady." He realized that insulting a countess wasn't going to ameliorate his situation. He untied the strings that held the purse to his belt and handed it to her.

Ela dropped the reins on her horse's neck, took the heavy purse in her hand and opened the strings. The bag bulged with silver pennies. "Most men won't see this much money in a year of hard labor," she commented. "And you've gathered it to your bosom in barely more than a day?"

"All the blessings bestowed upon me come from God, my lady."

"Indeed. Perhaps you'd like to make a gift toward the construction of our new cathedral here in Salisbury. I'm sure you saw the tower as you walked across the countryside." She turned to where the tower rose above the trees and indicated it with her hand.

"I like to think that the Lord, having raised me from the dead, has provided me with money to provide succor and comfort for my elderly mother."

Ela hadn't expected him to happily part with his newfound riches, and—unfortunately—she was hard pressed to find fault with his purported plan, even though she doubted his mother's very existence.

"Perhaps you should take control of his purse for safekeeping," suggested Haughton helpfully. "All manner of mischief may befall a man when he has a collection of coins loud enough to make a noise at his belt."

Bird protested that he was sure the Lord would protect him and even made to swipe at the bag of coins.

"You're so right, Sir Giles," said Ela, pulling it back out of Bird's reach. "As King's Coroner, I shall charge you with the protection of this bounty." She handed him the purse of coins. This was an ideal situation because if they discovered that John Bird was the perpetrator of a crime, rather than its victim, the money would be due to the crown as deodand. "I'm grateful for your suggestion."

John Bird sputtered ineffectually, then watched helplessly as Giles Haughton tucked the coins deep inside the folds of his cloak. "When will I get it back?"

"When you leave Salisbury," said Ela brightly.

"I'd like to leave at once!" he said suddenly, looking west as if he might climb down from the cart and immediately start striding for Devon.

"I'm afraid that won't be possible," said Ela. "We must find out who committed such a cruel and unprovoked attack on you. Now, if you will please concentrate hard on the events of that fateful day, perhaps we can get to the bottom of the matter this morning, and you can be on your way this afternoon."

They traveled across the landscape on narrow country lanes, and the jingling of coins now came from the purse slapping against Giles Haughton's thigh as he rode. Ela took some amusement in John Bird's obvious consternation at being parted with his bounty.

While much of the landscape was open grazing, sprinkled with sheep, there were thickets and copses that made it easy enough for a man to hide along the way. Bird pointed to a great hollow oak where he said that he tucked himself during the height of the search. They dismounted to examine the tree and found that the cavity inside it, littered with spent acorns and crushed leaf litter, was a convincing hiding place and Ela had no reason to disbelieve this part of his story.

Once they reached the stone circle and dismounted, Bird grew agitated. "Oh, I can hardly breathe!" he muttered, glancing around anxiously.

"This is where we found you, prostrate and lifeless to all appearances," said Ela, pointing to the spot near the middle of the circle where the body had lain, with the knife sticking out of its back.

"God be praised for raising me back to life to do his works on earth!" he called, as if a receptive audience might mutter an affirmative response. Ela, Haughton and the guards remained silent.

"I think you should lie there again, face down, and try to remember what happened to put you in that position."

Bird frowned and looked like he wanted to protest. He thought better of it, because he got down onto his knees, crossed himself, and spread himself out on the sheep-cropped grass in the prone position.

Interestingly, Bird lay down with his head and feet oriented in the right direction. Ela could still see the dead body clearly in her mind's eye, and he now matched it almost perfectly. A disoriented man, waking with a total loss of memory, might not know exactly which way his head was pointing when he returned to the area two days later. He hadn't seen himself lying down—or had he?

CHAPTER 4

Ela stared at the man lying on the ground, trying to decide what was different about how he looked right now, and how the body had appeared when she and Bill first saw it. "Is this the position you awoke and found yourself in?"

"I'm sure I don't remember too well, my lady," he mumbled, turning his head toward them. "My mind is all a-jumble when it comes to the events of that day."

"Since I saw the body myself, I can observe that you have exactly captured the pose that the dead body lay in. Indeed, I'm surprised at the accuracy of your memory, given the disorienting circumstances of your awakening."

Ela turned to Haughton. "Bill and I approached the stone circle from the south, and we spotted him lying here and rode up. He made not the slightest movement the entire time. We both dismounted and approached. Bill checked for breath and heartbeat and found neither. The knife appeared to be plunged to the hilt in his back, and his shirt was thoroughly blood-soaked as you've seen it already."

"This ground is so cold!" Bird turned his head in protest.

"And it's terrible to think of the blood pouring from my body. My very life soaking into the ground. Gives me the shivers."

"You can get up now," said Ela. "You said that you came into the stone circle to take shelter from the elements and rest?"

"Yes, my lady."

"I wonder why you would pick such an exposed and windy spot as this ancient circle of stones when, as we've already observed, the woods provide better cover and protection?"

"Well, I didn't come to lie out here in the middle. I hunkered up against one of the big stones of the inner circle. I thought I'd have more protection from wild animals up here, not to mention that if some villain wanted to set upon me I'd have a chance to see them coming."

"Apparently you were wrong about the villain," observed Ela. "You might have had better luck hearing someone coming in the woods where their footfalls would break twigs or crush leaves. Out here on the short grass, a man can move around as silent as a ghost. It's almost an ideal location for a footpad to lurk in search of prey."

He blinked rapidly. "I never thought of that."

"Which stone were you sitting under?"

"I don't entirely remember. It was almost dark when I arrived."

"If the sun was setting, then surely you remember which direction it set in?"

"That way." He jutted his thumb accurately toward the west.

"Then where were you in relation to the setting sun?"

He huffed a bit, then stomped over toward one of the stones. "It might have been this one."

"Show us how you sat and how you arranged your belongings. And what exactly did you have with you?"

Again, he grew flustered and started waving his arms in a gesture of helplessness. "Do I have to sit down on the cold ground?"

"Yes. We are trying to answer the question of how you came to be left for dead. Surely you want the answer as much as we do?"

For an instant, he looked at Ela as if he'd prefer to choke the life from her, but then he lowered himself down into a sitting position at the base of the stone. "I didn't have much with me. My purse with a few coins and a bundle with my spare tunic and leggings and a woven blanket I was bringing to comfort my poor ailing mother." He gestured up at the sky. "Would that they had left me the blanket to soothe her aches and pains from the cold."

"Did you wrap yourself in the blanket?"

He blinked, as if wondering whether this would make him look better or worse if he did. "Indeed I did, my lady. It's January and I needed protection from the cold."

"I wonder that you weren't wearing your extra tunic and leggings as protection against the icy winds. Surely that would be easier than carrying them?"

"Would that I had, my lady! But then my tunic would only have served to soak up my blood as I lay there, left for dead."

Ela noticed that, under his new gray cloak, he wore an entirely different, and rather nicer, tunic than they'd found him in. That one was plain, rough, undyed wool and this one was almost sky blue with a piped trim in red. "Where did you get this new tunic?"

"Mistress Fitch at the Bull and Bear gave it to me to wear, my lady. God be praised for her generosity. She said that her husband's love for roast meat and rich pastries had rendered him unable to wear it these last five years."

"What good fortune to find yourself in a tunic finer than the one you arrived in," said Ela. "And with such a bulging purse of coins, you could buy ten blankets for your dear mother."

"God is good, my lady," he said, twitching awkwardly. "Can I get up now? This cold goes right to my bones."

"Not just yet." Ela wanted him to squirm. Discomfort might make him irritable and incautious. "Did you fall asleep sitting there and leaning against the stone?"

"I suppose I did."

"And what woke you up?"

His hands flailed about a bit and he squinted into the middle of the circle. "I wish I knew. I don't remember another thing until I came to with a knife in my back."

"Did you pull the knife out?"

He blinked, clearly thinking. "I suppose I did."

"You suppose? You don't remember such a shocking event as pulling a sharp, bloody knife from the flesh of your own back?" Ela looked at Haughton.

Haughton took her cue. "It would have taken considerable effort to pull a knife out at such an angle. Would you please demonstrate the action for us?"

"Can I get up?"

"Were you standing or sitting or kneeling when you pulled the knife out?" asked Haughton.

"I don't recall."

"Then pick whichever pose you prefer, and pretend to pull a knife out of your back."

Bird stared at Haughton for a moment, mind working away behind his gaze. He got himself up to his feet, then reached a hand around behind his back, then made a plucking motion."

"Oh, no," said Haughton. "The knife was in the middle of your back, not off to one side like that." Haughton walked up to him and poked a finger into the middle of his back. "You'll need to grab my finger."

John Bird reached around again, the fingers of his right hand stretching and scrabbling for Haughton's finger.

"You can't reach it," said Haughton slowly. "Do you know why?"

"No," said Bird, still making a game effort.

"It's because the muscles of your shoulders and upper back are tight. It's quite common among men."

"I must have done it with my other hand," protested Bird. He lifted his left arm and groped and flailed and twisted and reached and couldn't grab Haughton's finger with that hand either.

Haughton pulled his finger away from Bird's back and looked at Ela.

"Are you suggesting that he couldn't have pulled the knife from his own back?" asked Ela.

"Of course, I can! Put your finger back there." Bird abandoned the effort with his left arm, which was even less flexible than the right. With some contortion and wincing and grimacing, he finally managed to grab Haughton's finger between his thumb and finger. "See!"

"Pull on my finger. Get it away from your back." Haughton pushed his finger into Bird's back, causing the man to exclaim and wriggle and pluck helplessly at the finger. "You don't have the strength to pull my finger from your back at that angle."

Bird grabbed his hand back and jumped away from the painful pressure of Haughton's fingertip. "I don't remember how I did it, but the pain must have given me the will and the way."

The difficulty or even impossibility of Bird plucking the knife from his own back gave weight to Ela's belief that such an event had never happened. But the fact remained that he did have a wound, albeit a minor one, on his back. She looked at Haughton. "If he didn't pluck the knife from his back, then how did he manage to stab himself there to inflict the minor wound that we found?"

Haughton shrugged. "He might have found a nail on a fence or barn to back up to or even stuck the knife blade-out in a dry stone wall. There are many possibilities."

"What are you talking about?" screeched Bird. "You can see as plain as day what happened."

"We can't," said Haughton quietly. "And you apparently can't describe it with any accuracy either."

Bird's eyes narrowed slightly. "Yes, I can. It's coming back to me."

"Oh?" Ela looked on curiously, wondering what tall tale he'd spin now. She admired Haughton's strategy of revealing Bird's physical limitations.

"As I climbed to my feet, the knife fell out."

"A knife, plunged to the hilt—almost the depth of a span—simply popped out of your back like a rabbit emerging from its burrow?"

"Perhaps the bones of my spine or ribs pushed it out," said Bird. His gaze darted from Ela to Haughton to see how his new effort was going over. "Plucked by the hand of God, it was! He released me from the jaws of death and gathered me to his holy bosom."

"That's quite an image," said Ela. Still, they'd have a hard time proving that something *didn't* happen unless they could prove what actually had happened. Bird knew that and intended to take full advantage of their ignorance of the truth, using God as his henchman.

"If your memory is now so clear," said Haughton, "where is the knife?"

Bird, now agitated and fidgety, looked around the landscape as if he might spy it glistening somewhere. "Perhaps it's still lying here in the grass. Or a magpie took it?"

"I'd like to see the magpie that could carry a knife in its beak. Would it grab the blade or the handle, do you suppose?" Haughton's eyes twinkled with amusement.

Bird started striding around as if looking for the knife in the grass.

"We searched the area thoroughly when the jurors came here in search of your corpse," said Ela. "We'd have found the knife if it were still here."

"Then where is it?" cried Bird, as if its disappearance was their fault.

Wherever you hid it, thought Ela. *Possibly near where you hid the body of the dead man that you killed.*

Something prevented her from uttering the words aloud, though. An instinct that secrecy and caution gave her an advantage that would be lost by putting Bird utterly on the defensive. They didn't have enough evidence to lock him away—yet—and she and Haughton needed to focus on finding the missing body.

∽

ELA GATHERED twenty guards and charged them—once again—with finding the body of a man of medium height and build, with brown hair and a fatal stab wound in his back. By late the next morning, they'd returned empty-handed and—she strongly suspected—muttering that they'd been sent on a wild goose chase.

She summoned Haughton to the castle to discuss how to proceed.

"We can't prove a murder was committed without a dead body," said Haughton. "At least I've never seen it happen."

"So, if a man disappears, and everyone thinks his brother

killed him—because they were seen arguing—his brother can't be tried?" She could imagine any number of scenarios where murder might be suspected without a corpse being present.

"You could bring him before a jury, but as long as he insisted that his brother had stormed off and not been heard of since, even the judge at the assizes would be hard-pressed to find him guilty in the absence of proof that his brother is dead. I've seen more than one suspicious disappearance, but I've not known anyone to be convicted in such a case."

"Do you think there is a body?"

Haughton rubbed his mouth with his hand. "Perhaps the man was simply unconscious but not dead."

"Then how do you explain the knife? And so much blood from a mere scratch on his back?"

"The knife could have become stuck in his clothing, and some men do bleed more than others."

"If I hadn't seen the sight with my own eyes, I'd be doubting it. But if Bill Talbot says he was dead, then I'm convinced of it." She glanced across the hall to where Bill Talbot sat across a table from her sons, earnestly discussing something with them. "There must be some explanation."

"You're not inclined to a supernatural explanation?" said Haughton. His brow lifted slightly, suggesting amusement. "One of God's holy miracles?"

Ela inhaled deeply. "Far be it from me to doubt the power of God to create miracles here on earth."

"But?"

"But I don't like John Bird and I don't trust him."

"You could arrest him on suspicion of murder. You could also possibly torture him into a confession." Haughton suggested it as gaily as if proposing a brisk ride across the countryside. "I daresay your predecessor Simon de Hal would have done something similar, at least until a suitable bribe could be produced."

"I prefer to leave Bird at large where we can learn more about him."

"You aren't worried he'll just disappear?"

"Not until I give his coins back." She smiled. "And you have them stored away for safekeeping. I have no doubt that he'll at least come to claim them before continuing his journey to visit his supposedly ailing mother. It seems that she's rallied and no longer needs his urgent attention. He doesn't seem to be in a rush to leave Salisbury."

"I suggest you have one of your guards dress like an ordinary man to follow him and report on his movements."

"The people of Salisbury would likely know he's a guard and might treat him with suspicion. Better to have a trusted juror who just happens to be on hand. Peter Howard would be a good one, but he's too busy baking bread."

"How about Matthew Hart? His son John manages most of his affairs now, but he's still sound of body and mind."

"Excellent choice," said Ela. "I shall summon him and charge him with the duties. As long as he's agreeable, he can start following John Bird immediately. And I intend to charge my guards with digging anywhere they see disturbed ground in the hope that we can uncover what I still believe is a missing body."

∽

MATTHEW HART WAS one of the older jurors, a mild-mannered man more inclined to harmony than argument. He lived in a house inside the castle walls and arrived in the hall barely a quarter hour after Ela had sent a messenger to fetch him.

"Have you heard of the man they say was raised from the

dead?" asked Ela, wondering if everyone in Salisbury was aware of the strange newcomer.

"Oh, yes. My wife told me that the Lord healed his wound completely—she saw it with her own eyes!"

"Where was that?"

"In the marketplace yesterday. A deep wound that gushed with blood and would have killed him is now barely a scratch. It's a holy miracle!"

Ela wondered if she'd chosen the right man for the job. Still, she knew him to be fair-minded and thoughtful. "I think there's a possibility that John Bird isn't who we think he is."

"He healed the widow Willard's earache, they say. My wife told me that when she returned from the bakery this morning."

Ela stared at him. "Well, that is already some interesting new information you've brought me. I shall visit the widow Willard myself and ask her about her experience. In the meantime, keep your eyes peeled. Come at the end of the day to tell me what you've learned."

CHAPTER 5

⌘

*E*la knew that Annie Willard, widow of old Tom Willard the blacksmith, lived in a tiny crooked house propped against the castle's outer wall. She hastened there on foot with a gift of fresh butter carried by Petronella, her oldest daughter still living at home, and two guards in tow.

A guard rapped hard on the door and they waited. And waited.

"Let me try," said Ela. Perhaps the widow was peeking out through a gap on the wall and intimidated by the official-looking party of visitors. "Hello? Dear Mistress Willard, it's your countess Ela and her daughter Petronella. We bring a small gift for you to enjoy with your daily bread." She leaned in to hear if anything stirred behind the scarred wood door.

"I'm coming! I'm coming!" said a thin voice from some distance away. "It takes me an age to get across the room, what with my legs."

"May I open the door?" asked Ela, wanting to save her the journey across her room.

"You could if it weren't barred and bolted, but my son is that cautious and insists I keep it locked."

After what seemed an eternity, Ela heard the sound of a piece of wood being lifted from behind the door and dropped on the floor with a thud. The door then scraped very slowly open over the plain earthen floor. Widow Willard looked exhausted by the effort and stood there teetering as if she might drop to the floor herself.

"Petronella dear, do put the butter down and help Mistress Willard to a chair." Petronella silently obeyed, and, with some help from Ela, they conveyed the elderly widow to a rickety chair that seemed almost as unsteady on its feet as she was.

"How is your earache, Mistress Willard?" asked Ela.

"What earache?" she replied. "Would you like a bit of bread and butter?" Her eyes sparkled in her rather wizened face. She was a very old woman, probably more than four score years. Her husband had been dead for at least two decades.

"Please, don't trouble yourself, mistress," said Ela. "So, you don't have an earache?"

"No, my lady. Should I? I'm a bit hard of hearing, but I can hear you well enough if you're close."

"Have you met a man called John Bird?"

Widow Willard frowned and looked as if she might be searching her mind for memories of a John Bird. "Can't say I have."

"It would have been in the last couple of days. He's not from Salisbury and just came to town."

"I haven't been out of this house in a week or more," said Mistress Willard, looking perplexed.

"Have you had any visitors?"

"My son comes every day, bless him. He brings me bread and butter and cheese on his way to market. He's a farmer, you know. His wife bakes her own bread, so they don't have to waste money at the baker. She sometimes brings their dear sweet children to visit."

"Anyone else? Perhaps a stranger?"

Widow Willard thought about this for a moment, then shook her head. "I wouldn't let a stranger in my house. My son told me not to open the door to strangers."

"Your son sounds very caring and thoughtful. But you haven't had an earache?"

"I don't think so. I do get a bit scatterbrained. At least my son says so."

Ela nodded, very confused. Did Matthew Hart have her confused with some other widow with an earache? "So, you haven't been in the market square yourself? Or to the Bull and Bear?"

Widow Willard blinked her eyes. "No. At least, I don't think so. Perhaps I have. You'd better ask my son."

Ela glanced at Petronella. "Your son is Richard Willard?"

"Yes, my lady. I'm sure you know my Dickie. He's one of the jurors of the hundred."

"I know him." He was one of the jurors who never seemed to be available to do his duty. She mostly knew him from an acrimonious dispute he'd had with a neighbor over a dog that had supposedly savaged his prized ewe. Since he couldn't produce the ewe or prove it had ever existed, she had not awarded him any damages. The incident had not improved Ela's opinion of Dickie Willard. "Where might I find him, do you suppose?"

"He just left this basket of eggs on the table this morning, so I'd imagine he's at the market selling eggs and butter and milk."

Ela wished they'd brought jam instead of butter since the widow clearly had a steady stream of butter. "You're blessed to have a son that takes such good care of you."

"That's what he always says," said Mistress Willard, with a gap-toothed smile.

∽

"Where did Matthew Hart get the idea that John Bird had cured a widow who hasn't left her house in a week?" asked Petronella once they'd stepped outside. "Perhaps he drank too much at the Bull and Bear last night."

"Matthew Hart is not one to over-imbibe or to make up stories. I must admit that I am rather mystified. Let's talk to Richard Willard and see if he knows anything about this story."

As they approached the marketplace, they could see a crowd gathered. A much larger crowd than you would find mid-morning on an ordinary weekday.

"It's Lazarus, risen from the dead," said Petronella, peering over their heads at John Bird. "But I can't hear what he's saying."

"Let's leave him be for the moment and find Dickie Willard," said Ela firmly. "He usually sets up his stall at the far end where his eggs and milk are in the shade of the nearby building." Sure enough, she could see his stall, with two customers waiting to be served while he wrapped up butter in waxed cloth belonging to a third customer.

Ela approached the stall and the farmer looked up from taking his customer's money. "My lady. Would you like some butter made fresh this morning?"

"I'd like a private word with you, but I shall wait until you've served these two customers."

"That's very humble of you," whispered Petronella.

"I'll take that as a compliment."

"It's intended as one, dear Mama." Petronella seemed content to wait as two local women took their slabs of butter and wrapped them in their own cloth and exchanged their pennies, rather flustered to have their countess waiting patiently behind them.

Dickie Willard wiped his hands on a cloth and came out from behind his stall. "How may I help you, my lady?"

"Master Willard, I heard that your dear mother was cured of an earache."

He smiled broadly. "Indeed she was! Quite a miraculous healing by our new visitor. She'd suffered from it for weeks. Now it's gone and she can hear clear as a bell. An act of God!"

Ela felt Petronella looking at her. She kept her gaze fixed on Dickie Willard. "I just visited your mother in her home, and she did not recall ever having had an earache."

He blinked very fast, and Ela saw color rising on his face. "She's very old, my lady. Very, very old."

"Indeed, she has attained a great age, with God's grace. And her mind seems remarkably sharp. But she did become confused when I asked her about the earache."

"She does get forgetful," he blustered. "I'm sure it's slipped her mind."

"Did she come to the market to experience this miraculous healing, or did John Bird come to her house?" She asked it pleasantly, as if she was simply curious.

"Uh, I, she came…No, he was kind enough to come to her house. She doesn't get about too well anymore."

"I did notice that. She had trouble crossing the room to answer the door, so I didn't imagine she'd have walked all the way across the village and battled the throng at the market to meet him." Ela peered at him. "Except that she said no strangers had come to her house."

Dickie Willard now looked very uncomfortable. He knew he'd been caught in a lie. He looked about him as if planning an escape route or hoping for another "miracle" to snatch him from this predicament. Then he turned back to her. "She must be mistaken. Her mind is not as clear as it once was."

Customers gathered at his stall, waiting for their turn to buy eggs and milk and butter. Ela gestured for him to return to his business. "I thank you for your time."

She turned and walked away quickly, with Petronella hurrying behind her. "He's lying!" hissed Petronella under her breath.

"I know. I shall have him struck from the jury rolls."

"You should have accused him right then and there!"

"That would create a stir that wouldn't serve my true purpose, which is to find out what John Bird is up to. I suspect Bird paid Dickie Willard to spread the story of his mother's supposedly miraculous healing. If I am to accuse him of that I'd like to do it in front of a jury and in the presence of John Bird, not in the marketplace in front of some confused housewives. But rest assured, his lie shall not go unpunished."

"Unless his mother really did forget," said Petronella mildly, looking across the crowd still gathered around John Bird. "And our local Lazarus does have healing powers. There are those who still doubt that Jesus fed the five thousand with loaves and fishes or turned water into wine. Do you believe those miracles happened?"

"Of course I do."

"Then is it utterly impossible that John Bird truly did rise from the dead and has now healed an elderly lady's earache?"

"It's not impossible, but I grow increasingly convinced that neither of those events happened. The difficulty is in proving what did happen."

A wail arose from the nearby crowd, and they both turned their heads. A murmur arose and people craned their heads to see better.

"What's going on?" whispered Petronella.

J. G. LEWIS

"Let's go see," said Ela quietly.

"My pain is gone!" came the wailing voice again. "This ankle's been sore for years and now it feels right as rain!"

"It's a miracle," said someone.

"An act of God," said another.

Ela couldn't see John Bird due to the crush of people around him. No one seemed to notice that their countess was present, as their eyes were all fixed on the woman exclaiming over her ankle.

One of Ela's guards stepped forward. "Part ways for your countess," he said gruffly. It was a moment before anyone even paid attention and shuffled aside a little. Ela might have felt offended by their lack of respect, but she was more intrigued by the mysterious healing that had apparently taken place in their midst.

Ela made her way to the front, behind her guard, who moved people aside. John Bird looked at her. She half expected him to look horrified or even turn and run, but instead he lifted his chin and looked at her in triumph. "My lady, just in time to witness the miracle of God working through these poor tired hands." He lifted his hands as if she might inspect them.

Ela realized that the shrieking woman was Lizzie Trout, a farmer's widow who lived with her son and his family in a nearby village. She did have a slight limp that she'd had as long as Ela could remember.

"Mistress Trout, is your limp gone?"

"I think so, my lady," said the astonished woman, eyes wide with shock. She wore a yellowed kerchief over her hair and a faded green gown. "Let me try walking." She shuffled forward a few steps, which was all the press of people would allow. Tears sprang to her eyes. "My pain is gone and my limp is too!"

"It's a holy miracle!" exclaimed John Bird. "By the grace of

God who's placed his trust and healing powers in the hands of this poor sinner."

"Can you heal my eyes?" called one old woman, whose vision was dimmed by a veil of whiteness.

"Please mend my aching back," cried Jack Denton, who'd been hunched almost double for as long as Ela could remember.

"Can you cure my son who's been sickly since he was born?" begged someone Ela didn't recognize.

All eyes rested on John Bird, who—although usually inclined to be in constant movement, waving his hands about and shifting from foot to foot—seemed to take in the attention with the stillness and composure of a man used to addressing a crowd. "God willing, I shall work his healing miracles on everyone who needs one, but for now I am tired and in need of rest."

He was immediately beset by offers of hospitality from those living near and far. John Fitch of the Bull and Bear was quick to renew his offer of a meal and ale and lodgings—which would ensure continued busy custom at his establishment. John Bird set off for the Bull and Bear with his entourage trailing behind him.

～

"I don't know what to make of him," said Ela frankly. She sat in the hall, at the table nearest the fire, sharing the midday meal with her children and Bill Talbot. "I thought him a charlatan, but if he's truly cured Lizzie Trout's lameness, then there's more to him than meets the eye."

She'd convinced herself that Bird had paid Dickie Willard to spread rumors about his mother's earache being cured. But having witnessed the miracle of Lizzie's healing, she now rather doubted his mother's memory.

Father Thomas had been hovering nearby, an excited gleam in his eye. "Sometimes the work of the Lord passes all understanding."

"Indeed, that is true," Ela was forced to admit. "I'm a mere mortal woman and cannot hope to grasp all the mysteries of the Almighty."

"He's chosen to make his presence known among us right here in Salisbury," exclaimed Father Thomas. The priest rarely made an appearance in the hall. A bookish, sensitive man, he probably found the noise and commotion unpleasant. Ela wasn't even sure where he usually took his meals, since he never claimed a place at her table, though he knew he was welcome.

But since John Bird had arrived, Father Thomas seemed as ever-present as the garrison soldiers. Perhaps he was keen to gather every scrap of news about the strange events unfolding in their midst.

Bill Talbot broke open a bread roll and spread some soft cheese on it. "He's certainly made himself very popular. That's no easy feat, as most people are wary of strangers."

"He has indeed," said Ela. "He seems a nervous, twitchy sort of man, but perhaps his ordinariness puts people at ease."

"There is something of the everyman about him," agreed Father Thomas with enthusiasm. His gray eyes sparkled in a way she'd never seen before. "Just like Our Lord when he came among the people as one of them."

Ela fought the urge to roll her eyes, then chastised herself for her arrogance in assuming that she was right and everyone else was wrong. Perhaps her own cynicism—brought about by her dealings with all manner of crimes and criminals in her role as sheriff—had made her too quick to see the bad in men instead of the good.

"I'd like to bring him before the jury again," said Ela. "And learn in more detail exactly what he's experiencing."

"Healing people is not a crime, surely?"

"Not if he's really healing them. If he's taking money with false promises or bribing people to lie about healings, that's a whole different matter."

"I heard the bishop wishes to interview him, to discuss the mystical events that are taking place," said Father Thomas.

"Does he? I'd like to meet with the bishop to discuss the matter before he does so."

"That's a wonderful idea, my lady." Thomas looked almost beside himself with excitement. "Shall I convey the message to him myself?"

"If you like." If the priest wanted to ride to the cathedral close, she had no reason to stop him. "If tomorrow morning is convenient, we can meet here in my hall after Prime."

∽

IN THE LATE AFTERNOON, shortly before dusk, Matthew Hart arrived back at the castle. Ela ushered him out of the hall and into the armory. She wanted to be sure he could talk in complete confidence. The older man looked around at the glittering array of polished weapons on the walls with some alarm.

"Were you able to follow John Bird and observe his movements?"

"That I did, my lady. I saw you in the marketplace myself at the moment that Lizzie Trout declared herself cured of her limp. Quite astonishing and humbling to see the workings of our Lord here in Salisbury." His eyes sparkled.

"Did you happen to see any money change hands between Mistress Trout and John Bird?"

He frowned. "Do you mean to ask if she paid for his services?"

"Possibly. Or if he paid her?"

"Paid her? Why would he give her money when he's curing her?"

Ela wasn't sure whether to expand on her deep suspicion that John Bird was paying select people to say they were cured, so he could perpetrate a fraud on the rest of the townspeople. "Did you see any money change hands between them?"

"I did not."

She wondered why he hadn't just said that in the first place. "Did you see him heal anyone else?"

"He healed…well, I suppose I didn't see it, but they said he healed old Steven Thicke of his gout."

Ela couldn't picture Steven Thicke. "Does he live inside the castle walls?"

"No. I think he lives on his son's farm. I haven't seen him in some time, myself."

"So you saw no healings other than Lizzie Trout, whose healing I witnessed myself?"

"That's about the length and breadth of it, my lady. John Bird seemed as astonished as everyone else about his healing powers and kept talking about the mysterious hand of the Lord in his life."

"Did you see anyone give him money?"

"Oh, yes, my lady! I think almost everyone in the village gave him a coin or two. For luck, you see! Almost an offering."

"Did you give him money?"

"Five pennies."

"Five? Why not just a penny? Or even a half-penny?"

Matthew Hart looked affronted. "Why, such a paltry

offering might insult him and by extension insult our dear Lord who's shown him such tender mercies."

"Quite." Did no one else think this man might be some kind of confidence artist? He seemed very skilled at parting people from their money. "How much money would you say he collected today, if you had to guess?"

He stared at her and his brow furrowed. "Why, this is like the guess-how-many-beans-are-in-the-pot contest at the summer fair. I couldn't say how much he collected since I didn't count it myself."

Haughton had counted the coins in the purse they took from Bird the previous day. It contained nearly three pounds. Bird apparently hadn't had any trouble replacing its contents with fresh loot shaken from the people of Salisbury.

"Please, be discreet with what I'm about to say to you." She felt some hesitation in confiding her suspicions. "But I worry that John Bird is not what he seems and that he's preying on the good people of Salisbury."

"How is that possible? We can see with our own eyes that he was raised from the dead."

"Someone lay dead in the stone circle on Salisbury plain. That I know because I saw the body myself. But I'm not convinced it was John Bird. He's a man of very average height and build. His hair color and length are quite unremarkable. I didn't see the dead man's face since he was face-down. I suspect another man lay dead in the circle of stones. I think John Bird hid his body, injured himself just enough to feign a stab wound, and assumed the dead man's identity to profit from this apparent miracle."

Matthew Hart looked utterly incredulous. "But there is no other body. We'd have found it when we searched the countryside for it on that first day."

"Indeed, the disappearance is mysterious. I have some of

my men digging in any areas of disturbed ground to see if they can find it."

"Have they found anything?"

"Not yet."

He hesitated for a moment as if choosing his words carefully. "It would be quite a trick to hide an entire corpse from the people of Salisbury. Doesn't it seem more likely that he's telling the truth?"

Ela did not think it was more likely. But, once again, she was in the minority in her suspicions. A situation that did not improve when the bishop visited her hall the following morning.

CHAPTER 6

"My lady, do you not believe in Our Lord God Almighty?" Bishop Robert de Bingham was a tall and well-built man in the prime of middle age, arrayed in all the trappings of success and wealth that you might expect to observe on a man who believes himself to be one of the most impressive specimens of his kind. A brocade-trimmed hat topped his still-thick and dark hair, hiding his tonsure.

Ela wasn't sure whether to dignify his question with an answer. The boldness of his question shocked her so deeply that if he weren't one of God's bishops and a powerful man in Wiltshire and even in all England, she would have chastised him soundly and ordered her guards to march him from her castle. "I believe my reputation for piety speaks for itself."

"It is true that you are known for your good works, my lady." His well-groomed fingers fondled the tooling on his silver cup of wine. "But I'm surprised that you choose not to believe the evidence of your own eyes and the conviction of the people of Salisbury."

"It is my job as the sheriff to investigate crimes. I saw a dead body with my own eyes. I am not satisfied that the dead body was that of John Bird."

"Do you not believe that Jesus Christ himself raised Lazarus from the dead?"

"I have never questioned the truth of God's word as written in the Holy Scripture," said Ela briskly.

"Then do you believe the Lord our God capable of repeating this miraculous act here in Salisbury?"

"Jesus Christ raised Lazarus from the dead. I do not believe that the Son of God is present in our midst," said Ela carefully. "Or at least I have not yet heard news of it." She knew she was in dangerous territory arguing theology with a bishop.

"Jesus Christ now sits at the right hand of the Father, instead of walking among us, but God's holy miracles are wrought in the lives of the saints. Think of the miracle of Saint Jerome, who healed three sick children who lay at the brink of death. Or St. Peter, who appeared in a vision to heal the wounds inflicted on St. Agatha as she lay in prison. These healings are proof of God's power to influence life among men, if he so pleases."

"Do you think that John Bird is a saint? Perhaps we should inform the pope himself." Ela tried to keep sarcasm from her voice.

"I have written to him already," said de Bingham. A smile spread across his mouth, revealing rather yellow teeth. "To inform him of the miraculous happenings here in Salisbury and to ask him how to proceed with documenting them. Perhaps the pope will even summon John Bird to visit him in Rome so he can meet him in person. I'd be happy to accompany him, even on such a long and arduous journey."

Ela stared at him, speechless, for a moment. Had John Bird so convinced the people of Salisbury that he was able to both give and receive miracles that he was about to be canonized as a saint—instead of tried for murder? Or did Bishop de Bingham, with more cynical motivation, see this as an opportunity to raise his own stature within the church.

"I fear you are hasty, your Grace."

"I move with all the speed that the Holy Church demands of me in such a striking circumstance." Bishop de Bingham narrowed his eyes and leaned forward. "And I am deeply shocked that you seem hostile to the saintly presence in our midst."

His voice contained the edge of a threat. Did he mean to complain to the church authorities that she was sowing doubt and discord and railing against Salisbury's new saint? Ela felt she was now definitely treading on dangerous ground and had better tuck her foot back beneath her robe for now.

"Far be it from me to question the presence of God among us. I hope and trust that he lives in my heart and yours and in all of the people of Salisbury. Perhaps you are not aware, Your Grace, that I am at present engaged in building not one but two monastic houses. I intend to take the veil in the convent at Lacock myself when the time is right."

"That is a relief, my lady, as I was beginning to wonder if you might be ready to lead a fight between the sacred and the secular right here in Salisbury!" An oily smile crossed his thin lips. "And I'm sure God's Holy Church and even the pope himself would take a very dim view of such an endeavor."

~

"Are you well, Mama?" asked Petronella after Bishop de Bingham had left. Ela felt deeply shaken by the encounter and his accusations that in suspecting John Bird of fraud she took up a role as the enemy of the church and all that was holy.

"Petronella, what is your impression of John Bird?" Petronella was the most devout person she knew. Her daughter likely had more genuine devotion to God than all the bishops of England combined.

"I admit that I was suspicious of him, partly because you sowed the seeds of doubt in my heart. But now that the bishop has spoken of him with such confidence, and even written to the pope about him, I feel more inclined to think him genuine."

That's what worries me. Ela didn't want to alarm Petronella by reliving her argument with the bishop.

"Bishops are very close to God, after all," continued Petronella. "And surely have deeper wisdom than those of us who are cursed to live a secular life."

"Cursed? Really, Petronella. You live a life of unusual luxury and comfort and you already know you will take your place in the cloister of the convent at Lacock once it's built."

"Why are you bringing that up again, Mama? I was talking about the wisdom of the bishops. Surely you agree that they are holier than, say, Sir William here."

Bill Talbot, hearing his name, looked up from the game of chess he was playing with her son Richard. "No doubt Bishop de Bingham is indeed holier than me," he said gallantly. "I would not seek to argue such a point."

Ela wanted to protest that bishops, for all their fine robes and theological study, were mortal men and as prone to the lure of the seven deadly sins as any other. Perhaps more so. Bishop de Bingham's predecessor, Bishop Richard Poore, had gathered wealth and power to his well-clad person as avidly as any noble in the kingdom. And Ela had herself uncovered a child slavery ring, operating under the gaze of an abbot, to supply the religious houses of Europe with innocent children to use for the most unholy and terrible purposes.

But she didn't want to seem—in her own great hall and surrounded by ears of all shapes and sizes—to be at odds with the church.

"Don't you agree, Mama?" pressed Petronella.

"I consider Sir William Talbot to be a hero of the highest order. He's saved my life on more than one occasion and has been a pillar of our household for almost my entire life. If I could make him a saint, I would," Ela replied. Bill looked up at her in surprise, and she returned his gaze with a smile.

"But not as holy as a bishop, though?" said Bill with a wry look.

"No, not as holy as a bishop," she was forced to admit. She had no motive to argue with Bill's answer, even though her faith in Bill was greater than her admiration and respect for even the Archbishop of Canterbury himself.

"Perhaps you should call John Bird before the jury again," suggested Bill, moving his rook several spaces on the chessboard.

Thank you, Saint Bill, for suggesting what I wanted to say—again—but am now hesitant to express.

"On what pretext?" asked Petronella, peering at him.

"Just to find out more about him, I suppose," said Bill, as if it meant little to him. "Where he came from and what he's done with the first few decades of his life." He looked at Ela. "You could even frame it as a sort of feting of him, rather than an inquisition. More an exploration of the incredible feats of healing that are taking place under our nose."

"Indeed," said Ela gratefully. "I think I shall do just that."

∽

THE JURY WAS SUMMONED to the hall the next morning to meet with John Bird and hear more about his newfound healing abilities. Ela even gathered three sick people in the hope that she could ask him to heal them on the spot and that the results might speak for themselves—one way or the other.

While it could often prove challenging to get jurors to appear when there wasn't a bleeding body or some other urgent crisis, today almost ten of them turned up in the hall, chattering amongst themselves and very interested in the day's proceedings. Their curiosity about —or reverence for—John Bird superseded their need to get their flour milled or shoe leather sewn or hides tanned.

Even the bishop himself arrived to hear the proceedings. He brought two clerical acolytes who secured for him the most comfortable chair in the hall, a throne-like painted wood chair that had belonged to her late husband and which Ela now usually kept for herself.

Bird himself did not look so effusive and cheerful. He also didn't bring his bulging new purse of money. He must have stashed it somewhere, perhaps the Bull and Bear, to prevent Ela from relieving him of its burden again.

Once everyone had settled into their seats along the trestle tables, with Bird on a chair in the middle, Bill Talbot called for quiet.

"Good morning," said Ela, "to all of you but especially to John Bird, who I am surprised to see still in our midst here in Salisbury. I thought you made urgent haste to visit your elderly mother who hovers on the brink of death?" she said pleasantly.

"I'm still recovering from my mortal wound," said Bird gruffly.

"But I had hoped that, by the grace of God, you are now

fully recovered." She leaned forward. "Or perhaps you have found a new urgent calling as a healer here in Salisbury?"

"God has indeed charged me with healing his sick here," agreed Bird, looking somewhat relieved. "And I am blessed to do his holy work."

"Quite so!" exclaimed the bishop. "And we are blessed by your presence, long may it continue." He looked sternly at Ela as if to scold her for browbeating their new saint.

Ela knew she would have to tread carefully.

"It is indeed astonishing and miraculous that you are now endowed with the power to heal, by God's mercy," said Ela to Bird. "What made you realize that your touch could heal? Or is it your touch?"

Bird shifted around in his seat, tapping his feet on the floor. "I had a dream, my lady. Or some might call it a vision." He glanced at the bishop, who looked back approvingly.

"What kind of vision?" asked Ela, wondering what kind of story he'd spout.

"A great, scaly dragon, my lady."

Murmuring rose amongst the jurors. Ela found herself thoroughly taken aback. She'd expected, perhaps, a vision of John the Baptist, or Paul on the road to Damascus, or even the Virgin Mary herself. The dragon took her and everyone else utterly by surprise.

"Did you say a dragon?" she asked, wondering if she'd misheard.

"Covered in scales from head to toe and breathing fire!" said Bird, sitting up in his chair and warming to the tale. "In the ring of stones where my body lay dead. It breathed its terrible fire, and the flames scorched the grass all the way to Salisbury!" His eyes glinted.

Speechless, Ela crossed herself. "God forbid," she managed finally. "Surely such a dragon is not a creature of God but of his greatest adversary?"

"Why yes, my lady!" said Bird, almost jumping out of his chair. "And I was charged with fighting this terrible creature. And with the help of God and his angels, I managed to pierce its heart with my knife and slay it before it could destroy the entire kingdom."

By now, Ela had regained her composure and reassured herself that such a tall tale was not only utter nonsense but must have surely revealed itself as such to every man there who had a brain in his head.

"Where is the carcass of this fearsome dragon?"

"The carcass?" A crooked smile creased Bird's face. "This was a dream, my lady. A vision in my head. I did not take up arms against a dragon on Salisbury plain."

"I understand that, Master Bird. But where did the dragon's body fall, in your dream or vision?" Perhaps she could reveal the cracks in his story through probing questions. "Did it crash to earth in the center of the circle of stones?"

"It did indeed, my lady."

She realized she'd made that answer too easy for him.

"Why there, do you think?"

"Why are the stones there, my lady? If we had answers to these questions, we would surely understand the mysteries of life."

"The historian Geoffrey of Monmouth states that the stones were erected by King Vortigern to commemorate the fallen dead of a great battle," said Ela, recalling the conversation she and Bill had before they discovered the body.

"Was Vortigern a Christian king?" asked the bishop. "Or a pagan savage?"

"He was a Christian," said Ela. "Though not a very good one if Monmouth's account of his sinful deeds is to be believed. You may have read of him in Bede's *Ecclesiastical History of the English People* or Gildas's *On the Ruin and Conquest of Britain*."

The bishop blinked as if he'd never heard of the books. "It has been some years since my studies at Oxford. I prefer to fill my head with the Word of Our Lord as written in his Holy Bible, not the scribblings of long-dead so-called historians."

"Quite understandable," said Ela, agreeably. "Though if you wish to read any of these texts, I have copies in my library."

The bishop's brow darkened. Had she gone too far in demonstrating her superior education? Probably she had. Knowing when to stop was not her strong suit.

But there was the matter of the dragon. "What color was the dragon in your vision, Master Bird?" she asked.

He blinked and fidgeted a bit. "Gold."

"Gold? In the ancient legends, there's a great battle between two dragons, a red one and a white one, that perhaps symbolizes the battle between the ancient Britons and the Saxon invaders."

"Did you bring us here this morning to inquire of the color of a dragon in a man's dream?" asked the bishop curtly. "I fail to see the relevance of this to the healing miracles God has wrought among us."

"I beg your pardon, Your Grace. I simply seek to learn the content of these amazing visions so that I may better understand what holy miracles are taking place here in Salisbury." Did her voice sound sarcastic? She hoped not. She turned back to Bird. "But let us turn our attention to the healings themselves. How many people have you healed so far?"

"I've lost count." He shifted in his chair.

"Is there anyone else here who could describe the healings that have taken place?" She looked pointedly at Matthew Hart, who she'd charged with following Bird and noting his activities.

Hart swallowed. "I've seen one, my lady. The same one

you witnessed with your own eyes. And I've heard tell of others."

Bird fidgeted in his chair.

"How many people would you estimate that you've healed, Master Bird?" She peered at him. "I don't need the exact number, but perhaps you could describe a few."

"Well, I don't remember everyone's names. I'm a stranger and you were all unknown to me a few days ago."

"We understand that," said Ela pleasantly. "And I saw the moment when Lizzie Trout remarked that the pain in her leg was gone and she could walk without a limp. But what other healings have you wrought?"

"There was one old lady whose deafness lifted away, leaving her able to hear the sweet song of the birds again."

"Remarkable," said Ela. "Could you or anyone else tell me her name?"

"She was a widow of great age. Willard, I think the name was."

"Oh!" Ela's heart quickened at the prospect of catching him in a lie. "I visited the Widow Willard myself yesterday after Matthew Hart told me you'd healed her of an earache. As it turned out, she didn't remember anything about the matter. I'm not aware that she was ever deaf."

Bird squirmed. "Deaf as a post, she was. A dear, sweet old lady. I dare say her brain's addled."

"Did you visit her at home?"

"I did indeed. Her dear son took me there. He has a stall in the market."

"Where was her house situated?" She hoped to catch him in his lie as she was fairly sure Dick Willard had just taken money to spread the story of his mother's healing, rather than taking him to the house.

"Inside the castle wall," said Bird confidently.

Ela fought a sigh. "Where exactly inside the walls?"

"My dear lady," the bishop cut in loudly. "I fail to see how the exact location of old Widow Willard's house is of any interest or importance."

"I'm merely trying to establish that he went there at all."

"John Bird is not on trial here this morning, my lady," continued the bishop. "So I see no reason for the accusatory nature of your inquiry. If he says he healed Widow Willard, and Widow Willard no longer has an earache or deafness, then it's reasonable to assume that our visitor is telling the truth. I won't countenance him being accused of lies and deception when there is no evidence of either."

If de Bingham weren't the bishop, Ela would have castigated him soundly and probably had him removed from her hall. Unfortunately, he was the bishop, and God's highest representative in Salisbury, so she bit her tongue.

"I would simply like to establish that an actual, verifiable healing has taken place." Ela tried to keep her voice as neutral as possible. "Has anyone seen Mistress Trout since her limp was cured?"

There was some muttering among the jurors, but no one had seen her that day. She lived some distance outside the castle walls, on her son's farm, and only came in when he brought her in his cart, so that was hardly remarkable.

"Perhaps we can try another approach," said Ela brightly. "I have here three infirm residents of Salisbury, all in urgent need of healing. Master Bird, would you be willing to try your hand at relieving them of their ailments?"

CHAPTER 7

"You speak as if the power to heal lies with me, my lady. Only through God's grace can I cure the sick." He sat unusually still. Ela noticed that although his speech wasn't that of a gentleman, it wasn't that of a serf or lowly peasant, either. He didn't speak like someone who'd grown up gleaning wheat fields in a lonely Norfolk backwater. He sounded more like the son of a burgher or tradesman.

"Quite so. But would you be willing to attempt such a healing, if the bishop thinks it appropriate?" Ela decided it would be wise to get the bishop's buy-in on this new endeavor.

He nodded and shifted in his seat, then sat tapping a toe on the floor.

"Bishop de Bingham." Ela looked at him with as much enthusiasm as she could muster. "Do you object to allowing John Bird to work a healing miracle in the lives of these poor unfortunates gathered in my hall today?"

"I have no objection at all, my lady," said the bishop with a beatific smile.

The bishop believes he is genuine. This relieved Ela. She was beginning to wonder if the bishop was in on the confidence game she saw unfolding inside her castle's outer walls.

She rose from her chair and walked over to another table, where the three sick people sat with members of their families in attendance. Two of them had been in the market the day that Lizzie Trout had proclaimed herself healed. "This is Jack Denton, whose back has become so stooped and bent that he can no longer stand upright." She signaled for Denton to do his best to stand. At his full, bow-backed height, his head barely reached Ela's chest.

"And this is Widow Marchwell, whose eyes are so clouded with a milky substance that she can no longer see more than the presence of light."

There had been a third person in the market that day, seeking healing for a sickly babe, but Ela did not have the heart to get a desperate mother's hopes up when she didn't believe for a moment that John Bird had the power to cure anyone.

"And this is Thomas Thicke, who's touched in the head these last seven years after being struck down by apoplexy. He can no longer form words, though before he used to be the best storyteller in Salisbury."

A look of great sadness flickered across Thicke's face. Ela felt sure he could still understand those around him, even if he could no longer express himself in words.

"If you—with the grace of God—can cure the ailments plaguing any of these three, I will be deeply in your debt and thoroughly convinced that your proclaimed healing gift is real."

Bird glanced shiftily at the three hopeful supplicants. "These ailments all seem very difficult to treat."

"I'd say they are generally considered impossible to treat," agreed Ela. "Except by some miracle. Are you willing to try?"

"I am."

His willingness surprised her. "Which will you heal first?"

"Let me see which the Lord guides me to."

A murmuring arose among the gathered jurors, but hushed as Bird stood and approached the table of invalids. He walked behind them where they sat at the table. "Are you all able to turn around so you're facing away from the table so that I may lay my hands on you?"

Each of them slowly turned around. They sat looking at Bird with some trepidation.

John Bird held his hands up in the air and slowly drew closer to Thomas Thicke, the man deprived of speech. He held his hands over Thomas's head and started murmuring words that sounded almost like a prayer, but not any prayer that Ela had heard. Perhaps in the absence of a religious upbringing or a history of church attendance, he was making one up.

She glanced at the bishop to see what he made of all this and found him staring at John Bird with rapt attention.

"Two pennies and one half-penny."

Ela heard the words but wasn't sure who said them. Did Bird have the gall to demand payment for healing here in her hall?

"Two pennies and one half-penny." This time she watched Bird's lips and they didn't move. He continued to move his hands over Thomas Thicke's gray hair.

"Two pennies and one half-penny."

"He speaks," said Bird. "Praise be to God."

"Praise be to God!" Exclaimed the bishop, leaping to his feet. "Praise be to the one, the only, the Most Almighty God who has shown his fearful and magnificent presence among us here in Salisbury today!" Ela could hear tears in his voice. He was deeply moved.

Ela was less so. She'd seen a jester put voices in the mouths of others by a trick of ventriloquism. Had Bird made the sounds but pretended Thicke was talking?

But she didn't see a way to object. The hall exploded in an uproar, with people falling to their knees, praising God. Their fervent prayers echoed off the beamed ceiling and bounced off the braziers on the walls. If she—even as Countess of Salisbury and sheriff of all Wiltshire—were to cast doubt on this apparent miracle, she knew the bishop and likely the jurors and even her castle staff would be horrified by her apparent apostasy.

"Two pennies and one half-penny."

Ela moved toward Thomas Thicke, crossing herself for several reasons all at once. For one, she hoped God was with them and not some other, more awful presence. For another, she hoped that John Bird hadn't pulled a fiendish trick on the people of Salisbury right here in her hall. For a third, which she was least proud of, she didn't want to appear at odds with everyone here in suspecting that this sudden miracle was born of trickery rather than true faith.

As she drew closer, she watched Thomas Thicke's mouth, and thus she saw with her own eyes when his lips rose and fell as he mouthed the words, "Two pennies and one half-penny."

"Praise be to God," she whispered. "But why does he keep saying the same thing." Thomas Thicke himself looked agitated. While he seemed excited to have some powers of speech return, it seemed clear that he was desperately trying to say something other than—

"Two pennies and one half-penny."

"That's what he was saying when he was struck down," called one of the jurors. "He was at his market stall, bargaining with Mistress Dyer when he suddenly fell to his knees and then flat on his face. When he came to, he couldn't talk at all but kept gaping his mouth like a fish."

Ela looked for Bird, who was now encircled by the bishop and the two friars he'd brought with him, and several other people. Bird himself looked rather shocked. His face had grown pale and he wasn't gesticulating with his arms. She watched as he turned and looked at Thomas Thicke, just as Thicke rose to his feet and bellowed, "Two pennies and one half-penny!"

Bird's as shocked as the rest of us, thought Ela. To his surprise, and certainly to hers, he'd wrought an actual miracle. If one of limited value to poor Thomas Thicke.

"The pope must hear of this," cried the bishop. "I shall write to him again at once, and I'd be pleased to host John Bird as my guest in the bishop's palace."

John Bird protested that he was quite comfortable in the Bull and Bear.

"I insist! You are liable to be exploited by unscrupulous persons once word of your miracles spreads to the surrounding towns."

John Bird looked around with some desperation. He probably knew he'd have a difficult time collecting money from hopeful townspeople if he was under the bishop's watchful eye. It was likely that the bishop intended to solicit donations for his own benefit.

"I think he should stay here at the castle," she said, speaking above the din. "Where we can offer him the protection of the king's garrison and keep him safe from harm."

John Bird looked panicked. "I must be leaving town to make my way to my old mother. Her time is short."

"Under these circumstances, I'm afraid that's impossible," said the bishop. "Why, you might be England's next saint!" The entire hall was still in an uproar. Ela could see there was no question of continuing the jury hearing and asking the more mundane questions she'd originally intended. The best she could do was keep him here and prevent him from fleeing her jurisdiction.

"I can send a carriage to bring your dear mother here to my castle," said Ela. "My men will set out at once to Paignton in Devon and bring medicines and provisions that she may be as comfortable as royalty. She shall rest in the chambers once occupied by Eleanor of Aquitaine here in Salisbury castle."

John Bird blinked and looked like he wanted to protest. Ela was almost sure that he had no mother at all, or at least not one on her deathbed in Paignton. So she was shocked by Bird's next words.

"All right. I shall take you up on your offer to bring her here. Perhaps I can heal her."

~

THE CHAMBERS once occupied by the late queen were swept, the green damask bed curtains beaten, and the bed dressed in fresh linens. Ela had never slept in the large suite of rooms herself. Her mother, Alianore, who had come to the castle as a young bride and befriended Eleanor during her years of captivity there, was rather superstitious and wouldn't countenance any family member sleeping in the late queen's rooms. It was too great a misfortune to be the wife of two kings and the mother of three more and yet to find yourself kept in confinement—even in considerable luxury—for nearly fifteen years.

Ela had opened the rooms to quite a few people over the years: traveling justices, bishops and nobles had all slept there. This would certainly be the first time they'd accommodated one of the common people.

A smaller room in the suite, with a tiny, high window and

a door that could be locked from the outside—just in case—was made ready for John Bird. Bird himself went to collect his belongings from the Bull and Bear, with an armed guard for protection at Ela's insistence.

The guard, a trusted longtime member of her household, was also instructed to report back to her if Bird collected any money or stowed any money or possessions somewhere else.

Bird arrived back shortly before dusk, looking rather downcast at being confined in the castle rather than raking in money at the Bull and Bear. His demeanor soon changed when the castle staff and the garrison soldiers flocked around him, asking for blessings and wanting to kiss his feet and making offerings of coins and little gifts.

Ela did nothing to stop them. She merely observed the scene and noted how hungry the people were for a sign—no matter how strange—of God's presence and his intercession in their lives here on earth. She resolved to visit Thomas Thicke tomorrow to see if he'd regained any further powers of speech, or shown any other improvements. For now, she could hardly doubt that she'd seen a miracle with her own eyes.

∼

THE NEXT MORNING Ela sat on the dais in her hall, receiving petitioners with their usual round of complaints and requests. John Bird sat likewise at a nearby table, humoring his acolytes by recounting the miracle of how he was raised from the dead in the stones of the ancient henge.

Suddenly a guard burst in through the great doors and ran up to Ela, red-faced and panting. "We've found some bones, my lady."

Ela glanced at Bird. Were these the bones of the man she

suspected him of killing? She didn't know what to think about the whole situation anymore. After yesterday's healing, she now half believed that God had indeed raised John Bird from the dead and that her doubt was a shameful sign of the poor quality of her faith.

"Where were they found?"

"By the bank of the river Avon south of Amesbury."

At least they weren't found inside the old stone circle. She didn't relish the prospect of disturbing the bodies of the dead warriors of King Vortigern. She'd always dismissed the tale of stones from Africa brought all the way from Ireland at the behest of an ancient king as foolishness, but since stranger things even than that had happened in the past few days, she couldn't rule the old stories out, either.

"Are you sure they're human bones?" There had been occasions when someone thought they'd found a human body, only to discover that a cow's thigh-bone could resemble a human one.

"They certainly aren't human. I don't know what they are, my lady. They're enormous! The bones of a giant or a dragon."

Ela's heart sank. Had John Bird's rambling nonsense about his dream of a dragon lit a fire in the imaginations of her guards? "Dragons and giants are creatures of myth and fairytale," she said quietly. "Surely there's some mistake. Perhaps they simply found stones of unusual shape?"

"It is very like a stone, my lady, but shaped entirely like a bone. It's one of the odd-shaped bones that run along a spine, and we've found the ribs and part of what looks like a leg of some sort. But it's huge. Like, if it were standing straight up it would fill this hall and bang its head on the rafters!" The man's eyes, even his whole demeanor, spoke of his shock and excitement over this discovery.

Ela wanted to cross herself. But, aware of all the eyes upon her, she governed herself to remain calm. "That is indeed mysterious. I would like to see these great bones. I shall finish with my petitioners and then ride over at once if you'd be kind enough to show me the way.

∽

Ela rode out with Bill Talbot and both her sons, as well as the usual phalanx of guards. She also summoned Giles Haughton to the scene to gain from his expertise with skeletal remains. She wanted to know if he could tell her what creature had left such impressive bones—if they were indeed bones at all.

"Perhaps it's the giant from Jack and the Beanstalk," said Richard cheerfully.

"That's a foolish story for children," protested his younger brother Stephen, who at fifteen considered himself very far from being such a mere child. "Everyone knows that giants used to live in Cornwall, far from here."

"Not so far that they couldn't walk this way taking a great many giant steps," said Ela.

"Don't tease him, mother," said Richard. "You know giants aren't real. You told me so yourself when Nicky was crying over one coming to his window at night years ago."

"That's what my mother always told me," said Ela. "But perhaps she was wrong?"

"I'm certainly curious to see these massive bones," said Bill Talbot, as they rode over a rise. "I've seen the remains of ancient sea creatures—great snails and fish a good deal larger than our own—frozen into stone near the Dorset coast. At the time, men said they were creatures from the darkest depths of the ocean that got washed ashore hundreds or even thousands of years ago."

"Frozen in stone, you say? How would that happen?"

"I'm afraid I couldn't say, my lady. None of us had seen such a thing before visiting that corner of Dorset. But when tapped with a hammer the dead creatures split and fell open exactly like the stone of the local cliffs."

When they reached the site described by her guard, Ela saw that the men were removing clay from the riverbank to reveal the stone beneath.

Giles Haughton had already arrived. "My lady, I wish I had got here before they had started removing the bones so I might have made a drawing of how they lay."

"Is it a human?" asked Ela with a frisson of unease. The spinal bones, four of which had been pulled from the ground and brushed almost clean, were each the size of a laying hen.

"It's too soon to say, my lady. But if it is, he would have been fifty feet tall."

Ela's sons jumped down from their horses and rushed to handle the bones with exclamations of shock and excitement.

"Do be careful, boys. They may be fragile."

"They're solid stone, my lady," said Haughton. "Though I suppose care should be taken that an edge doesn't break off. They lay embedded in an outcropping of similar stone, and have been chiseled from it."

"Do you know how bone turns to stone?" Ela asked again, hoping that Haughton might have more knowledge of the subject.

"I believe that the object itself rots away, as a dead body is wont to do, and the natural clay compresses in its place and turns into stone over time. If the body wasn't there, the stone would still be there, but without such an imprint on it."

"So they're ancient," asked Ela.

"Very ancient," replied Haughton. "Before the time of the Christ and even long before that."

Her boys oohed and ahhed, running their hands over the exposed rock face.

"I'm not sure whether to be relieved or disappointed that the guards found an ancient creature rather than a recent corpse," said Ela quietly.

"You still suspect John Bird killed a man?"

"I do. I think the corpse probably lies within half a mile of the stone henge. My guards are still digging anywhere there are signs of recent disturbance. So far, they've found nothing but animal bones and this...whatever it is."

"It's a dragon, mother!" cried Stephen. "It's not a giant at all. Look, you can see the leg bones." He pointed to an area of the stone face that had been cleared of clay. "They're not long like a human, they're short and with a steep angle, more like a rabbit."

"A monstrous rabbit?" exclaimed Ela. Now she did cross herself and only half in jest. "I always wondered why great rabbits the size of horses were so beloved of the scribes who draw strange creatures in the margins of their holy books. Will it have long ears, do you suppose?"

"Ears aren't made of bone, mother," said Stephen with some exasperation. "And all that's left here are the bones of this creature." Stephen turned to Giles Haughton. "Do you think it's a dragon?"

Haughton pretended to consider his question seriously. Or perhaps he did consider it seriously. It could be hard to tell when Haughton was joking. "I can't rule it out."

"And the miracle man said he saw a vision of one, breathing fire, right here in Salisbury," said Richard thoughtfully. "Perhaps these bones will come back to life?"

Ela looked at Bill Talbot, wondering what he'd been teaching her sons in their years of diligent lessons. Bill Talbot took the hint. "That is not likely, of course. Myth and reality do not often coincide. Myth is a realm where ideas are considered and theories tested."

"These dragon bones are certainly making me consider that dragons were once real," said Richard with conviction. "Even if they're all dead now. What are you going to do with the bones?"

"That's a good question," said Ela. She didn't want a pile of mysterious dragon bones in her castle keep. People would come to gape at them, possibly from all over Wiltshire and beyond, and create a nuisance underfoot.

"I'd be happy to take custody of them and put them in the mortuary if that suits you," offered Haughton. "I'm most curious to put them back together and see what kind of creature they make. It would be ideal if the entire rock face could be lifted and put there in one piece, but alas we don't have the wizard Merlin here to help us move great pieces of stone." Now his eyes did twinkle with amusement.

Ela was relieved to see that he hadn't entirely departed on a flight of fancy. "A man coming back from the dead, and now a dragon? Whatever will happen next?"

"Perhaps these strange happenings are a sign that Judgment Day is at hand," said Richard, who'd grown serious.

"I do hope not! Sir William said I could fight in a tournament next year," protested Stephen. "If I could just win a joust at a tournament I'm sure I wouldn't mind Judgment Day all that much. But it would be a shame to waste all the training we've done these past years."

Ela looked at Bill and they both laughed. Stephen laughed, too. Even Richard laughed. But then Bill said, "I shall say some extra prayers tonight for the protection of Salisbury and all England."

"And I shall thank you for it," said Haughton.

A guard came running up, red-faced and panting. "My lady,

a body has been found." He glanced at the giant bones. "A human one. Or the remains of one. A farmer has discovered it in his pig sty. He's brought what's left of the remains to the hall in a sack."

Ela crossed herself again and turned to Haughton. "God have mercy on that poor soul. We'll come at once."

CHAPTER 8

*E*la arrived back at the castle with Haughton and sent her sons off to attend to their studies with Bill Talbot. She didn't want a sack of bones emptied onto a table in the hall, so she asked the guards to escort the man to the mortuary, where she would meet him at once.

A guard introduced the farmer as Alfred Sebold. He was a man well into middle age, his gray hair covered with a leather cap. His weather-wizened visage wore an earnest expression. Ela recognized him in passing from the marketplace, though she didn't remember his ever having come to her hall on business.

"Good day, my lady," he said. "I'm sorry to bring you such startling and horrible news." He held out the crudely woven sack, which was damp and dirty and distorted by its grisly contents. Sebold looked at Haughton as if asking whether he should reveal the gruesome remains in the presence of a lady.

"Please place your bag on the table," said Ela, commanding both her features and her stomach to stay steady. "And the coroner will examine them."

Sebold heaved the sack onto the scarred wood table, where it settled with a dispiriting thud. A piece of homemade string held the ragged ends closed, and Haughton worked it open with his fingers.

The odor of the contents reached Ela's nostrils and made her stomach clench. These were not the bones of some long-dead creature emerging from the soil in the spring thaw. Whatever Alfred Sebold had in his bag had died recently enough to still be putrid.

Once he'd removed the string, Haughton carefully rolled back the ends of the bag, peeling it back from the bag's contents. He fished out a small piece of what looked like bone, but with ragged ends, and then a partial skull, mostly defleshed, but with an almost full head of hair.

Ela grabbed the edge of the table as a wave of nausea rose through her. The smell, combined with the half-eaten appearance of the human head, was too much for even her strong stomach.

"Are you well, my lady?" asked the guard, hurrying forward as if to catch her before she fainted to the stone floor.

"I'm fine, thank you," she said rather too curtly.

"Such a sight turns even my stomach," said Haughton soberly. "Despite my many years of experience handling death. And this is, without doubt, a human skull and recently dead."

"The hair is the same color as the man Bill and I saw lying dead in the circle of stones."

"And the same color as the hair of John Bird," observed Haughton.

"Is it, though? It seems a shade or two lighter." This man's hair—or what was left of it, plastered to the remains of his skull—had red tones and perhaps even some blonde strands. It was unquestionably brown, but Ela would describe it as light brown. "John Bird's hair is more of a solid nut brown. Let's call for Bill Talbot and ask him if this matches his recollection of the man we saw."

A guard was sent to fetch Talbot.

"He's been eaten by my pigs," said the farmer quietly. "I found it right inside the darkest depths of the sty. Might have been there for days. I don't normally go in there myself, as the roof is barely waist high, but the smell disturbed me. I thought a wild creature might be trapped inside the sty, so I bent down and climbed in. I found these remains right in the back. I wondered if someone hid in there and didn't realize that pigs will knock a man down and eat him whole."

Ela crossed herself and looked at Giles Haughton. "I don't suppose there's any way to learn if the man was alive or dead when he entered the pigsty?"

"Not from these fragmentary remains, I'm afraid. I am fairly confident that it's a man, based on the size of the skull and the length of what's left of the hair. He's not an old man, as there's little visible gray in his hair. Likely under forty and perhaps younger. Not a raw youth either, from the wear on his molars."

"Were there any items of clothing or other possessions found inside the sty?"

"I didn't see any, though I might have missed something. It's that dark in there and I was in a bit of a state, as you can imagine."

Bill Talbot arrived and agreed that the hair color did match the man they'd seen lying dead in the circle of stones.

"But I thought that man rose from the dead? That's what my wife told me," said the farmer.

Ela didn't want to start gossip that she disagreed with the bishop and nearly every soul in Salisbury, so she simply said. "There are certainly miracles and mysteries afoot. Let us accompany you to your farm so we can see the sty where you found these remains."

～

Ela asked Bill Talbot to come to the farm, just in case she needed to refer back to his memory of that fateful morning when they saw the body. They rode with Haughton and several guards and summoned jurors to witness the scene since their evidence might be needed for a future trial…of someone.

Alfred Sebold's small farm lay very close to the great stone henge but hidden from it by a thick copse of woods. The smallholding held an assortment of pigs and chickens and not much else. The pigsty was a low, tunnel-like structure made from bits of old scrap wood and half-heartedly thatched with rotting straw. She couldn't imagine how a man could climb inside it without getting down on all fours.

"It still smells rather putrid," observed Haughton. "I wonder if there are more remains inside?"

"Can we perhaps dismantle the structure, to better observe it in daylight?"

Farmer Sebold made quite a fuss about the trouble he'd had to build the sty, but Ela reassured him that she'd send men to reconstruct it, so he finally relented.

The farmer chased his pigs into a nearby pen of wattle fencing. Ela's guards then pulled the sty apart and reduced it to a pile of sticks and a heap of moldy straw. Haughton spotted several more bone fragments in the dark, malodorous mud and found a ragged fragment of green cloth.

"There's nothing here to aid in identification of the body," observed Ela, praying that her stomach would hold.

"We have a fair amount with the remains of the skull. Almost half the teeth are still in it."

"Unfortunately, Bill and I didn't see the dead man's teeth as he was lying face down."

"I shall keep his remains in the mortuary for now in the hope that we can find out who it is," said Haughton. "We can send out word that a body has been found and ask messengers and town criers to spread the word. Hopefully, a relative will come forward."

~

Two days later, a woman reported that her husband had gone missing. She'd walked from a good distance away, on hearing that the coroner sought news of a missing person.

"My husband went to meet a man about a cow. He took the money he'd got for selling the last of our grain from last year's crop. He said he would be gone for a bit as the cow was half a day's walk away and he'd have to walk back home with the cow, which—as I'm sure you know—is not always easy."

The woman, who identified herself as Ida Huntley, was younger than Ela but not in the first blush of youth. She wore rustic, homespun clothing, and had a baby in her arms and two young children tugging at her skirts. The busy atmosphere of the hall made her anxious at first, but she found her voice as she talked. "And I've been waiting for him to come home. I thought maybe he got drunk and—pardon me, my lady, but sometimes men do such things when away from home, don't they?"

Ela refrained from agreeing even though she knew it was true.

"But he's been gone for a week now and I'm worried. I've had to collect the wood and chop it myself—that's usually his work—and we've no cow to milk because our old one died, so I've had no butter and cheese for the children."

"Could you please describe your husband?"

"He's normal height, I'd say." She held up her hand, indicating as much. "Brown hair, brown eyes. Not thin and not fat. When I describe him, he sounds like every man in England, doesn't he?"

He also sounded just like the body Ela and Bill had seen in the stone circle. And like John Bird…

"Where's Dada?" asked the oldest girl, who wasn't more than six. She seemed to ask the question of Ela as much as of her mother.

"We're hoping to find that out as soon as possible," said Ela softly. "Does your husband have any distinguishing features?"

"Not really, my lady. His teeth do cross over a little in front. Just a very little, mind you. You wouldn't notice it if you were having a quick word with him."

Ela glanced at Bill. Neither of them had seen the dead man's teeth while he lay in the stone circle because he lay face down. She couldn't recall such a detail from the grisly remains of the skull found in the pig sty.

"Your husband started north of Avebury early in the morning. Would he have passed near the old henge on his way to Salisbury?"

"I suppose so, my lady."

"Who was he meeting to buy the cow?"

"My Jack told me he was a respectable farmer and the cow was a proven milker from quality stock. He said she threw the finest calves in Wiltshire."

"That does sound like quite a cow," said Ela. "Did its appearance match this marvelous description?"

"I don't know. He didn't have it with him."

A SURFEIT OF MIRACLES

"Did your husband mention the name of the man selling the cow?"

She hesitated as if searching her mind. "I don't believe he did. He said the man wasn't from these parts but had come here looking for a buyer for his cow."

"It seems odd, then, that he didn't have the cow with him when he came upon your husband. Did your husband say why this man wanted to sell such a valuable beast?" asked Ela.

"I suppose it was the same reason any farmer sells a cow," said the woman, looking at Ela as if she might be simple. "For money."

"Indeed. But he didn't have some story or reason behind it? I'm just trying to learn more about this person your husband went to meet."

"Not that I know of." The woman shifted the baby on her hip and looked about her, taking in the crowd of people in the hall. "I heard that there was a strange man in Salisbury, working miracles."

"There is," said Ela reluctantly. "A strange man." Despite her spoken promise to the contrary, she wasn't yet willing to admit to actual miracles being performed.

"I wonder if he might be able to work a miracle and bring my husband home?"

Ela wondered if the miracle man might also be the mysterious cow peddler. "I don't suppose you met this man, who promised your husband such a wonderful cow?"

"Well, I wasn't introduced to him but I did see him from a distance. My husband spoke to him in the lane. He told me he invited him in for a bit of bread and cheese, but the man said he was in a hurry to get back to his cow to take it to graze."

Excitement prickled Ela's fingertips. She still believed that a murder had been committed. Might they finally be close to identifying both the murderer and the murdered man? "Would you recognize the man if you saw him again?"

"I think I would, yes."

∼

Ela set out at once for the market square. She had it on good authority, from Matthew Hart and others, that John Bird was spending most of his days there. She'd attempted to keep him confined to the castle—for his safety, she'd said—but the bishop protested that the people needed to see God's work in their midst.

Ela approached with Ida Huntley, carrying her baby and with her two older children grabbing at her skirts. Bird sat on a chair in the middle of the market, between two stalls. People flocked around as if to taste his wares, but instead of butter or kegs of ale, he offered stories and blessings in exchange for their hard-earned money.

Ela glanced back at Ida Huntley. The woman looked about her nervously. She wasn't used to being far from her remote farm and surrounded by strangers, especially in the troubling circumstance of her husband's disappearance. She kept fussing over her children as if she worried about losing one in the throng.

"Do you recognize the man you saw at your farm?"

"Goodness, I hardly recognize myself in this crowd of people." Ida adjusted her kerchief.

"We shall walk through the market stalls. Do tell me if you see him."

They walked past a stall of baskets woven from reed and willow, and another with great cheeses wrapped in waxed cloth. Ida peered at the proprietors: the first was a girl of sixteen or so, and the second was an old man with a beard.

Next along their route was John Bird, whose crowd

dwarfed those at the other stalls. "Is this the man that was raised from the dead?" whispered Ida, with a look of panic on her face.

"Yes, it is." Ela searched her expression for signs of recognition. "Does he look familiar to you?"

John Bird's wardrobe had improved significantly since his arrival in Salisbury. Instead of a plain undyed tunic drenched with blood—his or someone else's—he now wore a thick gray cloak thrown back to reveal a rich blue tunic trimmed with red. A smart black wool hat covered most of his brown hair and his new leather shoes bore no road dust.

"Oh, I only just heard of him. I've never seen him with my own eyes before." The baby started fussing, and she rocked it up and down on her hip.

Ela felt disappointment sink through her. "So he's not the man that came to sell your husband the cow?"

Ida stared at her as if she'd lost her mind. "The miracle man? Why—" Then she frowned and looked back at him. "Well, the man who came wore plain clothes and this one is proud as a peacock. But I suppose the man who came was of middling height, and with brown hair...and this man has the same."

"He looks like Dada," said the oldest. "His hair's the same color."

"Be quiet, Annie," said Ida sharply. "Don't speak unless you're spoken to."

The girl's face crumpled. Her comment intrigued Ela. If Wulf Huntley looked just like John Bird then it seemed even more likely that he was the dead body that she and Bill had seen in the circle of stones that morning.

"What of his face?" Ela asked Ida. "Does this man's face look similar to your husband's?" John Bird had lamentably unremarkable features, without either striking beauty or notable ugliness. He had the perfect face and build for a man who wished to pass unnoticed in a crowd.

"I don't know. I'd like to say no, as his overall appearance is so different, but I can't be sure. I suppose I didn't get a good enough look at the farmer who came. I was a good distance away with some bushes in the way for some of the time."

Ela glanced at little Annie for confirmation, but the girl turned her head away and buried it in her mother's hip. Ela focused back on Ida. "But you couldn't be sure that it *isn't* the same man?"

Ida shifted the baby on her hip for the hundredth time. "I don't think I could."

"Did you hear the man's voice?"

"I didn't. I knew he was talking as I could see him making gestures, but what with the chickens squawking in the yard I couldn't hear a word."

"Gestures, you said?" Ela's ears pricked up. John Bird had an animated manner about him, always waving his arms about or shifting from foot to foot. "Do this man's gestures seem similar?"

Ida Huntley peered at John Bird. Who suddenly turned and looked right at her. She let out a tiny, almost inaudible gasp as if she'd been caught doing something she shouldn't. He stared at her for a moment, then spoke. "Sister, come here."

CHAPTER 9

Ida Huntley looked at Ela with panic in her eyes. "Me?"

"He means you, I think, yes." Ela wondered what John intended to do with the woman. Did he recognize her as the wife of the man he killed? She knew she was letting her imagination run away with her since she had no proof that he'd killed anyone at all. Still…

"Me?" Ida Huntley seemed reluctant to step forward into the crowd around John Bird, especially with her young children in tow.

"Yes, dearly beloved daughter of God, with your sweet ones gathered around you like the Madonna with her holy child."

Ela wanted to roll her eyes at Bird's flowery language. Did he think he now had the authority to talk like a bishop?

Ida hesitated for a moment, then stepped into the crowd, which parted as she moved toward Bird. He sat on a high wooden stool, the kind some shopkeepers sat on so they could see all around their market stall.

"What brings you to Salisbury today, dear sister?" His

hands, often waving wildly about, sat in his lap. Ida's children stared up at him.

"I come seeking news of my husband, Wulf Huntley, who has vanished into thin air."

Ela watched Bird's face closely to see if he'd react to the name. He didn't. Or at least not visibly. "Come, let us pray together for his safe return."

The crowd stirred and murmured for a moment before joining in as he led them in a prayer for the safe deliverance of Wulf Huntley to his wife and family.

Ela's lips remained still, even after she saw one or two people glancing at her to gauge her reaction. Normally, the sight of townspeople joined together in prayer would fill her heart with gladness and gratitude for the presence of the Holy Spirit among them.

This time, however, she felt the presence of an entirely different kind of spirit.

"Praise be to God for his intercession in our humble affairs!" boomed a voice from behind her. Ela turned with a gasp to see that the bishop had moved up behind her. "You are not joining the people in prayer, my lady?"

"The Lord hears my prayers without me uttering them in the marketplace," she replied quietly. How dare he question her piety in front of the people of Salisbury?

Bird's face lit with a smile for the bishop. "Dear Bishop de Bingham, join us as we pray for the safe and urgent return of this woman's missing husband. I feel sure that he will be back with us before sundown."

Ela suspected that he was already close by, his remains contained in a soiled linen sack now safely stored in the mortuary. Still, she murmured the words, "Praise be to God," along with everyone else so as not to draw further attention to her lack of enthusiasm for Salisbury's new "miracle man."

Ela saw people dropping coins into a basket near John

Bird's feet. They also brought offerings of food, including pies and cakes, which they unwrapped to show him. She watched as two cowled brothers, presumably there with the bishop, picked up the gifts and transferred them to a nearby wagon.

The crowd continued to pray aloud, and Ida Huntley with them. Ela decided to go visit Thomas Thicke and see how he was getting on after his seemingly miraculous healing.

∼

ELA LED her guards to Thomas Thicke's door. He lived in a small, crooked house near the castle's outer wall. The guard knocked three times before a rather harried middle-aged woman answered it.

"What do you want?" she snapped, before looking past the guard to see Ela standing outside the door of her home. She nodded her head. "My lady?"

"God be with you, Mistress. Are you Thomas Thicke's daughter-in-law?"

"Indeed I am, my lady. Ruth Thicke is my name. I was slow to come to the door as I had my hands in the bread dough and it took some trouble to get them clean." She wiped her hands on a piece of cloth.

"I apologize for interrupting your baking, Mistress Thicke. I came to see how your father-in-law is faring since he suddenly found himself able to utter words in the marketplace."

Ruth Thicke's face brightened. "He's doing so well, my lady! More animated than he has been in years, and new words returning every day."

Ela found herself rather shocked by this news. "May I see him?"

Ruth Thicke looked less than thrilled by the idea of

inviting a countess into her humble home, but she muttered agreement and moved to the side. "He's sitting by the fire. Might be asleep for all I know."

Ela approached the old man slowly. "Master Thicke, it's Ela, Countess of Salisbury, who brought you to the castle to meet with John Bird." She felt a touch of contrition that she'd brought him and the others there to prove that Bird was *not* a healer. "How are you feeling?" She braced herself to hear about two pennies and one half-penny.

"Well, my dear lady, well as can be!" He turned to face her, eyes sparkling.

"God be praised!" exclaimed Ela, shocked and chastened by her own lack of faith.

"It truly is a miracle," said Ruth Thicke. "He still tires easily, but he can speak in full sentences again. He even remembers a few snippets of Latin! We are so blessed to have a true healer among us here in Salisbury."

"Indeed we are." Ela blinked, trying to process this new information. Was John Bird truly manifesting miracles, as the power of God worked through him? He never claimed to possess any magic or sorcery of his own but gave full credit to the Lord. And if he did possess such powers, was he also risen from the dead by the grace of God?

Ela focused on Thomas Thicke. "How long had you been without the power of speech?"

"Nigh on eight years," offered his daughter-in-law, before he could get a word out. "And the Lord knows that the whole family has prayed many times that his cruel muteness might be lifted. We'd quite given up hope when your man came to us and told us about the new healer."

Ela had sent Bill Talbot on the errand to round up sick people to present to John Bird. "I'm so grateful that you had the good faith to attend and give him a chance to try healing you." Again she felt pure guilt about her original intention.

"The bishop has said that he might put together a party to visit the pope in Rome and Thomas might go with him," said Ruth excitedly.

"Goodness, what an opportunity for a pilgrimage to Rome," said Ela. The bishop had certainly wasted no time in sending news of the miracles in Salisbury to Rome, though it would likely be some days before his first missive even arrived there.

"I'm too old for such travel," uttered Thomas, who hadn't said a word since greeting her. "I don't want to leave my home and travel halfway across the world."

"Quite understandable," said Ela. "I'm sure you'd prefer to rest in the bosom of your family."

"They won't make me go, will they?" His pale eyes grew wide.

"I don't imagine that anyone would make you go against your will," said Ela. "Though the bishop can be very persuasive when he's set his mind to something."

Having reassured herself that Thomas Thicke's powers of speech were genuine, she returned to the castle.

On the way past the marketplace, she observed the crowd gathered around John Bird. He sat surrounded by his phalanx of holy attendants, commanded by the bishop.

So he is genuine. She still couldn't quite believe it. But perhaps snobbery had led her to expect a man chosen to be an instrument of God to be raised in a noble home and educated at Oxford, rather than the son of a farmer or a tradesman. Jesus himself was the son of a simple carpenter.

But when she returned to the hall, new information sowed fresh seeds of doubt in her heart.

"We traveled all the way to Paignton and asked high and low for the mother of John Bird." Two guards, still road-spattered and weary, stood in the hall. "We visited the surrounding villages and even the two nearest towns. No one had ever heard of her, or of anyone with the name of Bird."

John Bird had told them that his mother's name was Mary and that she still bore the name of Bird, though her husband had died some decades earlier.

"Please stay for meat and drink as I will likely want to ask you some more questions after I talk to John Bird."

"We went to every cottage, even the meanest and most remote, my lady," said one man, looking anxious at this promise of further scrutiny.

"I'm sure you did, and I thank you for your trouble. Do rest yourselves. I shall send word to your commander that I need you here for the time being."

She summoned Bill Talbot to fetch John Bird from the market and bring him here to hear this news about his mother. She wondered what his reaction would be.

Bill Talbot returned, alone. "I'm afraid the bishop insists that Bird is exhausted from his healing efforts and that he's returning to the bishop's palace for the night."

"The bishop's palace? But he's quartered here in the castle."

"The bishop protested that a holy man should not rest his head alongside the brutes of the king's garrison."

Once again, Ela found herself bristling at the Bishop's implied insult. "Was Bird not even curious to discover the fate of his ailing mother?"

"The bishop made noises about praying for her, that she might be found and restored to him at once."

"And Bird went along with this?"

"He led all of them in a prayer, my lady."

"In light of recent events, I half expect her to appear in

A SURFEIT OF MIRACLES

my hall tonight." She summoned Bill closer so that no one else could hear her. "Do you get the impression that Bird is genuine?"

"I must admit confusion, my lady. He seems such an ordinary man, perhaps even the type of man who would sell flour weighted with sand or poor quality wool bound up in tight bales with good wool peeking out at the ends."

"I had him pegged as a trickster," said Ela softly. "Trying to fleece the people of Salisbury for a few coins before disappearing into the night as quickly as he came. But his healing of Thomas Thicke does appear to be a true miracle."

"And we have no proof that he isn't the man we saw left for dead," said Bill. "So we can't rule out that he has risen from the dead."

"You've reached the same conclusions as myself. But still, I can't rest easy."

"The bishop believes him to be genuine. I'm sure of that."

"The bishop has spotted a cash cow," whispered Ela. "Is John Bird managing his own purse of money, or do the bishop's men sweep his bounty away before he can touch it himself?"

"A good question, my lady. Because if Bird isn't even enjoying the bounty of his miracles, he would have no motivation to continue with a pretense, if indeed it is a pretense."

"A pressing question remains, dear Bill. Whose bones were found in the sty?"

"I suspect they're the bones of Ida Huntley's husband."

"Yes." Ela's heart clenched. She'd let Ida Huntley hope that the "miracle man" could bring her dear disappeared husband back. "I'm afraid I didn't even tell her about the grisly remains in the sack. I was more concerned with having her look upon John Bird and tell us if he was the man who'd visited her husband to sell him a cow. She was starting to tell me that Bird's gestures reminded her of the man, then he called her to his side. I must bring her here and interview her again now that she's had more time to look upon John Bird."

"Perhaps you should summon her before a jury?"

Ela inhaled deeply. "Perhaps I should. This is a delicate situation, though. Bird has stirred the local people to his side. They think he's a saint in their midst. I can't accuse him of deception and murder without making myself look like a villain. And truth be told, I'm not sure whether he is saint or sinner."

"A man can be both," said Bill evenly. "On a battlefield, it can be hard to tell the difference."

"I shall pray on the matter."

∽

BY THE MORNING, after some prayer and reflection and no little scheming, Ela had formulated a plan. She called a jury and sent guards to fetch Ida Huntley to her hall to provide what information she could about her missing husband. She also summoned Haughton to bring the remains discovered in the pigsty and the farmer who'd found them.

At the same time, she summoned John Bird to the hall to discuss the matter of his missing mother. If events of both proceedings should happen to overlap, then so be it.

Ida Huntley arrived without her children. She looked distinctly anxious at being brought before a jury, even though only three of Salisbury's oldest and least busy jurors could be roused to turn their attentions to the matter of her missing husband.

"No one is accusing you of anything," said Ela quietly, as she watched Ida's shaking hands. "We simply want the jury to have all the available information about the situation."

Ida told them the story of the man who'd promised to sell her husband a valuable cow, and how Wulf had gone the next day to meet him. Ela resisted the urge to renew her question about whether the man who'd come to her house looked like John Bird. She didn't want to find herself accused of idle speculation or even open hostility toward their local saint. That could come later.

Then Ela asked Haughton to discuss the bones they'd found. Ida Huntley's face turned white as he described the state of the corpse. He then produced the remains of the skull with its full head of hair. The smell had diminished somewhat since the remains had dried out. Still, the sight was not for the faint of heart.

Ida took one look and crumpled to the hall's flagstone floor.

Ela summoned Elsie to bring smelling salts. It took some time to get Ida revived and seated in a chair. "How did—? What happened—?"

"I'm afraid that the victim appears to have been consumed by swine," said Haughton softly.

Ida Huntley let out a whimper, and Elsie—hovering over her—tried to offer comfort. "But how?"

"The remains were found in a farmer's pigsty. It's possible that he took shelter there and found himself overcome by the pigs, but in my opinion, it's more likely that he was killed elsewhere and deposited there so the remains would be eaten and the crime concealed."

Ida, now shaking uncontrollably, couldn't form words. Every attempt came out as gibberish.

"Can you be sure that this dead man is your husband?" asked Ela, as gently as she could.

Ida nodded. Once her sobs subsided, she managed to say, "His two front teeth…you see."

Ela steeled herself to look at the skull, which had at least been cleaned of dirt from its undistinguished grave. The two front teeth remained, and one of them did cross very slightly over the other, just as Ida Huntley had described the previous day.

She glanced up to see that John Bird had arrived in the hall with a large entourage, including the bishop, at least two priests, and a veritable phalanx of brothers. Quite a few townspeople followed in their wake, presumably hoping to witness a miracle or receive the benefits of one.

Ela turned back to Ida Huntley. "My deepest sympathies on the untimely death of your dear husband, mistress. As sheriff, my immediate concern is to identify his killer and bring him to trial. Do you have any suspects?"

Naturally, she was hoping that Ida Huntley would immediately raise the matter of the mysterious stranger with the valuable cow. "None whatsoever, my lady." She seemed to have regained her composure, though she dabbed at her eyes with a handkerchief Elsie had brought for her. "He didn't have an enemy in the world. He was the kindest and gentlest man you ever met."

"Jurors, do you have questions for Mistress Huntley?" Ela asked hopefully.

The jurors were distracted by the commotion on the other side of the hall, where John Bird, now seated in a chair, gathered his followers around him like Christ when he fed five thousand hungry followers.

Matthew Hart looked at the other two jurors. "Wasn't there another man who went to buy a cow and got swindled out of his money?"

Thomas Pryce, the old retired thatcher, scratched his head. "I do believe I heard something like that. Cheated out of three pounds he was. Turned up with his money and there was no cow, then he was beaten and robbed. That was over Andover way if I remember right."

"Two or more years ago, though, wasn't it?" said Peter

Hogg, a farmer possibly even older than the other two jurors. "I'd almost forgotten it. Never did get his money back."

"Who was robbed?" asked Ela. She didn't remember the case, which would have occurred while John of Monmouth was sheriff.

No one could remember the man's name, since he wasn't local and hadn't been in Salisbury since.

"And was the culprit caught?"

"Nay, my lady," said Pryce. "No one knew who he was. His description fit half the men in Wiltshire."

"It certainly sounds like a very similar crime, but in this case, his victim ended up dead. It does seem odd that anyone would attempt to repeat such a heinous crime so close to the location where he got away with it once before."

"Criminals are greedy and greed leads to stupidity," muttered Peter Hogg. The others nodded in agreement. Ela had to admit that she's seen quite a few cases where men— and women—had repeated crimes, even ones that had gained them fines and time in the stocks.

"We need to find the man who suffered this crime so that he can provide us with a description of the perpetrator. His name will have been recorded in the rolls and I shall examine them myself."

She glanced over at John Bird, then back at Ida Huntley. "You are now acquainted with John Bird, who appeared in Salisbury at the same time as your husband disappeared." She paused, to let the coincidence sink in. "He's here in the hall right now. Does he look familiar to you?"

CHAPTER 10

Ida looked somewhat alarmed. "I did meet John Bird in the market with you yesterday, my lady. So he looks familiar from then."

"But, at that time, I asked you if you had seen him before…and you weren't entirely sure. And now you've had time to reflect. Does he look familiar?"

"No, my lady," said Ida Huntley without any hesitation.

Ela's heart sank. Even if Bird was the man Ida saw outside her house, talking to her husband about a cow, he'd had ample opportunity to bribe her or just convince her of his innocence since yesterday's marketplace encounter. The way he'd ushered her over at the very moment Ela had hoped to obtain an identification was suspicious in and of itself.

"You'd never seen John Bird before yesterday?"

"Never, my lady."

"Thank you, mistress." She asked the jurors if they had any questions for Ida Huntley, to help them in their search for the man who killed her husband, and they asked her a few more questions about what he looked like and what his voice sounded like. If anyone of them noticed that the description fit John Bird almost perfectly, they kept the thought to themselves.

Gathering her strength, Ela asked Bill—who sat at her right side—to bring John Bird over to them.

"Thank you, Mistress Huntley. You may take a seat."

"May I leave now?" Ida Huntley looked anxiously at the jurors as if she half expected them to accuse her of something. "It's my babes, my lady. I don't like to leave them alone this long."

Shock rang through Ela. "Your children are alone in your home?"

"Annie is quite capable of watching them but only for a short time. She won't be able to comfort the baby when she starts crying for the breast."

"Your children are far too young to be left unattended." She couldn't keep the scolding tone from her voice.

"My husband is gone missing and I have no other relatives."

"No neighbors?"

Ida hesitated. "We live in an isolated spot, my lady."

"No friends?"

Ida's lip quivered. "No, my lady."

"Good Lord, you must return to them at once. Please, if you are summoned again, bring them with you rather than leave them unattended." She ordered the guards to help Ida Huntley return home as fast as possible, and she saw Ida insisting to them that she was fine alone, and didn't need an escort, as they left the hall.

Ela let out a sigh at the thought of those poor children left alone in whatever hovel the family occupied. She prayed there wasn't a fire burning or a pot of water left unattended that a babe might fall into. Bishop Poore, with whom she'd had many differences, had made such dangers a frequent subject of his sermons and no doubt saved many lives in and around Salisbury. She resolved to visit Ida and make sure the family wouldn't starve now that their provider and protector was gone.

∼

ELA LOOKED up to see John Bird standing in front of her. "You summoned me to your hall, my lady." Dressed in his new finery, he looked more like a visiting noble than an itinerant robber.

"Indeed I did, Master Bird. My men traveled to Paignton to retrieve your mother and bring her to my castle, where we have a chamber prepared. They found that no one in Paignton or the vicinity had ever heard of her." She watched his face closely as she spoke.

Not a muscle twitched in his face, but his hands did fly up in a gesture of surprise. "I do pray that she hasn't been taken from us before I could reach her."

"If she was, it wasn't in Paignton," said Ela. "My men spoke to the local priest who assured them he had no parishioner by the name Mary Bird, living or dead. My men went to all the surrounding villages and even remote cottages and no one had heard of her."

"'Tis passing strange. She sent word to me not three months ago telling me to make haste because her time was short. It breaks my heart that she's gone and so soon forgotten by those around her!"

Ela wasn't quite sure where to go with this new line of nonsense. She looked at the men with him, holy brothers in their plain robes. Their blank faces gave her no answer. "I had a chamber prepared for her but it appears she won't be needing it. And it seems that you'll no longer need the chamber we keep for you if you're now in residence at the bishop's palace." She wanted to get a sense of whether he was there willingly.

"I'd welcome the chance to return under your roof to enjoy your generous hospitality, my lady," he answered, suddenly animated, his hands waving. "But the bishop is most insistent at keeping me in his care. Perhaps you could have a word with him?"

Ela had her answer. No doubt the bishop was taking his money and likely had no intention of giving it back. "Far be it from me to contradict the will of our holy bishop. I'm sure he has the best interests of yourself and all Salisbury in mind as he keeps you close to his hearth and heart." She kept a straight face and enjoyed the look of frustration that flickered across his.

"I must leave for Paignton to see what became of my dear mother." No doubt Bird realized that his days of making easy money in Salisbury were at an end and wished to depart—under almost any pretext—as soon as possible.

"It seems that such a journey would be in vain," she said with feigned sadness. "Perhaps the bishop might be persuaded to offer a Mass in memory of your dear departed mother." Bird looked like he wanted to argue. His lips twitched a few times. "I could have a word with him about that, if you like?"

"I shall speak to him about it myself," he muttered.

"Perhaps you'd like to meet with the people here in my hall, instead of the chill air of the marketplace?"

Panic flickered across his face. "Nay, my lady. The common people may be intimidated by the great stone walls of your keep. Better that I greet them where they pass to buy their daily bread."

"As you wish."

Ela watched him turn and walk out of the hall, five or six brothers hot on his heels. She wanted to laugh. If John Bird had come to Salisbury to shake coins loose from its residents, he'd been most successful. But between her and the bishop, she felt sure that Bird wouldn't be leaving Salisbury with even a clipped half-penny in his shoe for his pains.

If he left Salisbury. She certainly didn't want him to do that while she still suspected him of killing Wulf Huntley. And she wanted to know if he was the man who'd tried to defraud people out of money for an imaginary cow, so she had to find a way to keep him here until a previous victim could be found and persuaded to come to identify him.

∽

Worried that Bird might flee her jurisdiction, Ela begged the bishop to take great pains to protect him from harm. The bishop assured her that Bird was comfortably settled in a second-floor chamber, where no one might climb to harass him, and that sturdy brothers stood outside his door at all hours of the night.

∽

A study of the jury rolls for 1229 revealed that a man named Rolf White had been tricked into bringing three pounds to pay for a good milk cow, then beaten and robbed when he arrived at a remote crossroads to collect his new beast. Rolf White was located in a nearby village and brought to Salisbury to meet with Ela the following morning.

Since she was unable to conjure a pretext to get John Bird back in her hall so soon, Ela resolved to take White to the marketplace to lay eyes on him. If White positively identified Bird as the man who robbed him, she intended to call a jury and have Bird arrested.

White had a thick head of carrot-colored hair and a face

with small features crowded together in the middle of it. Though broad in build, he was lumbering rather than nimble, and Ela could see how a robber might find him a satisfactory victim.

She greeted him and commiserated about the terrible crime he'd suffered two years earlier.

"He hit me over the head that hard, my lady. I didn't think the pain in my head would ever go away."

"Could you describe the man who robbed you?" Ela had made sure to have Bill Talbot close at hand, in addition to two trusted guards, so she'd have witnesses to anything he said.

"Well." He scratched his red head. "He was shorter than me, but not too short, with brown hair of middling length."

"Dark brown or light brown?" asked Ela, hoping to get as specific as possible.

"I'd say somewhere in between dark and light."

"Did he have a heavy build, or slight?"

"In the middle. Muscled, but not large."

Ela couldn't help a tiny surge of excitement. "Would you recognize him if you saw him again?"

"I most certainly would, my lady. His face is scarred into my mind like a burn."

∾

ELA APPROACHED the marketplace with some trepidation. Once again, she was here to try to prove their local saint to be not just a sinner but a hardened criminal. She knew she had to be furtive about her purpose, even with White himself.

"As we enter the marketplace, I'd like you to look around and tell me if you see anyone that reminds you of the scoundrel who stole your money."

The marketplace was as busy as she'd ever seen it. Late January was usually a quiet time, far outside the growing season, but not this year. Tradesmen from miles around had got wind of John Bird bringing fresh custom into the town. They brought their cheeses, strings of smoked sausage and casks of salted fish, crates of live chickens, and baskets of root vegetables and piled them high on their stalls. The stalls now hunkered together cheek by jowl, so one could barely see the cobblestones of the marketplace.

Ela glanced at Dickie Willard, who'd boldly lied to her about his mother being cured, no doubt because Bird had bribed him to do so. Willard met her gaze for an instant then looked down at his wares.

"Is that the man who's been curing people?" said White, looking at Bird.

This was their first mention of the "miracle man." She probably shouldn't be surprised that his reputation has spread to every remote hamlet. However, she didn't want White to assume him innocent if he was the man who robbed him.

"Some call him that," she said quietly. "And thus he's dressed in fine robes that he didn't own a few days ago. Look very closely at his face and the way he carries himself and ask yourself if he looks familiar."

White turned to stare at her. "You think he might be the swindler?"

"I do not wish to put thoughts in your head, Farmer White. Please, take your time and make up your mind on the matter." She tried to sound nonchalant, as if it meant nothing to her, one way or the other.

John Bird looked at her, in the way people do when they realize they are being watched. Then he looked at Rolf White. Ela half expected him to summon White to his side as he'd done with Ida Huntley, and she gathered herself to insist on him staying with her.

But John Bird simply looked back at the person before him, a woman on her knees imploring him—in hushed tones—to heal some ailment.

Ela glanced at White impatient to know his thoughts.

"He's not the man who robbed me."

Ela's heart sank and she fought the urge to protest and insist that he look closer. "What makes you so sure?"

"Just not his face. I've got a good memory for faces." White continued staring at Bird. "The man who robbed me took his time selling me on the many merits of his imaginary cow. You could have milked three cows in the time he waxed on about her. I had ample opportunity to see every detail of his face and features. The man who robbed me had cheekbones that were a little higher, and his face was just a bit longer and narrower. Also, his teeth crossed over each other very slightly in front and—"

"His teeth?" A surge of excitement rose in her.

"Yes, his front teeth. One of them lay just a little on top of the other as if his mouth was too small for them as they grew in."

Ela frowned, suddenly very confused. The man with the crossed teeth—the skull found in the pigsty—had been positively identified as Ida Huntley's husband. He was another victim of the cowless trickster, not the perpetrator himself.

Or was he?

"Come, we shall return to the hall. I wish for you to speak with the coroner."

"The coroner? I'm not dead, thanks be to God."

"No indeed, Farmer White, but another man is who fits the description you've just given. I'd like you to look upon his remains."

J. G. LEWIS

~

Ela awaited Giles Haughton's arrival impatiently. It was entirely possible that Wulf Huntley's bones had already been buried, or worse, that they'd been given to his wife, Ida, for burial and would have to be retrieved from her care.

Haughton set her mind at ease. "The remains are still in the mortuary, sealed in a clay pot to best preserve them until such time as the investigation into his death is complete."

"Rolf White was robbed by the man who claimed to have a cow for sale. A very similar situation to the one Ida Huntley described. But he says the man who robbed him had front teeth that overlapped."

"It's not an uncommon feature, my lady. If you look closely you'll see that my own teeth overlap to some degree."

Surprised, Ela peered into Haughton's mouth, which he arranged in a rictus grin to best display his teeth. She'd certainly never noticed anything unusual about them. "I suppose I see what you mean, but it's very subtle. I'd never have thought to mention it if I was describing you."

"God willing, you'll never need to describe me for someone looking for me as either villain or victim," said Haughton with that characteristic twinkle in his eye. "But let me unseal the jar to show Huntley's remains to Farmer White."

The wide-mouthed clay pot was covered with a waxed cloth bound on tightly with twine. Haughton unwound the twine and lifted the cloth to reveal the contents. "It's but a skull and little else," he cautioned Rolf White.

"Never fear, I've butchered enough animals in my time that I have a strong stomach." Still, Ela could sense Rolf White bracing himself for the unpleasant sight.

Unwrapped, the grisly remains sat on the mortuary table. Long strands of brown hair and dried shreds of flesh still clung to parts of it. Most of the lower jaw was gone, but the front of the upper jaw sat intact in the skull.

"Aye, that's him. I said I have an eye for faces. That's the teeth of the man who promised me the cow, and who beat me and robbed me. I can't say I'm sad to see him in this condition as I dare say he had it coming. Who is he?"

Ela glanced at Haughton, wondering if they should tell him. Haughton cleared his throat. "We believe this skull belongs to a local man named Wulf Huntley. His wife reported him missing some days ago. She said he'd gone to meet a man who promised to sell him a cow."

Rolf White blinked at him. "I don't have the sharpest mind in all Wiltshire, but something doesn't fit here."

"Indeed it does not," said Ela. She looked at Haughton. "Do you think Ida Huntley was lying?"

"I suppose she'd hardly come into your hall and say that her husband went out to rob a man and didn't come home."

So, it was the swindler who lay dead in the stone circle that fateful morning. What did he have to do with John Bird? Ela felt deflated. She'd pinned her hopes on a positive identification from Rolf White and now she had to start all over again. "I suppose if this man made a business of swindling others out of their hard-earned money, there might be more than one man in Wiltshire who wished him dead."

"I dare say, but I didn't kill him," said White, perceiving the new direction of her thoughts. "I didn't know who he was or where he was from, and I hadn't seen him since."

"I suppose we should compile a list of men who claim to have been robbed by Huntley," said Ela. "Perhaps one might have a special motive to end his life. Also, I shall pay a visit to Ida Huntley to see what information I can tease out of her."

CHAPTER 11

Early the following morning, Ela set out with Petronella and four guards to visit Ida Huntley. Since one of her men had driven Ida home from her jury interview yesterday, they knew where she lived. Ela already intended to visit the family to learn what alms they needed. Now she had a lot of other questions on her mind.

"What forest is this?" asked Petronella as the cart took them deeper into it. The bare branches cast harsh shadows in the winter sunshine. The road dwindled to a cart track and Ela feared it would narrow into a footpath.

"It's part of the Chute Forest that extends for many furlongs in every direction."

"It's where the outlaw hid, isn't it?"

Ela remembered her strange encounter with the outlaw a few years earlier, during her first term as sheriff. "It is indeed. It's dense and broad and empty enough to hide a band of outlaws."

Petronella glanced over her shoulder as if brigands might spring from behind the encroaching tree trunks. "Why would she live out here so far from civilization?"

"If her husband was a thief and they're living as squatters on someone else's land, that would explain the remote location."

They did have to dismount from the cart for the last leg of the journey. The guard who'd dropped Ida home had insisted on accompanying her to her door, so he knew which track to follow to find her remote home.

Ida's house was on top of a rocky mound encircled by brambles except for a small opening. The Huntleys had chosen a desolate spot unlikely to be invaded by the king's hounds and horses as they hunted in the forest.

The tiny cottage was fashioned from narrow logs sticking straight up from the ground like a paling fence. No daub or whitewash covered the mossy bark of the strange shelter. The roof seemed composed of crisscrossing branches and cut turf rather than thatch. Still, the construction looked solid enough. A wisp of smoke rose up through the roof, hinting at a fire inside.

A guard knocked on the door and announced Ela's presence. Ela overheard some commotion and a baby fussing inside before the door—made from old timbers likely repurposed from another building—scraped across the earthen floor to reveal Ida Huntley's shocked face. "My lady—"

She held the infant in her arms and the older children hung back in the dark shadowy interior of the cottage.

"God be with you, Mistress Huntley," said Ela, trying to sound pleasant and not like an inquisitor. She didn't want to frighten the children. Also, Ida Huntley might have no knowledge of her husband's criminal activities. "How are you and the children faring today?"

"Not well, I'm afraid, my lady, since my husband went to buy a cow and came back without one, we have no milk or cheese or butter."

"Did you have a cow before? I mean, one that died?" She

looked at the leafless, wintry thicket surrounding the house. There was no sign that a cow had ever lived there, let alone recently.

Ida Huntley blinked as if trying to remember if she had or hadn't. "Not for some time, my lady. It took my husband some months to save up enough money to buy one."

She's lying. Ela had watched enough liars to see the telltale signs in her face. If she'd had any reason to be suspicious of Ida Huntley before now, she'd probably have seen those same signs back at the castle. There was no reason to prevaricate.

"I spoke with a man named Rolf White who was robbed by the same swindler a little over two years ago. He was able to describe him in great detail. He told us that the man who beat him and stole his money had front teeth that overlapped very slightly."

Ida's face twitched and she shifted the baby on her hip so suddenly that Ela wondered if she'd almost dropped her in shock.

"We showed him the remains that you positively identified as your late husband's, and he confirmed that they belonged to the man who robbed him."

"But that's impossible," protested Ida Huntley. "It's a mistake. He's confused—"

"Go away!" shouted the oldest child, who peered out from behind her mother. She stared directly at Ela. "Go away!"

"Shh, Lizzie. Go sit by the fire." Ida Huntley's face now creased with worry.

"But she's saying bad things about Dada."

"I'm sorry to bring this matter up in front of your children," said Ela, "But it appears that you deliberately misled me when you came to my castle and told me that your husband had gone to meet a strange man with a cow that probably didn't exist. It seems that instead, your husband was the man with the imaginary cow."

Ida Huntley's lip quivered.

"Did you know your husband robbed people?"

Ida looked down at the dark earthen floor and nodded her head.

"How many people did he rob?"

"I don't know," she whispered. "He didn't want to do it, but it was too hard to eke a living from the forest in the winter."

"This is the king's forest."

Ida looked at her, her face taut with misery.

"Why are you living in the king's forest?"

The baby began to cry. "We had no choice. We were sent away from our village seven years ago after he argued with the lord. And he only shouted at him because Sir Peregrine insisted on having his bride rights."

"Bride rights?" Ela had a horrible feeling that she knew what Ida referred to.

"The right to take each new bride's innocence before her wedding day."

Ela felt fury rise within her. "Your former lord had no such right. Such a thing is not the law of the land and is abhorrent in the eyes of God."

"That's what my Wulf said. That Sir Peregrine was a pig and deserved to be butchered."

Ela froze. "Did your husband kill him?"

"Nay, but he wanted to. When he learned that Sir Peregrine was coming to my parents' house to fetch me, he fought Sir Peregrine off with a pitchfork. Wulf wouldn't let him near me despite my parents pleading with Wulf to let Sir Peregrine take me, as it was the custom. That night Sir Peregrine's men set fire to Wulf's house and drove him out of the village. I went with him."

Ela wanted to ask if Sir Peregrine had still managed to have his wicked way with her and if she and Wulf had ever officially married, but neither of those probing and intimate questions seemed appropriate under the circumstances. "I'm so sorry to hear of that. How did you end up here?"

"We just kept walking until I got too tired to walk. It's such a quiet spot that no one ever comes here."

Ela looked around the thicket again. "The king hunts in this forest and it's patrolled by his wardens of the eyre. Though I suppose this knot of woods is too rocky and uneven for galloping horses. But how do you survive?"

Ida went silent.

Poaching. If she confessed, Ida could be tried and possibly even hanged for poaching in the king's forest. If her husband had killed a deer or a pig the penalties were most severe, but even a stolen quail's egg could get a man locked up in the dungeon.

"You can't stay here."

"I suppose I could go back to my parents," said Ida, looking at her two children. "But they told me I was a fool to go with Wulf after what happened, so I'm not sure they'll take me back, especially with three mouths to feed."

Ela could hardly believe that the girl's parents would prefer for her to submit to the carnal lusts of their lord, but she knew such horrors were not entirely rare, even in this age.

"Where are you from?"

"Shalbourne."

The village was several hours' ride to the north of Salisbury. Ela sighed. "You must return with us to the castle for now."

Ida's face tightened. "Will you lock me in the dungeon? What will become of my babes?"

"Oh no, you won't be locked up. We shall find a place for you all to stay until better arrangements can be made. There's always work to be done in the castle for you to earn your bread. If your youngest is old enough to wean, you could be a wet nurse."

"She's old enough, but I've no food for her. I daresay I could suckle someone else's child if it meant food for mine."

Ela's stomach shrank at what she'd suggested. She wouldn't like to press another woman's babe to her breast as a means to earn a living, but there were advantages. "Being a wet nurse pays well. At least as wages for women are counted. I shall ask the doctor if he knows of any mothers in need."

∽

IDA HUNTLEY'S few meager possessions—a cooking pot, a hairbrush, and some hand-carved utensils, were bundled inside her faded clothes and loaded onto the cart. Ela advised Ida that her men would be back to dismantle the hut so that it wouldn't attract the attention of the wardens or offer shelter to some unsavory character in the future. If Ida Huntley felt pain at leaving her remote forest life behind, she hid it well.

Back at the castle, Elsie went to find a room where the young family might rest until Ela could contact the doctor about finding work for Ida as a wet nurse, or the bishop about the possibility of shelter in an almshouse.

∽

ELA WANTED to confront Bird directly to ask him if he'd killed Huntley but knew she couldn't risk calling a jury and accusing him in front of all Salisbury. He'd almost reached the status of a saint in the town, even though the bishop's urgent letters to the pope likely still hadn't arrived in Rome yet.

She decided to wait until sundown, which was still early at this time of the year, when Bird and his acolytes would be safely back at the bishop's palace. She planned to visit the bishop ostensibly to discuss the matter of Ida Huntley and her children. While there, she hoped for an opportunity to speak to Bird alone.

Ela set out with Bill Talbot and her guards just as the sun set. A bright almost-full moon illuminated the landscape after the sun disappeared behind the hills. She liked riding at night but got little opportunity to do it now that great responsibility curtailed all her activities.

The leafless trees allowed moonlight to shine down full on the road, which stretched before them like a silver river toward New Salisbury. Their horses' breath steamed in the cold darkness, and their jingling harness broke the stillness of the night.

"Bill, what's the matter?" She could see he was on edge and kept looking around them as if brigands might spring out of the bushes.

"You know how I feel about riding at night, my lady." His voice had an accusatory tone.

"You and William used to hunt at night!" she reminded him. "And I know you've taken my boys out to do the same."

"They're all trained swordsmen."

"And I am but a weak female who will need you to spring to my defense? You do have a point."

"There is nothing weak about you, my lady, but you do lack a sword, for one thing."

"Rest your trust in the Lord, dear Bill. If he wants me to reach Salisbury unmolested, then he shall protect us on our journey."

She could swear she heard Bill sigh, and he didn't look any less vigilant after her admonition that he should trust the Lord more fully.

Braziers lit up the courtyard of the bishop's palace, and candles gleaming in the windows presented a most welcoming aspect. Ela could hear choir boys singing in a chapel nearby, and the sound warmed her heart.

"I do miss having the bishop's palace and its chapels and cathedral within our castle walls," she said softly to Bill. "I'm not sure I shall ever recover from the pain of seeing them dismantled like the ruins of an ancient civilization."

"Beauty has risen from the ruins in the majesty of the new cathedral, My lady," said Bill woodenly.

"I know, I know. No one can believe it got built so fast, not even myself. Much as I resented Bishop Poore for conceiving it, he has left a miracle in our midst. I'm sure he wishes he were here to enjoy it." Bishop Poore had been translated to Durham two years earlier. Ela wasn't entirely sure why, but she knew it was unlikely to have been his idea when he had built an entire town around his new cathedral, with a peerless palace, an excellent school, and almshouses that set the standard for all the kingdom.

She and Bill dismounted. One of the guards knocked on the door and announced that Ela had arrived to see the bishop.

"After dark?" said the tonsured monk at the door. No one responded, which rather answered his question. "I shall see if he's at home."

At length, the monk ushered them in and seated them in the parlor. The new bishop had less luxurious taste than Bishop Poore. Instead of rich tapestries and shining silver, the parlor contained only a few plain chairs and a large wooden cross on the wall next to the fireplace. They accepted cups of wine, and Ela even sipped hers. She couldn't think of any compelling reason for Robert de Bingham to poison her.

"Countess Ela." The bishop greeted her with some

surprise. "What brings you here after dark? Nothing is amiss, I hope?"

"The days are so short at this time of year, Your Grace. Sometimes I find it's necessary to avail myself of the evening hours to conduct my business. Today I learned of a young widow living as a vagrant in the woods with her three young children."

"Oh, dear." The bishop looked suitably concerned.

"Naturally, I couldn't leave them to starve, so I brought them back to my castle. I know your predecessor Bishop Poore concerned himself deeply with the protection and education of young people, including the less fortunate, and I wondered if you might be continuing his good works?" She smiled, hoping she'd backed him into a corner.

"Well, of course, naturally, my dear lady. The church concerns itself with the welfare of its indigent parishioners. She's a widow, you say?"

"Yes, I'm afraid her husband was recently found dead. I'm still not sure what fate befell him—" She didn't intend to share the details of her current theory. "But I believe he was murdered. The family is not originally from this area, and the widow and her children have been left quite friendless and alone."

"Perhaps it would be best if she were to return to the bosom of her family."

"Ah, you think as I do, and I suggested as much. However, they fled their previous home because the noble lord who held it wished to make this poor woman the victim of his sinful lusts."

"Oh, dear."

"So naturally, I can hardly recommend that she return there as a defenseless widow."

"Indeed not." His thin face wrinkled with concern. Ela wasn't sure whether it was a concern for Ida Huntley's fate or concern for his purse at having to support an indigent family with church alms. "Though naturally, it is easier for us to find a place for a single man than for an entire family headed only by a woman."

"Is there any space in the new row of almshouses that are under construction?"

He cleared his throat. "I believe those are all spoken for."

"By those in greater need than a poor bereaved mother of three very young children? The youngest is but a babe in arms."

Bishop de Bingham made an appropriately mournful expression.

"I'd hoped that if a place could be found for her in the village, where there are other women available to watch her children, she might find work as a wet nurse. She's still in milk."

The bishop frowned and she felt him recoil. Perhaps the idea of a young woman as a milk-producing animal appalled him.

"It would be such a blessing for her children to grow up in an atmosphere of Christian fellowship and prayer. I fear they might otherwise have become young wild creatures of the forest!"

"Are they boys or girls?"

"All girls, I'm afraid." Ela knew that boys would have been of far greater potential interest as members of the choir or future students at the school. "But, they can learn to be good stewards of home and hearth and an asset to their future husbands." These poor girls would not have the dowry available to them to choose a life as holy sisters, so there was no sense in suggesting that.

"I will make inquiries, my lady. I'm afraid that's all I can promise for now."

To Ela, this seemed progress enough. "I would make a generous donation toward their support and succor."

His face brightened. "Your generosity and good works are well known in these parts, my dear lady."

She thanked him and resolved to turn the conversation to her next object of inquiry. "How fares John Bird?"

The bishop's face lit up. "His good works do not cease to amaze us! I have seen Thomas Thicke with my own eyes, speaking in full sentences as if he were never struck dumb at all."

"Truly wonderful, Your Grace. I saw the same myself. Have there been other healings?"

"Oh, several."

"Who? If you don't mind saying?"

He frowned and appeared to search his mind for a moment. "Well, they're so legion that I've quite lost count."

Ela suspected that as long as the coins were still pouring in, the quantity and even quality of any miracles performed were not so important. "Is John Bird here in your palace?"

"Why yes, my lady. I believe he said that he wished to spend the evening in silent prayer."

No doubt so that he wouldn't be forced to attend all the services for each of the canonical hours. "Might I speak to him for a moment?"

Bishop de Bingham looked taken aback. "For what purpose?"

Ela knew better than to confess she still suspected him of murder. Instead, she looked down at the floor and prayed that the Lord would understand and forgive a little white lie in the service of truth and justice. "It's a private matter, Your Grace. About an ailment I'm suffering from."

"Oh, dear. Rest assured that my prayers will join his for your full and speedy recovery, my lady." He hesitated, perhaps hoping he might come up with a pretext to deny her

A SURFEIT OF MIRACLES

a meeting with Bird. Apparently, he failed to find one. "I shall have one of my men knock on his door to see if he's available."

"Please don't trouble yourself. If one of your men can show me to his door I'm quite happy to announce myself." She glanced behind her to make sure that Bill was still there. Not that she had any doubt that he would be. Bill maintained a pleasant but impenetrable expression and—for the ten thousandth time—she congratulated herself on having such a stalwart companion at her side.

In very little time, Ela found herself upstairs and standing at the door of Bird's chamber. She thanked the monk who'd brought them there and dismissed him with a small donation of alms. She'd also brought an offering for Bird. One she was fairly sure he wouldn't refuse.

Bill knocked on the door. "Ela, Countess of Salisbury, is here to see you."

There was silence. Then a rustling noise. "I'm in prayer."

"We have brought the purse of money that Giles Haughton has kept safe for you."

Another silence, this time followed by a scraping sound like someone rising from a chair. They heard footfalls as he crossed the wooden floor on the other side of the door.

Then the door creaked open and John Bird stood before them, in finely woven undergarments, with an expectant expression on his face.

CHAPTER 12

"May I come in?" Ela asked politely.

Bird glanced into the room behind him, perhaps to see if there was anything he should hide. "You should give me the purse first."

"Oh, I don't think so," said Ela sweetly. "I have some questions for you."

"I don't believe you even have it on you," said Bird gruffly. He looked rather haggard. Being a local saint expected to heal all and sundry from dawn until dusk must be exhausting.

Bill produced the purse from a scrip hung over one shoulder, but when Bird reached for it he quickly pulled it out of reach. "All in good time, Master Bird. Answer your countess's questions."

"You've already quizzed me on everything under the sun, and I've demonstrated my healing powers in your hall."

"Ah, but many questions remain. If your mother lives in Paignton, why had no one ever heard of her there? Why did you arrive in Salisbury soaked in blood but with only a scratch on you? And a new question arises—" She hesitated, fixing her gaze on him, hoping to make him uncomfortable.

"What?" He looked agitated, now shifting from foot to foot and lifting his hands in a gesture of frustration.

"It appears that the man found dead in a pigsty was not simply the victim of a crime but also its perpetrator. He operated an occasional scheme whereby he would convince men that he was possessed of a marvelous cow, heavy with milk and capable of producing the finest calves in the land. Then when they arrived to see and buy this magnificent beast, he robbed them."

"What has this to do with me?" Bird glanced at the purse in Bill's hand.

"What indeed?" said Ela softly. "If you rid Salisbury of such a foul villain, you'd no doubt be doing its residents a favor. We suspect he's robbed half a dozen people, given that men are often unwilling to admit being duped."

"I couldn't care less if he robbed anyone, or didn't rob them."

"If he did rob someone, and was returning to his home with money he stole from his victim, we suspect he was murdered for his ill-gotten gains."

Bird threw up his hands in a gesture of frustration. "If, as you say, the man who killed him did you a favor, then perhaps you should seek him and offer him a key to the city."

"Perhaps I shall," said Ela, keeping her gaze fixed on his.

His eyes darted to the purse again. "I don't know that man, and I didn't kill him or steal his money." He looked back at her. "Do you have any other questions?"

"If you had killed that man and stolen his money, then where would you have hidden the murder weapon and the stolen money, I wonder?"

Now Bird did flinch slightly. *He's guilty.* She still had no proof, but she was as sure of it as she was of her own name.

"If I'd killed a man, do you not think I would have taken my money and fled Salisbury long before dawn? Why would I hang around to find myself an object of suspicion?"

"That is an interesting question, Master Bird, and one to which I do not yet have the answer. I suspect that a lack of non-blood-soaked clothing may be part of the reason. You could hardly flee the scene looking like you'd just fought in a battle. Blood stains don't remove easily without vigorous scrubbing with a good soap and you did not have that at hand."

"And he knew we'd seen the body," said Bill to Ela. "And would launch a murder investigation."

"Indeed," said Ela. "So, I suspect that you saw an opportunity to quash our investigation and line your own purse by rising from the dead to fleece the people of Salisbury. You just didn't reckon on the town having a sheriff with such a deeply suspicious nature."

"The bishop takes a dim view of your continued suspicion of God's holy work," said Bird, his hands quieting. "He knows that the Lord has brought me back from the dead and gifted me with healing powers."

Ela recoiled inwardly, knowing that what he said was true. "Here's another question. If you were raised from the dead—for the body that Sir William and I saw that morning was indeed thoroughly dead—then who killed you?"

"You already asked me that and made me re-enact the scene. If I knew, I would tell you."

"But you don't even seem to care to find the man who tried to murder you."

Bird rocked back on his heels. "I let the Lord guide my actions."

"So, you care nothing that a murderer may still roam the streets of Salisbury? I'm afraid I cannot rest my head easily in that circumstance. Would the Lord not want such a miscreant brought to justice?"

"He'll be brought to justice on Judgment Day," said Bird evenly.

"Indeed he will," said Ela slowly. "Indeed he will."

Bird twitched slightly, perhaps contemplating the fate of a murderer at the gates to God's kingdom. He wasn't a stupid man. She suspected him of a level of cunning she'd rarely seen before. And how was he healing people? Even if all the other miracles were no more than mirages, Thomas Thicke had his powers of speech back again.

Still, one thing intrigued her. "Does the bishop hold the money that you make for safekeeping, as I did?"

Bird fidgeted. "He does."

"How unfortunate."

"I don't imagine a man of God's Church would seek to cheat me."

"He has great expenses," said Ela with a half-smile. "Supporting the poor of the parish and keeping our great cathedral in fine beeswax candles and imported incense. And then there's the exorbitant cost of the remaining building works! The major work is complete, but there's still much expensive stone carving and ironwork to be done. I wouldn't be surprised if the bishop considers the people's donations to you as payment for your keep here in his palace."

Bird cleared his throat. She could see she'd touched a nerve. "Can I have my purse now?"

"It would be churlish of me to refuse it since I did promise it to you." She gestured to Bill to give it to him, which he did with obvious reluctance.

As they left, she noted with satisfaction that the house was well staffed with holy brothers coming and going in all directions. Given that sacred services and the preparations for them took place throughout the night, it would be difficult, if not impossible, for Bird to sneak out of the bishop's palace even under cover of darkness.

～

OVER THE NEXT FEW DAYS, Ela was too busy to worry much about John Bird. Bones from the giant skeleton continued to emerge from the ground. Haughton took great pains to observe the process and to arrange them in the mortuary so he might study the strange, giant creature that had left them buried so long ago.

The locals got wind that dragon bones were being unearthed, and they lined up to gaze on them with much oohing and aahing. John Bird, seizing on this new find, pointed out that he had dreamed of a dragon and that he was sure that this creature from his visions must be a sign from God.

"Did he dream about the dragon before or after the skeleton was found?" asked Ela of Bill one evening, as they sat discussing the mysterious chain of events. They sat in chairs near the fire, eating roasted nuts and sipping spiced wine.

"I'm fairly sure it was before," said Bill.

"Does that not strike you as odd?"

"You think he had some kind of premonition?"

"I don't know how to explain it otherwise," said Ela. "I hardly suspect him of planting the bones there himself, and I can't imagine he'd have known about them."

"And they are dragon bones?" Bill cracked a walnut and put the pieces of shell on his napkin.

"Haughton says that he can't be sure they're a dragon, but the limbs and spine do seem to at least somewhat echo the drawings of dragons we've all seen in manuscripts over the years."

"How astonishing. I was sure they were merely creatures of myth."

"Me too," admitted Ela. "And I'm still not sure they aren't, but I don't know how else to explain this extraordinary find."

"And I suppose we must congratulate John Bird because if it wasn't for our hunt for a missing human body, we'd never have found it."

"It is indeed very strange. I do wonder if the Lord has brought John Bird into our midst for some purpose that I can't yet perceive."

"Well, if he killed that Huntley fellow, I dare say he rid Salisbury of an iniquitous villain."

Ela sighed. "I suppose you're right, but I grieve for his poor widow and fatherless children. Ida now has a position in the household of the D'Auverley family. Marian D'Auverley gave birth to a babe and her milk has proven insufficient. Ida can live there with her children while succoring the D'Auverley's newborn infant." It had been surprisingly easy to find a place for Ida, who was quiet and uncomplaining about the matter. She prayed the woman's young children wouldn't suffer too much from all the upheaval. "Perhaps Ida will find a permanent place in her household. They just built a new wing onto their manor and have increased their staff. I wouldn't be surprised if Ida and the children even have their own room. It's certainly better than the poor babes being raised like young wolf pups in the forest."

"Indeed, my lady. Your good works are like miracles. The bishop should write to the pope about you instead of John Bird."

"Oh, Bill, don't say such nonsense. I find that much of the time I'm simply trying to stave off disaster."

"You're still worried about Bird, aren't you?"

"I am indeed. I wish we knew more about him. I'm quite

sure that everything he's told us is a lie. And if he did kill Huntley—presumably to rob him—then he's quite capable of killing again."

"Meanwhile, the bishop is pursuing his beatification."

Ela sighed. "I see the advantages of having our own saint here in Salisbury. Such an attraction would draw pilgrims from all over Europe, let alone Wiltshire. I'm sure the bishop has visions of great hospitals filled with beds to serve the travelers."

"I'm sure he doesn't mind his own name being read aloud in the pope's chambers either."

"Bishop de Bingham is not cut from the same extravagant cloth as his predecessor," said Ela under her breath. Bishop Poore had gathered great wealth and property to his bosom, and been one of the king's closest advisors, wielding power others could only dream of. "I believe he's a man of faith and conviction, but temptation can appear in strange forms."

∽

BY THE END of the week, another victim of Huntley's cow swindle turned up. He didn't come forward of his own accord, but he'd once confided the incident to a neighbor, who now spread the word across Salisbury. The man's name was Robert Bexley, and Ela summoned him to the castle to tell his tale to a jury.

Ela asked Giles Haughton to attend, and—perhaps impatient to pore over the mysterious bones in the mortuary—he wondered why. "Was there a death? It seems that Huntley's game was deception and robbery."

"Huntley himself is dead," said Ela under her breath. "And anyone he stole from is a potential suspect."

A man well into middle age, Robert Bexley possessed a grim aspect that included a deep groove between his eyebrows. It gave him the appearance of constantly frowning in disapproval. "I don't understand why I'm here," he said, once the jury took their seats and a hush descended.

"Speak when you're spoken to," said Bill Talbot brusquely. "And only when you're spoken to."

Bexley wore the plain homespun clothing of a farmer. His weathered skin spoke of a lifetime outdoors. He looked down at the stone floor after this admonition.

"Farmer Bexley," said Ela. "You're here because we seek information about the recently deceased Wulf Huntley and are informed that he robbed you two years ago."

"I didn't kill him," said Bexley, a little too fast. Ela heard Bill inhale to scold him again, and she touched his arm to stop him.

"No one has accused you of killing him. We seek to learn more about his criminal scheme. Did he offer to sell you a cow?"

"Waxed on about this cow as if it were the last good cow on earth," said Bexley. "He had a way with words, I'll give him that. More fool me to believe him."

"Do you keep a herd of cows?" asked Ela.

"I'm a sheep man, myself, but I keep a milker for the wife to make butter and cheese. Our old cow wasn't producing as well as she did in her younger days, so I thought it might be time to turn her into meat and buy a new one."

"Did Huntley approach you in the market?"

"Oh no. I can't say I ever saw him in the market. He came right to the door of my farmhouse and introduced himself."

"Did you not think it odd that he didn't have the cow with him?"

"Not really. It's not easy to move a cow. They have a mind of their own and weigh a ton. If I were selling mine, I'd be inclined to find a buyer by word of mouth before I dragged my beast all the way to market, then found myself having to coax it home again. He told me the cow grazed at his farm on the other side of the valley."

"Did you find it strange that you didn't recognize him?"

"Can't say I did. Salisbury's a busy town, especially with the cathedral and the whole new town going up these past few years. I see new faces every time I come to market."

"So he came to your house and described the cow. Did you settle on a price?" she asked.

"Yes, we negotiated and I beat him down to three pounds. He was asking four to start with." He looked pleased with himself for a moment, then seemed to remember that his victory in bargaining was over an imaginary cow. "He told me to meet him halfway and I could look the cow over before I made up my mind, which seemed reasonable enough. I thought maybe I'd find a fault or two in how she was put together and knock another pound off the price. Especially once he'd already walked her halfway to my farm."

"Where did you meet him?"

"We met at the crossroads where the shaft of the old stone cross still stands. He told me the cow was off grazing just past the hedgerow and ushered me into the hedgerow…" he paused, and a dark shadow seemed to cross his face. "He punched me in the stomach so hard I couldn't catch my breath. Caught me off guard, it did! I'm a bigger man than him and I didn't see it coming or I'd have knocked him for six. Then he thumped me over the head with something like a wooden club. I had a bruise there for weeks. Everything went black. When I woke up, he was gone and so were my three pounds and the tooled leather purse my wife had just made for me."

"I'm sorry to hear that," said Ela. "Why didn't you report it?"

"I felt like a right pillock falling for a story like that. I didn't want anyone to know I'd been fooled."

"Three pounds is a great deal of money," commiserated Ela. "Apart from your injuries."

"It is indeed! But I admit I was ashamed that I let a smaller man get the better of me and I didn't want others to know about it. If I hadn't confided to my neighbor when he asked about the bruise on my temple, I'd have kept the secret between me and my wife."

"I understand," said Ela. "But if you'd come forward sooner you might have prevented others from suffering the same fate."

Bexley contemplated that for a moment. "I heard others came forward and the thief still wasn't found. No one knew who he was. He used a false name with me. Said he was Tommy Weathers. I knew they were searching for the swindler but I didn't know where he was any better than they did."

"He was living illegally in the king's forest," said Ela. "In a most secluded spot."

"So me coming forward wouldn't have helped much then, would it?"

Ela sensed Bill tensing up beside her, and again she touched his arm to let him know she didn't need his intervention. "Thank you for your testimony, Farmer Bexley." She looked at the jurors. "Does the jury have any questions?"

The jury willing to devote their valuable time to learn about an unreported crime from two years ago was composed of only three trusty stalwarts, older men with time on their hands.

Thomas Pryce, the old thatcher, cleared his throat. "Did you ever see the man who robbed you again after the incident?"

"I did not," said Bexley. "I dare say he'd have ducked out of sight if he saw me coming."

"If you had seen him," continued Pryce. "What would you have done?"

Bexley seemed to consider this. "I'd have wanted to give him a piece of my mind."

"And perhaps get your three pounds back, I'd imagine," said Pryce.

"What man wouldn't?" agreed Bexley.

"And perhaps exact a little revenge for the way he set upon you," said Pryce, egging him on.

Bexley grew wary. "It's not my place to seek vengeance. I'd have reported him to the sheriff." He looked at Ela, perhaps hoping for confirmation that he'd said the right thing.

Ela did not suspect Bexley of Huntley's murder. He'd already demonstrated that he was a man who preferred to lick his wounds in mortified silence rather than to create a fuss. "Any further questions?"

"Huntley could have left you for dead when he clubbed you over the head, couldn't he?" asked Peter Hogg, the mostly-retired farmer. "I bet he didn't stick around to see if you stirred again."

"He wasn't there when I woke up," admitted Bexley. "But I'd hardly expect him to be."

"So, he might have killed you."

"Fortunately, he didn't. I did have a headache for a few days. But I had no desire to kill him if that's where you're heading."

"His method of robbery does sound like it comes with a high risk of killing the victim," said Ela. "I wonder if there are any unsolved murders that we might now attribute to him. I shall have a clerk examine the rolls from the last few years."

"There was a man found dead on a lane near Dinton," said Pryce. "A little over a year ago, while John of Monmouth was sheriff."

Illness had forced Ela to resign her role as sheriff for three years. Happily, John of Monmouth had been a just and decent sheriff during her absence. She'd watched some of the trials since they'd still taken place in her hall, but she'd been unable to keep up with the details of every incident in Wiltshire.

"I recall it well," said Haughton. "He'd been clubbed over the skull. It seems he'd tried to make his way home with his injuries, but bleeding in his brain felled him on the road. His wife said he'd told her he was going to market, but he wasn't found on the road between his house and the local market. He was discovered on a different road altogether."

"An encounter with Huntley is a distinct possibility," said Ela. She wondered if Huntley's young widow knew she'd been married to a monster. For all her difficulties, she was lucky to be rid of him. "It's frustrating that he can't be tried and punished for his crimes."

"At the very least he can be cast out of the walls and buried with the heathens and sinners."

"That would have been his fate anyway," said Ela, "due to his poverty and lack of connections." She asked again if anyone had questions for Bexley. No one did, so she told him he could go. He hurried out of the hall, clearly mortified by the whole proceedings.

After he'd gone, Dickie Hardwick, the retired butcher, cleared his throat. "There might be a dozen or more other victims of Huntley with a motive to smash his skull and feed him to the pigs."

The jurors agreed and one muttered that it was a fitting fate for such an evil man.

Ela didn't want to let the jury depart without planting one very specific flea in their ear. A flea that might bite her if not handled very carefully. She took a deep breath and looked around her before speaking.

CHAPTER 13

"I can't help but observe that the murder of Robert Huntley seems to have happened on the very day that John Bird arrived in Salisbury." Ela felt her heart pound as her statement lingered in the air. The jurors looked at her as if nonplussed.

Thomas Pryce scratched his head. "We don't know what day Huntley died, do we? His chewed-up remains weren't found until several days later."

Ela glanced at Haughton, hoping he might contradict this.

Haughton inhaled slowly. "It's true that I can't pinpoint an exact date of death due to the state of the remains."

Ela looked at Bill. She wanted desperately to suggest that the body she and Bill had both seen in the stone circle was the corpse of Robert Huntley—not the about-to-be-risen body of John Bird as everyone seemed to believe.

She silently pleaded with him for a moment. Bill stirred in his chair and looked confused, and she regretted not feeding him the words she'd like him to say beforehand. Or would that violate the principles of a jury hearing?

"Are you suggesting that John Bird might have killed

Huntley?" asked Peter Hogg, who'd been scratching his head for some time.

"It's not impossible," said Ela hopefully. "We know so little about him. He seems to have arrived out of nowhere and to have an astonishing talent for separating the people of Salisbury from their money."

"It's because he's working miracles," said Hardwick. "No one can argue with that. I've seen the miracles with my own eyes! I was able to chew the fat with my old friend Thomas Thicke for the first time in donkeys' years. I doubt that God would gift a man with the power to heal if he was a killer."

The other two jurors murmured in agreement. Ela's heart sank yet again. She glanced at Haughton, wondering about his opinion on the matter. He cleared his throat quietly, then pointed out that they had no actual evidence to suggest that John Bird had a hand in the murder of Huntley.

"But Bird doesn't have an explanation for the crime in which he was supposedly stabbed. He just says he doesn't remember anything. Did Huntley try to rob him and he fought back?" She hoped desperately to establish some connection between the two men in the minds of the jurors.

"Well," said Haughton, looking apologetic. "We're not even sure that Huntley was attacked, let alone deliberately murdered. He might have tried to hide in the pig sty and been assaulted by the pigs. It wouldn't be the first time I've heard of such a thing."

"Aye, Widow Dingle was killed by her pigs not ten years ago! I remember it like it was yesterday. Her son found her gnawed to shreds in her garden."

Ela crossed herself.

"Pigs do have very sharp teeth," agreed Peter Hogg. "And some of them have an aggressive temperament."

"Yes," agreed Pryce. "And in this case, they gave a villain

exactly what he deserved. A fitting end to a man who preyed on the people of Salisbury."

Ela looked at Haughton, wondering if he'd weigh in. Instead, he seemed to be deliberately avoiding her gaze.

Abandoning all hope of implicating Bird—at least for now—Ela dismissed the jury. She asked Haughton to wait and kept Bill Talbot at her side.

Before she could even start airing her exasperation, Haughton looked at her in what—for him—was a rather stern manner. "My lady, you know I respect your judgment on many matters, but I fear you are looking for a crime where one doesn't exist."

Ela looked at Bill in desperation. "But we saw the dead body in the stone circle! Didn't we, Bill?"

"We did indeed."

"And that man could have just as easily been Huntley as Bird, because they have similar stature and coloring, and even their features aren't dissimilar."

"It's a shame we didn't think to look at his teeth," said Bill.

"Yes, but we had no idea he was about to disappear. We went straight away to fetch a jury."

Haughton still looked doubtful. "I've seen a man look dead on the battlefield and come back to life when he wasn't expected to."

"I've seen it as well," agreed Bill. "Knocked unconscious with no appearance of breathing, then climbing to his feet like one risen from the dead."

She'd lost even her two closest allies. "You think I'm foolish to persist in suspecting Bird. There's something about the man that sets my teeth on edge. I'm sure he's more cunning than he seems."

"Not cunning enough to stop the bishop taking all the donations, though," said Bill with a smile. "So if he's after financial reward he'll soon grow tired of his current tricks."

"So you think they're tricks?" asked Ela.

"I don't know what to think," said Bill. "There does seem to be something to them. The people of Salisbury are a suspicious lot and wouldn't hesitate to tear him apart if they didn't believe he was genuine."

"What about you?" Ela asked Haughton.

He shrugged. "As the coroner, I'm forced to work with the proof I see with my own eyes or touch with my own hands. The evidence of him being a healer who was miraculously raised from the dead is currently stronger than the evidence to the contrary."

"Then I suppose the best we can hope for is that he'll tire of his new role and leave Salisbury." Ela hated the idea of a criminal going unpunished.

"The sellers at the market will be very unhappy to see him go," said Haughton. "He's brought more foot traffic to the town than the feast of St. Stephen. And if he's declared a saint, Salisbury will become a pilgrimage destination."

"Imagine Roger Poore's face when he learns that Salisbury has become a pilgrimage site in his absence." She took some pleasure in imagining Bishop Poore apoplectic with frustration that someone else would reap the rewards of all his cathedral-and-town-building efforts.

"You joke, my lady, but this is a serious matter." Haughton did look uncharacteristically serious. "I don't imagine Bishop de Bingham will look kindly on your efforts to lock his new proposed saint up in the castle dungeon."

"Perhaps you think it's more likely that I'll find myself in the castle dungeon for persisting with my efforts." She said it in jest, but neither Haughton nor Talbot smiled. And the silence spoke for them.

Chastened, Ela drew in a slow breath. "I appreciate your candor and will school myself in humility." She looked at Haughton. "I bow to your years of experience as the coroner and your knowledge of the need for solid physical evidence to prove a case."

"As I respect your zeal for justice, my lady."

"A zeal that I must temper with practicality."

Both Haughton and Talbot looked relieved. Perhaps they had worried about being expected to draw their swords to keep her from being placed in her own dungeon by the religious authorities. Was such a thing possible?

Most likely it was. And she would do well to mortify her pride in her ability to punish sinners when ultimately their fate lay in the hands of the Lord.

∽

Three days later, Bishop Robert de Bingham came to visit Ela in her hall. Arriving, as usual, with a veritable army of monks, he now sat in a chair by her fire, sipping on a cup of her best wine. "The process of having a marvelous event accepted by the church as a true miracle is quite an elaborate one! Naturally, the pope makes the final decision. I'm not entirely sure of the procedure, but I believe there is a special council of cardinals who investigate suspected miracles and pronounce them true or false."

"And these men would travel from Rome and interview Bird?"

"Either that or Bird would travel to Rome, under my care, of course." This was not the first time he'd expressed the idea and Ela felt sure he was nurturing the possibility. She could hardly blame him. She'd dearly love to make a pilgrimage to Rome. Many people of faith dreamed of such a journey.

"Which do you think they would be more impressed by, Bird rising from the dead or him healing the sick?" Ela humored the bishop since he was a powerful and important man and she couldn't afford to contradict him more often than was necessary.

"It is astonishing that there is more than one miracle to choose from, is it not?" De Bingham's rather kind brown eyes glowed with excitement. "Such a feast of God's glory right here in Salisbury."

"Indeed, Your Grace. We are truly blessed." It wouldn't help her cause—of seeing John Bird exposed as a fraud—to have the bishop see her as an enemy of his pet project.

"And when he's ascended into Heaven he may yet be declared a saint!"

"I know it was my father's fondest hope that Bishop Osmund might be made a saint," said Ela.

"He was the chaplain of William the Conqueror, was he not?"

"I believe so," said Ela, "And as Bishop of Salisbury, he built and consecrated the first Salisbury cathedral. But Bishop Poore raised the matter of him becoming a saint and his proposal was rejected. I suppose Osmund's chances of being raised to sainthood have probably been buried along with his greatest creation." The cathedral that had been Ela's childhood spiritual home lay razed and ruined, most of the stones carted off to form the foundations of the grand new cathedral just two miles down the road. "I dare say that Bishop Poore might find himself in line for sainthood for planning and building our magnificent new cathedral!" De Bingham looked rather enthused by this idea.

God forbid! She suddenly suspected that Bishop Poore might have been moved to Durham to prevent just such aggrandizement. She wouldn't be at all surprised if King Henry himself had commanded the bishop's move just to curtail his power and influence. She stifled a laugh as she pictured Bishop Poore dropping hints about the possibility of his future sainthood.

"To be sure, Bishop Poore is a great man, but I haven't heard of any miracles being attributed to him." Why had the bishop come here this morning? Ela had a line of petitioners forming just inside the doorway, waiting to see her on one urgent-to-them matter or another. "Is there something I can help you with?"

The bishop frowned. "Well, it's Bird himself. He seems to be growing restless and making noises about going to visit his mother."

Ela's interest was piqued. "My men searched high and low for his mother and found no trace of her."

"Thus he's concerned that she's come to harm." De Bingham frowned. "In my view, if an elderly lady has disappeared without a trace it's quite likely that she's resting peacefully in the arms of God. I don't wish him to go traipsing across the south of England on a wild goose chase when he has such important work to do here."

"He wants to leave Salisbury?"

"Just temporarily, of course. He accepts that Salisbury is his spiritual home."

"But you don't want him to leave."

"Indeed I do not! I'm worried that mischief may befall him. A man who can work miracles is very valuable."

"A goose that lays golden eggs," said Ela brightly.

"Yes." Then his face twitched. "Well, that's not exactly what I meant, but he's bringing lost sheep back into the fold of mother church. We've had country people visiting the town and the cathedral who haven't set foot on sacred ground in years."

"That is certainly a benefit of his presence. Do you propose to keep him here against his will?" She certainly didn't want Bird leaving to make mischief—and possibly even murder—in another part of Wiltshire. They still had no real idea who he was and where he came from. No part of his story had stood up to scrutiny despite messengers being dispatched to Norfolk to learn more about him. No one had heard of him there any more than they'd heard of his mother in Paignton.

"Against his will? Oh, dear me, I do hope not. I was hoping we might find a way to make his time here in Salisbury more pleasant. I had the idea that we might try to arrange an audience for him with the king." He spoke softly, and again she saw the gleam of hope in his eyes.

"The king?"

"Henry III is a man of deep faith, as I'm sure you know."

"He is, that is true."

"And he spends much time in the vicinity of Salisbury, between his estate at Clarendon, the hunting lodge at Ludgershall, and the castle at Devizes."

"He is certainly fond of this most pleasant part of the world."

"And, if I'm not mistaken, he's your children's cousin."

"Yes, my husband was his father's brother." Half-brother, but why quibble over fractions?

"Am I wrong in thinking that perhaps you have a little influence with our dear king?" Again, his eyes sparkled with excitement.

Ela found this whole idea quite perplexing. "Are you sure Bird wants to meet the king?" If he was the trickster and charlatan she suspected, he'd probably run a mile from such an encounter.

"Well, naturally, I haven't mentioned it to him. I didn't want to get his hopes up if the idea were to prove fruitless. Do you think King Henry might be interested in meeting a man who is lately risen from the dead and is working miracles in our midst?"

Would he? Ela suspected that Henry might indeed like to meet a man directly touched by the hand of God. On the other hand, she did not believe Bird was that man. The king was still young and impressionable and she didn't want to expose him to a potentially ruthless criminal. "I shall have to think on it, Your Grace. In the meantime, I'm still concerned with finding the man who tried to murder John Bird."

The bishop looked perplexed.

"Bird was found stabbed and soaked in blood. Even though he has been brought miraculously back to life by the power of God Almighty, as sheriff it is my sworn duty to bring his attacker to justice."

"Quite so," said de Bingham. "Do you have any suspects?"

"I rather think that Wulf Huntley might have been the one who attacked him."

"The cow swindler?"

"That's the one. He beat and robbed his victims when they arrived with money."

De Bingham frowned. "But why would John Bird want to buy a cow? He doesn't live in these parts. He'd hardly want to lead a milk cow all the way to Devon."

"I agree, and I don't think that he fits neatly into Huntley's usual scheme. But he did say that he was robbed. Huntley may have noticed him as a traveler and reflected that travelers often carry money. Perhaps he saw occasion for a crime of opportunity."

De Bingham listened, then sat silent as if his mind was working. "After robbing Bird—killing him!—he heard people coming and went to hide in the pigsty, where the Lord visited a fitting punishment upon him."

While this was not quite the scenario that Ela imagined, it was certainly a possibility. Huntley may even have initiated the encounter and then found himself overpowered or outwitted by a more cunning and capable scoundrel.

"It may have been Huntley that attacked him, but we can't be sure. His attacker may still be here in Salisbury. Thus it is imperative that Bird not leave the area until the crime is solved to my satisfaction."

"Oh." De Bingham blinked. "So you wish him to stay here, even if he'd prefer to leave?"

"Exactly, Your Grace."

Bingham looked cheered by this news. "Well, goodness knows I do want to keep him here. I will have to assure him that it's for his own good and the good of all Salisbury. I hope the news about our local sensation will reach the pope soon, if it hasn't already. I eagerly await his reply."

"Do let me know what the pope has to say on the matter. This is certainly a very interesting and auspicious time for Salisbury." She wanted de Bingham to think she was on his side in anxiously waiting for the pope to recognize Bird as a miracle in their midst.

She glanced over at her petitioners. Her head throbbed with the beginnings of a headache, and she wanted to get started on this important part of her daily business. "There are townspeople awaiting an audience with me."

"Ah, yes, so there are. Thank you for meeting with me and do let me know if you think the king would like to meet with our honored guest."

"Indeed I will."

∽

AFTER MEETING WITH SEVERAL PETITIONERS, Ela's headache grew more intense. She excused herself to attend the Sext service, hoping that quiet meditation would bring her relief. It didn't, and once the service ended, she headed to her solar for an uncharacteristic afternoon nap.

"Are you alright, my lady?" Elsie's voice woke Ela from her slumbers.

Ela sat up in a panic. She hadn't meant to fall asleep in the middle of the day. "What hour is it? Have I missed the bells for Nones?"

"You certainly have, my lady. It's past sunset and the children are eating their supper."

Ela scrambled to the edge of the bed to get up. Her head pounded worse than ever.

"You were deeply asleep. I spoke to you several times before you woke up."

"I don't know what got into me," said Ela. She shivered. "The room is so cold."

"It's not, though. It's hot as the cook's oven. I've kept the fire going for you since you looked so pale when you came to lie down."

Ela glanced at the roaring blaze. "That's very thoughtful of you, Elsie." She put her feet on the floor, which felt cold as ice even through her stockings.

"Let's get you dressed for supper. You sit right there while I do your hair." Elsie stuck four pins between her lips, shook out Ela's veil and slung it expertly over one arm, then took her barbette in one hand and fillet in the other. Ela sat, still and grateful, while Elsie arranged her headwear with practiced ease.

"You're a marvel, Elsie. What would I do without you?"

"Your hands are shaking." Elsie took one of Ela's hands in hers—a rather bold move for a servant—but Ela didn't protest. Her hand was indeed shaking. "You're trembling all over! I think you have a fever, my lady."

"That would explain my headache." Her head throbbed unevenly, like a cartwheel bumping over stones on a cobbled road.

"I think you should stay in bed for now. I shall see to the children and make sure they all eat their supper. I'll bring you a cup of soup if you'd like."

"Perhaps that is a good idea," said Ela, letting her head

sink back onto the pillow, veil and all. Suddenly keeping it upright seemed far too much effort. "Tell the children I'll look in on them later."

"I'll ask the cook to fix you some tea for your fever."

"Thank you. She'll know what to make." The cook had made many herbal preparations over the years, of both her own and Ela's invention, and her pantry contained many medicinal herbs. Perhaps a warm posset with an infusion of feverfew would help. If that didn't work…

∿

"My lady! My lady, wake up!" Ela heard Elsie's voice and became aware of tapping in the vicinity of her hand. She opened her eyes with great effort and saw Elsie's form—rather blurred—looming over her. "She's awake! Oh, dear me, my lady. It was an effort to wake you. You've slept like the dead. I kept checking during the night to make sure you were still breathing, but Cook and I had decided that if you were still asleep by the bells for Lauds we would send for the doctor."

Thank you, Elsie. Ela thought the words but didn't hear them fill the air of the room. Perhaps they hadn't traveled the distance from her brain to her lips.

"Her eyes have closed again!" she heard the urgency in Elsie's voice. "I'm that worried. It's not like her at all!"

Ela tried to think of something to say to reassure Elsie that she was fine, but the words, or perhaps it was the thoughts, were just a little too far out of reach.

"I'll head for the doctor's house," she heard Bill Talbot say. "And bring him back here myself."

"I'll fetch the smelling salts," said Elsie. "How's little Nicky doing? Is he still feverish as well?"

Ela felt her mind grasp the news that her youngest son

was ill. She opened her eyes again, but everything was an unfocused swirl of light like the surface of a pond at midday. She could barely make out the shapes of Elsie and the youngest children's nursemaid, who stood in the doorway.

"He's hot as a poker. He's trying his best to be brave, but he says his head hurts something terrible."

Ela struggled to push herself up onto her elbows, but her covers felt like a full suit of chainmail, heavy and pressing down against her limbs. "What's…what's wrong with Nicky?" she managed at last, in a thin, rasping voice.

"Oh, my lady! You're awake again. He's feverish, like you, and says his head hurts. Just wants to sleep and sleep. And he's saying strange things like he's having fanciful dreams."

Ela replied with great effort. "Let the doctor see him first."

"Yes, my lady. Don't fret yourself, I'm sure it's just a passing fever and you'll both be up and about in no time."

Yes. Ela heard the word in her mind, but again it failed to make the long journey to her lips. The doctor was coming. Doctor Goodwin was well versed in treating all kinds of ailments and would know at once whether they just needed to sip some calming tea and rest or whether they were in danger. And Ela knew from experience that he wouldn't lie to her about the latter.

CHAPTER 14

Doctor Goodwin was alarmed by the heat and intensity of Ela's fever. He told her that she and her son were both at risk of seizures and that measures should be immediately taken to cool them with cold water from a clean well.

Elsie rushed out to find someone to fetch the water and called for clean linen cloths. Soon she and another girl were dipping towels in the cold water and draping them across Ela's forehead and limbs. At the doctor's urging, they removed her clothes down to her fine chemise and laid the cold, damp cloths directly on her undergarment, soaking through the thin fabric. Soon Ela found herself shivering uncontrollably as the cold chilled her to her core.

"Oh my, I'm not sure this is good," said Elsie. Ela didn't seem to be able to respond. It was as if she could hear them from the other side of a wide river. "Cover her up while I find the doctor. He's in with Nicky."

She felt Rosie, a young serving maid, pull a sheet across her to cover her. The girl's young face was taut with worry, her big gray eyes wide, as she peered directly into Ela's eyes as if trying to see if anyone lay within. Ela continued to shiver violently, completely unable to stop the convulsive motions, though she remained vividly aware of them and could hear her teeth chattering together.

The doctor didn't come at once, though she could hear his voice in the distance. He must be attending to Nicky, which worried her. She tried to shift her feet to the side of the bed so she could stand and go to him, but her legs—still shaking—were so weak she could hardly move them at all.

"Rest easy, my lady," said Rosie, stroking her hand. "I'm right here with you."

Ela wanted to thank her for her kindness. This poor girl was barely older than her youngest daughter Ellie but managed the calm and composure of a seasoned nurse. But the sound of her chattering teeth was the only noise Ela's mouth could seem to make.

By the time the doctor came back, her shivering had subsided somewhat to just the occasional twitch. His face, though, was gray and grim. "I'm afraid your son has suffered a series of seizures, my lady. I believe they're due to his very high fever."

Panicked, Ela struggled to sit up.

"Don't rise, my lady," continued Doctor Goodwin. "We've cooled his body to where the seizures have calmed and I believe he's unharmed. It's essential to keep his body from overheating. You're at risk of seizures yourself." He placed his hand on her forehead, and she watched his frown deepen. "More cold water, please, girls," he said to Elsie and Rosie.

"But it made her shiver so! Her teeth rattled and I thought her bones would break," protested Elsie with desperation in her voice.

"It's essential to cool the blood to prevent it overheating and causing paroxysms of a worse kind."

~

Elsie and Rosie worked hard to keep Ela cool while giving her sips of Cook's herbal preparations, all of which had been cooled in the chilly winter air before serving.

Drifting between sleep and wakefulness, Ela found herself beset with terrible dreams. Foremost was one of a great dragon, rampaging through the countryside around Salisbury. Gold and shimmering in the light, it snatched unwary people up with its great claws and set fire to thatched roofs with blasts of its fiery breath.

She could feel the hot breath on her cheek, singeing her hair, until she opened her eyes and saw Elsie standing over her, face white with worry. "Thank goodness, my lady! You were crying for help and I couldn't wake you."

Ela recoiled from the idea that she'd been talking in her sleep, let alone pleading for help from a figment of her imagination. "It was a nightmare," she breathed, glad to hear that the words did seem to be audible and not just in her head. "I am glad to be awake."

"You're still feverish, and that can produce outlandish dreams," said Elsie.

"How is Nicky?"

Elsie opened her mouth, then closed it again. Then she looked behind her as if for reassurance or news from someone else. No one was in the room.

"Elsie! Tell me, has he taken a turn for the worse?"

"He's still feverish, my lady," she said quietly. "And now Ellie and Petronella are feeling ill as well."

Panic welled in Ela's chest and a prayer rose to her lips. "Has the doctor seen them?"

"Yes, my lady. Neither of them is as hot or sick as you and Nicky. Not yet, at least."

"I must go to them!" She struggled to rise and made it as far as her elbows before sudden dizziness overwhelmed her.

"Petronella wants to come in and see you. The doctor was against it as he doesn't want any pestilence to spread, but since she's sick now too…."

"Is she well enough to come here?"

"I think so, my lady."

"Then let her come." Ela let her head fall back on her pillow as Elsie headed for the door. She knew Petronella wouldn't stint on giving her an honest report of how Nicky and Ellie were doing.

Petronella appeared in her doorway a few moments later, face flushed and feverish, wet tendrils of hair escaping from the plain kerchief she always wore. "God be with you, dear Mama."

"He is, my love, He is always with me." Even though she was lying down she felt dizzy and her eyes had trouble focusing. She didn't want Petronella to know that, though. "I'm being very well taken care of and I'm sure I'll be back on my feet soon. How are you feeling?"

"I'm fine, Mama." She could tell her daughter was lying. Petronella was stoic to the core. She took pleasure in suffering as she felt the physical mortification aided her spiritual development.

"You're a brave girl. How are the little ones?"

"They're not so little now, Mama, so don't fret too much." Ellie was eleven and Nicky twelve, which still seemed very young and fragile to Ela. "Nicky's plagued with terrible dreams and Ellie's fever keeps rising. We must pray hard for them."

She and Petronella prayed a decade of the rosary together, with Petronella saying the words and Ela mostly too weak to utter them, then they sat in silence for a while.

"Mama," said Petronella, with a question in her voice.

"Yes, my dear?" It was hard to find the energy to make a sound.

"Do you think we might ask the miracle healer here to lay his hands upon us?"

"John Bird?" The name shot to the forefront of Ela's consciousness. In her feverish state, she'd quite forgotten him and his strange deeds.

"Yes. I know you think he might not be genuine, but can you explain the healings that have taken place? Look at Thomas Thicke! And there are others, too. What if he's truly touched by God and blessed with the power to heal?"

"God can heal us without the intercession of John Bird."

"I know." Petronella seemed to think about that. "But..." She looked at her mother. "It would be almost a sort of test. If he can heal Nicky's fever, and stop him from convulsing, then we'd know he's genuine and not a fraud."

"I'm not sure he'd want to heal us, given my public suspicion of him."

"If he's a man of true faith he won't balk. That would be another test."

Ela tried to lift her hand to touch Petronella, but the effort proved too much. "I admit, I am intrigued by your suggestion." Whether Bird came or not would be telling, and if he failed to heal any of them, Ela would have more arrows in her quiver if the occasion presented itself to accuse him again. Right now, her investigation of him had ground to a halt.

"Of course, if he heals us all, we will know that God is truly working miracles among us, through him." Petronella looked hopeful that this might be the case. "Perhaps this sickness is a test of our faith? Could the Lord be angry that we've doubted his good works here on earth?"

Ela's heart squeezed. What if—God forbid—one of them was to take a turn for the worse and even die? Would

Petronella and others blame her for not turning over every stone in the hope of a cure? Would the bishop and all his monks mutter over her lack of faith in turning from a true healer in their midst? "If you think it's wise, and if the doctor isn't opposed, then I shall send for him."

∽

Ela wondered if Bird would agree to attend to her and her children. Richard now had a fever as well. Only Stephen had so far been spared its ravages. But her guard returned from the bishop's palace with news that Bird would come at once and that the bishop would offer special prayers for the health of Ela and her family.

Ela rose from her bed and Elsie arranged her hair with a fresh veil. Enough of her strength had returned that she could walk from room to room and speak without too much effort. She told each of the children that Bird would be arriving to—hopefully—help them heal, and to please welcome him graciously despite their illness.

Bird arrived with two monks as attendants. Ela had wondered if the bishop would come too and was at first surprised at Bird's shrunken entourage, then she realized that even holy brothers were likely not enthused about exposing themselves to a raging fever.

She kept her distance from Bird, not wanting to expose him to contagion. "God be with you, John Bird. I thank you for visiting us in our illness." She tried to fill her heart with loving gratitude for his presence. He was taking a personal risk by visiting a house stalked by illness.

"God is indeed with me, my lady. May his mercy and grace bring healing to you and your family."

He'd certainly learned how to say the right words, thought Ela. And even his expression had the appropriate gravitas. Each time she saw him, he looked and sounded more like a bishop than a wandering trickster.

She ushered him into the first room, where Ellie and Petronella lay in their beds. Petronella usually slept alone, in the smallest room and on the floor by choice, but she'd offered to keep Ellie company in her illness and had then become ill. Little Ellie's cheeks were flushed and her eyes glassy. Petronella looked pale and listless.

"Your daughters," he said. "How old are they, pray?"

"Petronella is twenty-one and Ellie is eleven."

"Twenty-one! She's of marriageable age and not yet married," he exclaimed, looking at Petronella. Ela half expected Petronella to reply with indignation, but she was too weak. Her expression didn't even change.

"She intends to take the veil," said Ela. "And devote her life to Christ."

"A most worthy course of action," said Bird, without conviction.

"Would you like to see my sons?" Ela already felt deep regret for inviting him here. Even pretending that she thought he might heal her made her feel deeply uncomfortable.

"In good time, my lady. I'm told that you became ill first?"

"Yes, and I still have the fever. Don't come too close."

"If the Lord wishes me to suffer with the fever he will smite me with it. If he doesn't wish it, he will protect me." His extravagant hand gesture as he said this reminded her of the animated man who'd first appeared in Salisbury three weeks earlier. Otherwise, she'd barely recognize him. "Please allow me to approach you and lay my hands upon you."

Ela silently let him approach. He placed both hands on her forehead. His fingers felt cool against her still-burning skin, even through the thin fabric of her veil. She shivered at the sensation, then stiffened with horror that his touch affected her. He began muttering something. She tried to make out what he was saying, but the words sounded unfamiliar like he was speaking a foreign language. He continued babbling away, now with his eyes closed, until she began to sway and Elsie rushed forward and grabbed her arm.

"My lady, are you feeling faint?"

"I am a bit," admitted Ela. "Perhaps you could help me to a chair." Anything to get away from Bird. She looked at him. "What were you saying?"

He looked at her without much expression. "I can't say I know, my lady. The spirits speak through me."

"He's speaking in tongues," rasped Petronella, suddenly animated enough to sit up in her bed. "Like those filled by the Holy Spirit." Petronella stared at him with new reverence.

Ela had never heard of anyone outside the Bible—including John Bird—speaking in tongues before and wasn't inclined to put much faith in it. Perhaps it was some new party trick he'd come up with to keep the masses entertained.

"Do you feel better, my lady?" asked Elsie.

Did she? Now that she was seated she didn't feel worse, she could say that much. "I do hope so, dear Elsie. Thank you for your efforts, Master Bird."

"I shall attend to young Petronella now."

Petronella sat on the edge of her bed, her gown wet with perspiration that testified to the ferocity of her fever. Bird walked up to her and placed both his hands on her shoulders.

"I can feel the spirit of the Lord within you, Daughter of Christ," he said solemnly. Petronella's eyes closed and again he began to mutter in the strange language. Petronella shuddered slightly, but he held her steady. Petronella's lips even began to move, but no sound came out. After some moments of this, he lifted one of his hands and made the sign of the cross over her head, then stepped back. "Rest easy, for you will soon be healed."

Ela blinked, still too ill to rally her thoughts and understand what was going on. Was this elaborate fakery, or was the Holy Spirit using John Bird for a sacred purpose?

Bird laid his hands on the other children in turn, and on two of the servants who'd now also taken ill. After he was done he came and stood before Ela. "My work here is done. May you all be healed by the power of God."

Ela muttered something, she wasn't even sure what. He stood there expectantly.

He wants money. Such a thing was not unexpected or shocking, but quite conventional. "I shall send an offering to the bishop's palace," she managed. His face fell, but not that much. He'd grown used to seeing riches fly right past him.

"I'm surprised you're still here in Salisbury," she said, surprising herself with the utterance. Perhaps she was still delirious enough to release her private thoughts into the air. Since she and Bill gave Bird his purse back, she thought he would at least attempt to leave. "When you seemed so intent on finding your mother."

"The bishop has taken a great interest in me," said Bird. "He's strongly opposed to the idea of my leaving Salisbury, even for a short visit."

"How do you feel about that?"

"I can't say I blame him. I'm as surprised as he is about my ability to heal through the grace of God. Perhaps he thinks my powers are localized to Salisbury and may disappear if I move."

"Do you not rankle about being kept here against your will?" Ela couldn't understand why he stayed if he wasn't getting to keep all the offerings.

"Rankle? Against the softest bed I've ever slept in, meals fit for a king, and the ability to cure the sick? I'd surely be an ungrateful man if I resented those things, my lady." She couldn't tell if he was being genuine or if there was an edge of sarcasm in his voice. Somehow he managed to dance right between the two possibilities.

"I see your point, Master Bird. And perhaps the prospect of a pilgrimage to Rome promises adventure in foreign lands and accolades beyond imagining."

"Who knows what the Lord has in mind," said Bird pleasantly, with one of his bold hand gestures. "I certainly hope the health of you and your family is part of his earthly plan."

"I thank you for visiting us and doing your best to heal us. I shall have a messenger send you word of how we fare."

∽

ELA'S FEVER BROKE FIRST. Then Nicky's. Then Petronella's and Ellie's and Richard's. Soon they were all recovered, risen from their beds and back in the hall, eating Cook's best fare. The servants recovered, too. The doctor reaffirmed that they were all out of danger. He said he'd never seen so high a fever —one dangerous enough to cause seizures—vanish so quickly and completely.

All agreed it was a miracle wrought by God through the hands of John Bird. All except Ela, who—doubtful sinner as she was—couldn't help but wonder if the fever would have passed of its own accord and that once again John Bird had enjoyed a remarkable streak of good luck.

She sent word to him that they were all cured and thanked him profusely. She also told the messenger to give him a purse containing three gold coins in such a way that no one else would see it. Part of her genuinely wanted to reward him for coming to the castle to cure a woman who had accused him—more than once!—of murder and who dealt tenderly and warmly with her very ill children.

The other part of her wanted to give him enough money to make the prospect of escape more appealing. While he didn't seem to rankle at his current existence in the gilded cage of the bishop's palace, she didn't imagine he'd want to stay there forever.

Bird spent less time out in public. Ela suspected the bishop didn't want him mingling too much with the common people who might, by their extravagant demands, find him disappointing or cast doubt on his powers.

The bishop had plans for John Bird. Plans involving the pope, the Vatican, and the bishop himself, and he likely didn't want John Bird to spoil them. Ela hadn't forgotten the bishop's plan to introduce John Bird to the king, but her illness had given her an excuse to ignore it for a while.

"I wonder if John Bird will become the first saint buried in Salisbury cathedral?" asked Petronella, who'd regaled everyone with tales of their miraculous healing.

"The poor man would have to be dead for that," said Bill Talbot. "So I'm sure he'd be grateful if we have to wait patiently for that occasion."

"Such a holy man is probably itching to sit at God's feet!" exclaimed Petronella. "I know I would be. Imagine being chosen as proof of God's miraculous powers!"

Ela's younger children did not doubt that John Bird was a living saint of some sort. The speed of their recovery from so consuming an illness was a miracle of sorts. But Ela reminded herself that she'd started to feel better before Bird came. She'd been able to converse with him and walk from room to room. One day earlier, Elsie told her she'd been babbling and incoherent, drifting between sleep and wakefulness like a newborn babe.

Ela couldn't help thinking that her recovery might have been every bit as swift and complete without the intercession of John Bird. Of course, now she would never know.

∾

The next day the bishop visited, aglow with excitement. "The pope has deigned to reply! I have a letter with the Vatican seal upon it."

Ela smiled warmly. Or at least she hoped she did. She envied the deep and simple faith of apparently every single person around her. Why did she still doubt John Bird's gifts? Was there a terrible flaw in her soul that would keep her exiled permanently from the Kingdom of Heaven?

"Such a swift reply!" she said brightly. "He must be pleased by your good news."

"Indeed he is, though the letter contains instructions that rather took me by surprise."

CHAPTER 15

The bishop coughed into his closed hand before continuing. "It appears that there is a rather lengthy process of documentation and discussion that must be performed to determine if a miracle is truly an act of God."

"What kind of documentation?" This suspicion on the part of Mother Church warmed Ela's heart. She felt less like a Doubting Thomas.

"There must be a committee of four commissioners, nominated by the Holy See—including one bishop, myself of course—who must make a record of the miraculous events, then send a report to the Vatican." The bishop's face had flushed with excitement. "Apparently it is quite common for the King to be listed as one of these commissioners. The depositions of sworn witnesses to the miracles must be recorded with great accuracy. I do hope we are able to find ample evidence for these notes from eyewitness accounts. It seems churlish to ask John Bird to perform more miracles on command."

Ela composed herself. "I think it would rather be churlish

to question the Pope's wisdom on the matter. I feel sure John Bird won't object to simply performing more of the healing miracles he's already become known for. I shall call him to my hall."

"He must be most pleased to know that he has saved your family from the grip of a cruel fever."

"We are all deeply grateful to be well again." Ela was now fairly sure they would have recovered without his intervention. She'd since heard of a few similar cases inside and outside the castle walls, and not one person had suffered death or permanent effects from the high fever.

"I dare say you'll want to make a generous donation in gratitude for your healing."

"I did," she said evenly. "It was delivered into Bird's own hands."

The bishop's hopeful expression flickered. "The bishopric is taking great pains to provide a comfortable stay for our honored guest and we are incurring considerable expenses, as you can imagine."

"I can indeed." Ah, greed. It underlay so many human activities. "I will discuss the matter with my steward."

Jake, the young apprentice porter, rushed up to her. He'd recently started helping his grandfather Albert. "My lady, a man called Hugo Marsh wishes to speak with you urgently."

"Can you not see I'm engaged with the bishop?" Ela didn't like being interrupted when speaking with a person of importance. Young Jake was still learning the ins and outs of his position.

"Begging your pardon, my lady, but he says it's a matter of life or death." Jake's wide eyes underscored the urgency of his words. Ela glanced toward the great doorway of the hall. A man stood there, dressed in the clothing of a farmer or even a serf. As she looked over, he turned and met her gaze with an intensity that shook her.

"Then I think you must send him to me at once," she said. She glanced at the bishop, hoping he'd take his leave.

"I shall wait, my lady," said the bishop. "A matter of life and death cannot be delayed."

Jake beckoned the stranger to come across the hall. As he walked, Ela noted that he was a man in middle age, but not old. He had an earnest, clean-shaven face and light brown hair poking from beneath a worn leather cap. When he reached Ela, he pulled his cap from his head, revealing a rather oily scalp. "May God protect you, my lady."

"And you. What is your urgent business?"

"My name is Hugo Marsh. I come here because I heard tell of a man promising miracles and healing. I've run across someone who claimed such gifts before."

"Oh yes?" Ela's ears pricked up. "Have you met John Bird before?"

"I believe I have, my lady, though he called himself Daniel Witchett. He stayed at my brother's inn some eighteen months ago. He ran up a bill, eating and drinking and staying in the best room—"

Ela held up her hand to stop him. She wanted to be sure of something before they went any further. "Have you seen John Bird with your own eyes? Can you confirm that he's the same person?"

His face fell. "No, my lady. The description of him fits very well. He had brown hair and eyes and was of a typical build."

"Such a description fits you as well, Hugo Marsh."

Hugo glanced down at his homespun tunic as if to confirm this. "I suppose it does. But this man was a trickster who promised the impossible and collected sums of money for medicines that didn't work."

"We must have you look upon John Bird to determine whether he's the same man."

"I heard he's sometimes in the marketplace here in the castle, so I went there, but he was not to be found."

"He's in his room in my palace in New Salisbury," said the bishop, who'd been watching quietly until now. "But I find it hard to believe that this identification is a matter of life and death."

"If he's the man I think, then he killed my brother." Hugo Marsh stopped talking as a wave of emotion washed visibly over him. "Left him dead on the floor for his wife to find him at first light."

Ela's nerves jangled. Did she finally have definitive history on Bird that would prove her seemingly unfounded suspicions correct? "Why would he kill your brother?"

"My brother, Piers Marsh, was after him to pay his bill. Witchett had run up a costly sum and kept asking for more rich fare and fine ale without parting with a penny of the money he'd taken from the people of the village."

"Which village was this?" If Daniel Witchett truly was John Bird, there should be many witnesses to his former identity.

"Wiggiford Mill, my lady. It's on the border of Wiltshire and Hampshire." Ela didn't know the village even by name.

"And how long was Daniel Witchett living there?"

"He arrived just before Lent and escaped, leaving my brother Piers dead, on Whitsunday eve."

"I'm grieved to hear of your loss." He'd been there for almost four months.

"I reported it to the sheriff of Hampshire, but the villain had vanished without a trace. When I heard of this new stranger in Salisbury, swearing that he can heal people and other such nonsense, I latched onto the idea that it might be him. If it is him, you have a murderer in your midst." He turned to the bishop. "And that's why it's a matter of life and death."

The bishop's shocked expression altered into a hopeful one. "It can't be the same man, for John Bird has a true gift for healing! Our countess can vouch for it herself. He healed her entire family and herself from the grip of a fever cruel enough to cause convulsions. I feel sure that he's genuine. The pope himself is pleased to hear of the miracles and blessings occurring in Salisbury since John Bird has arrived."

Ela stared at the bishop for a moment. Could he simply ignore everything that Hugo Marsh had said and refuse to let this man see Bird at all? She knew she needed to manage this carefully. "Poor Master Marsh is most distressed at the death of his brother. He's now taken hold of the idea that we have his brother's killer living among us in Salisbury. Would it not ease his mind to lay his eyes on John Bird and reassure himself that the miracle worker among us is not the same man?"

The bishop pondered this for a moment. "Our guest might be offended by such grave suspicions against him."

"Surely, if he's innocent, he'll be as concerned as we are that he be absolved of all suspicion. Just a quick look will surely confirm that he's not the same man." She wanted the bishop to feel confident that his precious miracle man—and his newly cultivated correspondence with the pontiff—wouldn't be endangered. "Since the day draws on, perhaps we could ride together to your palace and set all our minds at ease?"

She hoped she didn't look too eager.

"I suppose that might be possible. Though we still have matters to discuss regarding my correspondence with His Grace the Pope." He glanced at Marsh to gauge his reaction. No doubt he expected Marsh to be awed by the grandeur of his correspondence.

Marsh, agitated, looked from one to the other. "I'd like to go at once. If he gets away, I'll never forgive myself."

"It can't be the same man, surely?" said the bishop. "Let's not be too hasty. We can arrange a meeting tomorrow, under more official circumstances. I hate to disturb him in his chamber when he might be in prayer."

Ela's heart sank slightly. She could hardly storm the bishop's palace and drag Bird out. The authority of the church trumped even hers as sheriff. "I could call a jury here tomorrow morning and Hugo Marsh can share the awful news of his brother's death. You can introduce John Bird and we can confirm that he isn't the same man."

"Tomorrow morning?" Marsh looked distraught. "Wherever shall I stay?"

"There's an inn called the Bull and Bear," said Ela. "If you have the money to pay for it." She didn't want to offer him a bed at the castle if she could avoid it. It wouldn't do to have a reputation for putting up petitioners and strangers from across Wiltshire.

"Aye, I can pay." His face had sunk. "Should I be here at first light?"

"Yes. And the jury shall hear the details of your brother's death so that, if Bird is not the man you knew, we can take steps to find your brother's killer."

"That prospect gives me a mote of peace, my lady."

"Until tomorrow, then."

Ela listened to the bishop describe the three days of fasting and prayer that the commissioners should undertake before beginning their inquiry. Ela wondered if King Henry III, pious though he was, would partake in such abstinence outside of Lent, if he even agreed to be part of this commission. She could see that the bishop believed absolutely that Bird was genuine. His excitement about sharing further good news with the pope animated his gestures and made his eyes sparkle.

All the while she hoped that his dreams would be dashed

when Hugo Marsh pointed a confident finger of accusation at John Bird in the morning.

∽

ELA ARRANGED for a messenger to contact several members of the jury in the hope that they could rouse a few men to hear Hugo Marsh's tale of woe.

The jurors arrived at first light, as arranged, and Ela found herself growing annoyed that Hugo Marsh himself was nowhere to be seen.

"Is he sleeping in?" asked Peter Howard, who'd left his daughter in charge of the bakery to be there.

"The beds at the Bull and Bear aren't that comfortable!" exclaimed Matthew Hart. "I hear they're lumpy and flea-ridden as Bill Taff's old donkey."

"I shall send a messenger to rouse him," said Ela.

The messenger crossed paths with John Bird, who arrived at that moment with a good-sized entourage from the bishop's palace. The bishop himself was busy with other matters, probably not wanting to be present when his pet was under public scrutiny. The bishop did seem quite concerned lately about Bird growing disgruntled and possibly wanting to quit the palace, so perhaps he was worried that this morning's meeting would only foment Bird's annoyance.

All sat in the hall, where the servants produced a small breakfast of freshly baked rolls and soft cheese.

They sat long enough that Ela had begun to silently curse Hugo Marsh and think him a liar and a troublemaker. Then the door to the hall creaked open and a gust of icy winter wind crossed the room fast enough to shiver the flames in the fireplace.

The messenger Ela had sent out ran back into the hall, his hair tousled and his tunic awry. His reddened cheeks suggested he'd run back from the Bull and Bear. He hurried up to Ela and stood there, as if afraid to talk. Understandable, since staff were instructed not to speak unless they were spoken to.

"What's amiss?" she asked, heartbeat quickening.

"He's dead, my lady!" The man's breathless voice underscored the horror of his words. "Strangled, it looks like. Awful bruises on his neck! Tongue sticking out like a great purple thing."

Ela crossed herself. "Please summon Giles Haughton to attend the body at once. Tell him I shall meet him at the Bull and Bear and I shall bring the jury with me." She looked at the jurors, all startled by this shocking turn of events. Then she called for the captain of the guard and told him to close the gates so no one could enter or leave Salisbury Castle. "The killer may still be at large."

She looked at John Bird, who appeared unperturbed by this horrible news. "Where did you sleep last night, Master Bird?"

"In my chamber in the bishop's palace, my lady. I slept like a babe." The placid look on his face had almost a smirking quality to it. The bishop must have told him that in the morning he would be coming to her hall to meet Hugo Marsh before a jury. If he was indeed the killer of Marsh's brother, he might have killed Hugo Marsh during the night to stop Marsh from identifying him.

But how? Bird's room was on the second floor of the bishop's palace. And the palace was in new Salisbury, two miles from her castle. And the castle was gated at night, with guards stationed along the walls. The Bull and Bear itself sat in the center of the cramped village inside the castle walls, not an easy place to sneak in or out of.

Unless John Bird did possess supernatural powers, it seemed almost impossible for him to have killed Marsh.

A SURFEIT OF MIRACLES

∾

Ela insisted that John Bird accompany her to the Bull and Bear. Bird protested that he preferred to return to the bishop's palace to pray. Ela insisted that the guards escort him alongside her, and she whispered to them to keep a very close eye on him.

Angry, Bird demanded that a monk hurry back to the bishop and tell him of the disrespectful way he was being treated by the sheriff. A brother nodded and hurried away.

Ela marched through the town, with the jurors and Bird trailing close behind her. As they walked, strangers hurried up to Bird and tugged at his clothes, begging him to heal their lame husband or sick child or blind mother. Bird barely acknowledged them. Silent and fuming rather than saintly, he did not seem at all happy about going to the Bull and Bear to view a dead body.

CHAPTER 16

Ela arrived in the upstairs chamber of the tavern to find Giles Haughton bent over the body. The small room, tucked into a roof peak, was barely large enough for a bed. There certainly wasn't room for Ela and the jury and John Bird to enter. Ela summoned John Bird to the front of the small crowd gathered at the top of the tavern's stairs.

"Good morning, Sir Giles. The dead man was supposed to attend my hall this morning so he could lay eyes on John Bird and tell us whether Bird was the man who killed his brother."

Haughton stood up quickly and stared at her, then Bird. "He accused Bird of murder?"

"He heard that we have a man in Salisbury who claims to be a healer. He said a similar man stayed at his brother's inn and refused to pay his bill, then killed the brother and fled. I tried to have the bishop take us to John Bird last night, but he protested that it was too late and he didn't want to disturb his guest. Bird knew he was to come to my hall to meet this newcomer this morning. But as you can see, the stranger—Hugo Marsh of Wiggiford Mill—did not survive the night to meet with John Bird."

Haughton looked hard at John Bird. "Is the dead man known to you?"

Bird didn't even glance at the body. "Never seen him before in my life."

Ela now took a moment to look at the corpse. Though dressed in the same clothes he'd worn in her hall, Marsh now looked utterly different, his face bloated and discolored. Deep purple bruises on his neck instantly betrayed his mode of death. "He was strangled."

"Yes. The marks of individual fingers are visible on his neck," said Haughton.

Ela glanced at John Bird's hands, which twitched suddenly. Bird didn't have particularly large hands for a man. Like everything else about him they were unremarkable. But now she did notice a scratch on one of them. "Master Bird, how did you come by that scratch on your hand?"

Bird snatched his hand up. "The cat in the bishop's palace took a swipe at me."

Haughton looked at Bird's hand. "Come over here and let me see the scratch. A cat scratch can easily become infected."

Bird looked like he'd rather gnaw his arm off than extend it toward Haughton. "The dead body is giving me the shivers," he said, avoiding looking at it. "I don't want to come anywhere near it."

"Ah, yes, perhaps I'm too used to the sight of death," said Haughton. "I shall come to you." He walked to the doorway and snatched Bird's hand without hesitation. He studied it and turned it over. "This is no cat scratch. It's more of an abrasion, as if your hand scraped against a stone wall or floor. And two of your nails are ragged."

Bird tried to snatch his hand back, but Haughton held it tight. "When I swatted at the blasted animal, my hand flew back against the wall. Hurt like fire. It was the damn cat's fault."

Haughton let his hand go rather slowly. "Not a scratch, though. An abrasion that was the result of a struggle…." He looked at Ela.

"With a cat!" insisted Bird.

"We must tell the bishop to remove this dangerous cat," said Ela. "It is a hazard to life and limb." She wondered if there even was a cat in the bishop's palace.

"It's just a cat," snapped Bird.

"When did the bishop tell you about this morning's planned meeting with Hugo Marsh?" asked Ela. How much warning did Bird have that an old enemy was now in Salisbury?

"He mentioned it sometime last evening," said Bird, after some hesitation. He knew the truth would be easy to confirm by asking the bishop.

"So, you knew there was a stranger in Salisbury who suspected that you might be the man who killed his brother?"

"I don't recall why the bishop said the man wanted to see me. He just told me to come to the hall at first light."

Ela glanced at Haughton. Any man claiming that he didn't remember something that happened yesterday was probably lying.

"Were you not concerned about the reason for it?"

Bird sighed heavily. "No one seems to give me any choice in what I do from day to day. I'm chivvied hither and yon and paraded in the marketplace like a prize pig. I half wish I wasn't touched by God and turned into a living saint."

"I don't believe there's any such thing as a living saint," said Ela quietly. She didn't want Bird thinking he was somehow invincible.

"The bishop seems hell-bent on making me a saint or some such. He now has a long list of tasks I must perform for the pope and his cardinals." Bird sounded bored or irritated by this prospect. He also seemed to have half-forgotten the man lying dead on the bed with his purple tongue sticking out.

"A calling by God is not an easy path," said Ela coldly. "Any martyr could tell you that." Since she strongly suspected Bird had chosen the path for purely material reasons, she didn't feel an ounce of sympathy for him. "Your reward will be when you sit at the hem of His robes."

Bird looked like he wanted to spit on the floor. He grew agitated and started to fidget. "Are you done with me? I don't know this man." He cast a wary glance over at the limp body of Hugo Marsh. "I've never seen him before in my life. I don't even know why you brought me here."

"God knows all and sees all," said Ela, glancing at the corpse. "Do any members of the jury have questions for John Bird?"

None of them did. If Bird weren't Salisbury's most cherished resident, with his name on the lips of the pope himself, Ela would surely have arrested him. She didn't like to arrest anyone without direct evidence, since a man could sicken and die in the castle dungeon. But, building on her suspicions about John Bird and the mysterious way his accuser had died, she felt increasingly convinced of his guilt.

She glanced at Haughton, wondering if he might invent some clever pretext to arrest Bird. Haughton lifted his chin and peered at him. "I may need to question you further, so don't leave the vicinity of Salisbury."

"I shall ask the bishop to make sure our honored guest is kept comfortable and secure," said Ela, sliding as much steel as she could into the words. "Guards, please escort John Bird back to the bishop's palace and guarantee his safety by remaining outside the building until I send further orders."

The guards shuffled off with Bird and the straggle of monks who'd followed him.

Haughton summoned the jurors to enter the cramped room as best they could. They ducked under the low ceiling and shuffled past him, wincing and scowling at the gruesome sight of the strangled corpse.

Haughton lifted Marsh's right hand and observed that his knuckles were abraded much like Bird's hand, as if they'd scraped against a wall or floor. "He tried to fight off his attacker, but I don't think he put up much of a fight. He was likely surprised and overcome before he could make a proper resistance."

"How did the killer get in?" asked Matthew Hart. "Surely the lads and girls that work at the inn sleep downstairs in the tavern when it's closed?"

"I believe the assailant came in through the window," said Haughton. A small window stood open behind them, allowing a constant stream of cold winter air into the already chilly room. "It has oilcloth rather than glass, and, as you can see, the oilcloth has been cut."

John Bird had already proved himself a very cunning man. Ela could easily see him hatching such a scheme. "John Bird stayed here at the Bull and Bear when he first arrived in Salisbury. He may have stayed in this very room. He'd know how the windows are made, and may even be familiar enough with the roof gables to navigate them in the dark."

"My lady," said old Thomas Pryce. "I don't mean to offend, but John Bird is a man of God! He was far outside the castle walls and in the bishop's palace in new Salisbury when this murder was committed. I find it hard to imagine that he could penetrate the castle's outer walls, let alone climb into a second-story window. How would he even know which window to climb in?"

"His knowledge of the inn and its current guests,

perhaps," said Ela. "While I shrink from accusing him directly, I don't want his seemingly miraculous healing powers to blind us to any wrongdoing he may have committed either here or elsewhere."

The jurors grunted and shuffled. Ela could tell they were more inclined to side with John Bird than with her continued—and to their mind unfounded—suspicions. Still, she did not intend to let the matter drop. "I shall ask the castle sentries if anyone entered or left the castle between the hours when Bird learned of the new arrival and when the body was discovered." There was at least some nodding and agreement to this proposal.

"The dead man's next of kin must be informed of his death," said Haughton.

Ela nodded. "Marsh said he came from a small village called Wiggiford Mill, on the border between Wiltshire and Hampshire. I shall send a messenger to seek his next of kin and bring them the sad tidings." Hope rose in her chest. "And if a relative of Hugo Marsh's can be found, or a neighbor who remembers the strange man who stayed at their inn, he could confirm whether John Bird is or isn't the man who stayed among them."

˷

The castle sentries had failed Ela in the past. Unless they saw a full-scale invading army on the horizon—an event happily absent from Ela's life so far—they were more inclined to play dice up on the ramparts rather than closely observe the dark ground below.

The sentries at the gate couldn't be sure if anyone had entered or not entered during the night. They were full of excuses about changing guards and eager to shift responsibility onto anyone but themselves. Even the garrison commander couldn't confirm that not one single soul had entered or left the castle.

"The gates are supposed to be closed and locked from dusk to dawn," said Ela with a frown.

"But my lady," said the captain of the guards, a youngish man with a snub nose. "Sometimes a tradesman is held up on the road by a broken spoke in his cartwheel or the like. Would you have us keep a man—well known to us and trusted like a friend—outside the castle walls in the dark all night where he might catch a chill in the winter's cold?"

Ela inhaled. "I can see that there might be exceptions, but the guards in this castle are from all over the country. They can hardly be expected to know every soul who lives within these walls."

"The sentries are charged with using their discretion, of course. And anyone suspicious would be detained for questioning."

"And who—suspicious or not—did indeed enter the castle last night?"

No one could produce a firm answer, either in the affirmative or the negative. "Your refusal to say that no one entered the castle suggests to me that someone did enter," she said to the garrison commander. "Since a murder has been committed in our walls—and the killer is still at large—I demand a full accounting of every soul who entered or left these gates between dusk and dawn."

∽

AT LENGTH, it was determined that three people had entered during the evening, and only one had left in the morning. The three were: a farmer by the name of Tenner who came hurrying up shortly after dusk to visit his ailing sister; an alewife named Una who'd taken two kegs of ale to the bishop's palace and whose donkey had lost a shoe on the way home; and, finally, a visiting cleric named Father Cedric, who'd traveled from Canterbury to meet with Father Thomas.

The sole person leaving before dawn had been an older woman making a drunken nuisance of herself outside the guard tower. The guards had put her outside the gate and told her not to come back until she was good and sober.

"Fetch Father Thomas," said Ela at once. "Did the old woman come back after dawn?"

"Nope," said the two guards who'd finally admitted to ejecting her. "Probably still wandering around half sozzled."

"Did you recognize her?" asked Ela.

"Can't say I did, but she had a hood on over her hair, and her face was sooty with smoke. Could barely see anything but her teeth."

"What did her voice sound like?" she asked.

"It was that deep!" exclaimed one of them. "More like an old man than a woman—" He broke off, realizing the critical mistake he'd made. "You think it was a man?"

"Unless you can find a half-drunk old woman wandering the fields outside the castle, I'd bet your next year's salary that it was a man," said the garrison commander. He raised his hand as if to strike the guard, then glanced at Ela and lowered his hand.

"How tall was she?" asked Ela.

"About the same as you, my lady," said the guard looking thoroughly chastened. Ela sighed. Tall for a woman, she was close in height to John Bird.

Father Thomas soon confirmed that he had certainly not expected any visitor from Canterbury and that no one had arrived to meet him.

"John Bird has met Father Thomas," said Ela. "On more than one occasion. Living at the bishop's palace, he also has access—if covertly—to ecclesiastical robes. I strongly suspect that he came here, strangled Hugo Marsh, stole a woman's clothes, changed into them, and made his escape."

"Such an entry and exit is uncommonly complicated, my lady," said the garrison commander.

"John Bird is cunning enough to convince the town of Salisbury that he rose from the dead."

"Do you believe he should be arrested?"

"I do. Unfortunately, he's established a reputation as a near saint, so I suspect an arrest warrant would create a backlash of opposition. I must gather further evidence before accusing him outright. Your guards and their accounts will likely prove crucial to that effort."

～

HAVING DETERMINED how Bird entered and left the castle, Ela's next project was to determine how Bird might have made his escape from the bishop's palace—despite being on the second floor in a building full of monks coming and going at all hours.

She brought Giles Haughton with her to the bishop's palace. She wanted his weight of expertise and authority so she wouldn't appear to be pursuing some petty personal vendetta against Bird.

After initial formalities, Bishop de Bingham greeted her warily. "I've heard of the crime committed against your visitor of yesterday."

"Indeed, Your Grace. It is most strange that a man newly arrived in town and a stranger to all of us—or should I say almost all of us—should be murdered in his bed. Might I inquire what time you told John Bird of the stranger's arrival and my request that he come to the castle to meet him?"

The bishop frowned. "Why, I suppose I told him around

A SURFEIT OF MIRACLES

dusk. I entered his chamber to invite him to Vespers but he preferred to remain in silent prayer. He begged me to leave him in peace for the rest of the night."

I bet he did.

Ela had already trod the route to Bird's chamber when she came to return his purse of coins. "Might I see where his window lies on the exterior of the building?"

"Whatever for, my lady?"

Haughton cleared his throat. "It's part of my investigation, Your Grace."

"To look at the placement of a window high in the wall?"

Haughton gave the slightest nod in response. He obviously considered the question to be impertinent as well as rhetorical. After a small harrumph, the bishop led them outside the building.

"That's his window up there." The bishop pointed to a neat glass window of fine quality, like most of the fixtures of the extravagant palace his predecessor had built for his own enjoyment. The wall was smooth cut stone, with few footholds.

The window was high enough off the ground that in jumping from it a man might risk serious injury. Hard cobblestones covered the ground below. She and Haughton looked up at the window in silence for a moment, while the bishop fidgeted as if he wished to spend his time on more important matters.

"He might have lowered himself out of the window by a length of fabric. Perhaps even the ecclesiastical robes he was seen in," said Haughton at last.

"What?" The bishop looked shocked. "You're not surely suggesting that our guest exited through his window, scaled the walls of Salisbury Castle, and murdered an utter stranger all because of a proposed meeting?"

"No, Your Grace," said Haughton calmly. "We have

already determined that he walked in and out of the gates of the castle after dark and before dawn."

"I don't believe it!" exclaimed the bishop. His face grew red. "Even if such an exit were possible. How could he get back inside his room?"

A puzzling dilemma indeed. "Let us concern ourselves first with his exit. We suspect he stole a set of ecclesiastical robes and presented himself as a visiting cleric when he arrived at the castle. Please have your men search your stores and see if such vestments are missing."

The bishop blinked in disbelief. "You are making a lot of assumptions, my lady."

"It is my duty as sheriff to test theories in order to solve crimes. Giles Haughton's years of experience guide my efforts. Will you search for the vestments?"

He hesitated for a moment. "Yes, I shall. But I feel sure that John Bird remained alone in prayer as he mostly prefers to do when he isn't going out among the people."

Ela now wondered if this might not be the first time Bird had left his room during the night. Who knew what mischief he might have committed at night and in disguise? She recalled a report two days ago of a drunk man returning from the tavern and being robbed of his purse by a beggar.

"I'm sure you'll discover that an entirely different man killed the newcomer," said the bishop. "I'm compiling a list of men who might serve on the commission to investigate John Bird's miracles. Would you like to hear the names I intend to suggest to the Holy See? I flatter myself that, as John Bird's host and patron, I shall be chosen as one of their number."

Ela fought the urge to roll her eyes. While she was trying to prove that John Bird was a double or even triple murderer, the bishop still clung to the idea that he was a future saint. She schooled her face into placid interest as best she could. "Please, do share all the exciting details."

CHAPTER 17

The distraction of John Bird and the new murder and all the pilgrims now flocking to Salisbury had not stopped the work of excavating the giant skeleton from the riverbank. As the collection of bones grew, they soon outgrew the confines of the mortuary.

Ela agreed that a tent might be set up to contain them on the grounds of the old abbey, now reduced to its foundation stones, that her sons sometimes used as a jousting ground. Servants erected a tent usually reserved for tournaments, and Haughton supervised as they reassembled the massive bones under the striped canopy.

Soon visitors started to arrive to see the great creature, and there was much discussion about its origins and appearance.

"A scaled dragon!" exclaimed one self-proclaimed expert who'd traveled from London. "Likely green in color."

"How do you know it was green?" asked a nearby man, "when there's nothing left but the bones?"

"Everyone knows that dragons are green," said a farmer's wife who'd arrived to view the spectacle with her husband.

"The miracle man had a vision of a dragon with scales all of gold. Doesn't it seem likely that this is the dragon he saw in his mind's eye?" asked one of the jurors, Stephen Hale, the cordwainer, who'd become fascinated by the find.

John Bird came to the tent and expounded at length about the mystery and magic of the long-dead creature. He kept the audience enthralled with tales of its fiery breath that once scorched the countryside around Salisbury and laid waste to settlements of the primitive humans who once lived there.

Since that part of Wiltshire was indeed littered with remains of walls and tombs and old round houses, and since English legends bristled with tales of fearsome dragons, it was hard to argue with him.

"The dragon returning to Salisbury could be a sign that the second coming of our Lord is nigh," said Bird in sonorous tones. His fine robes, and the weeks spent in luxurious quarters, gave him an air of confidence and gravitas that he hadn't possessed when he arrived in Salisbury. "All would do well to make peace with the Lord their God so their soul may travel safely to Paradise!"

Ela watched with a mix of disgust and admiration as these urgent warnings transmuted into showers of coins collected in baskets and coffers that the monks carried for him. Bird must rankle at the bishop putting his fingers into these generous takings. Perhaps the bishop was letting Bird keep more of his "earnings" to keep his pet prodigy content and malleable. Ela made sure that at least two guards followed Bird everywhere he went, as she did not intend to let him slip away.

∽

Messengers sent to Wiggiford Mill returned with news: Indeed there had been a stranger staying there who'd disappeared in the night leaving an unpaid bill. He'd spent his time in the village telling fortunes and selling portions from a keg of foul-smelling "healing" liquid that seemed to have effects similar to very strong drink. Charming and friendly, by most accounts, he'd made more friends than enemies.

The innkeeper's wife and son were devastated to learn that Hugo Marsh had now been murdered. The messengers tried to persuade the mother and son come back to Salisbury with them, in the hope that they could identify Bird as the same man who'd stayed in Wiggiford Mill. They both protested that they could hardly leave their business and home in the hands of the pot boy or the kitchen girl.

The guards returned with this news but without mother or son.

"Can we bring Bird with us to Wiggiford Mill?" asked Ela, frustrated at yet another delay. Worried that Bird might kill someone else, she grew increasingly anxious to see him formally accused of murder.

But Bird was otherwise engaged in apparently curing people's headaches and easing their limps and even turning vinegar back into wine. Ela couldn't understand how he was doing it. She suspected that the miracles were wishful thinking or products of the imagination of those around him. She tasted the "wine" and found that it still tasted remarkably like vinegar to her critical tongue.

Still, the bishop was aglow with delight and penning more missives to the pope about their miraculous guest and his holy gifts and even about the mysterious "dragon" that had emerged from the ground in his presence.

Ela wanted to protest that she was the sheriff and that if she wanted Bird to travel to Wiggiford Mill, then, by God, he would go there. However, the entire church establishment was in a stir of excitement over Bird. If the man entering the castle that fateful night hadn't actually been a cleric from

Canterbury, now clerics were flocking from Canterbury and Chichester and Oxford, and even as far as Ely and York as word of the miraculous events in Salisbury spread throughout England.

Ela sat at dinner with Bill Talbot, lamenting the impasse she found them in. "If I accuse John Bird of murder, I'm dashing the bishop's hope of being feted in Rome. You can see the joy people feel at the notion that God is doing his work here on earth in the person of John Bird."

"Their joy is a delusion," said Bill, after taking a sip of his wine.

"You know that, and I know that, but can we prove them all wrong and destroy their hope and happiness? I wasn't born yesterday. I'm well-schooled in the world of court politics. As William Longespeé's wife I could hardly avoid it. I know that the religious establishment has its own rules of order and etiquette. I'd surely be contravening them by declaring their beloved Saint John to be a foul murderer. I must somehow get the bishop on my side."

∽

BUT THE BISHOP was flying far too high on his newfound fame and glory to even hear Ela's doubts about Bird. "The king's secretary has written to me to arrange a meeting between himself and dear John!" He clapped his hands together with glee. "I must give you all the credit, my lady, for making it happen."

Ela blinked. She certainly couldn't take any credit, since she hadn't breathed a word about Bird to the king. Barely a week had passed since the bishop had mentioned a possible meeting. He must think that she'd moved on his request with great urgency.

Is it wise to introduce our king to a man suspected of murder?

The words echoed in her head but she didn't dare utter them. She intended to pursue her investigation of Bird and didn't want to risk being told to cease and desist.

"Will the king come to Salisbury?"

"The king has invited us to attend him in his palace at Clarendon in two days' time," said the bishop, wreathed in smiles. "Such an auspicious event for us here in Salisbury! I shall share this fresh news with His Holiness."

Ela wanted to be happy for the bishop, who was overjoyed to be in correspondence with two of the most important men in Europe, in addition to having a supposed holy man living under his roof. But misgivings ate at her.

If her suspicions about Bird were correct, his evil matched his cunning. The king himself—or members of his court—might be in danger if Bird somehow sank his hooks into them. At the very least, the king's reputation might be tarnished by association with such a character when the truth came out.

If the truth did come out. That responsibility fell on her head and she felt its weight like a millstone around her neck.

"I'd like to come with you on your visit to the king. He is my children's uncle and very dear to me. I'd be happy to see him." She smiled brightly.

The bishop's cheery expression faded. He probably didn't like the idea of anyone attempting to muscle in on his moment of glory. "I shall let you introduce our visitor and take the lead in all matters," she added. "You will barely know I'm there."

"I'm sure we'd all be most grateful for your presence," said de Bingham, flatly. "We plan to leave from my palace shortly after dawn tomorrow."

"So soon! I shall have my horses readied early so we can travel with you." She didn't want to give Bird a chance to escape en route. Arrogant as he was, even he might not be confident that he could pull the wool over the eyes of a monarch.

The bishop agreed with poorly disguised reluctance. Ela intended to bring Bill Talbot and a phalanx of guards who'd be instructed to keep a very close eye on Bird.

∾

THE FOUR HORSES hitched to Ela's carriage blew steam in the cold morning air, and the tiny bells on their harness jingled with their impatience.

Ela would have preferred to ride, but a visit to the king required the sort of elaborate, fur-lined, finely-trimmed garments that wouldn't permit her to sit comfortably astride. Thus she was condemned to bump along the icy and rutted roads on wooden wheels.

Bill, gallant as always, stood ready to accompany her in the carriage, though he too would far rather have been on horseback. "This meeting of Bird and the bishop with the king is like a runaway horse. Any attempt to stand in front of it would end with us getting trampled and left for dead."

"I know," said Ela, "which is why I didn't protest it. I still worry that we're bringing a murderer—a double murderer—into the king's palace. I shall not forgive myself if anything goes awry."

"We shall ensure that it doesn't."

∾

THE SHORT JOURNEY to Clarendon was happily uneventful. Ela had worried that Bird would be given a horse to ride and might seize the opportunity to gallop off. The bishop had instead arranged for a comfortable carriage for Bird, himself, and several senior clerics. Ela was mightily relieved that Bird would be contained and surrounded en route to the palace.

"Did you tell the king we were coming?" asked Bill, as they entered the tree-lined lane that led from the road toward the king's country retreat.

"I did not," said Ela. "I saw no need. He'd expect a sizable entourage, so a few more warm bodies on this cold winter's day should make no difference. And again, I didn't want to be cautioned not to come or prevented in some way, perhaps by Bird himself."

"Sensible," said Bill.

Considerable fanfare greeted their arrival at Clarendon. Grooms and servants rushed out to take their horses and to assist them in dismounting from the carriage. Bird and the Bishop had just dismounted from their own similar conveyance. The whitewashed palace glowed in the winter sun, and hardy trees and bushes in pots ornamented the courtyard and entranceway.

The porter led them into a large chamber with elaborate scenes painted on the walls. He announced their names in order of rank, with Ela's read first. When the king entered, everyone bowed low and a hush fell over the chamber.

Henry III was the fourth king of England in Ela's lifetime and her favorite by quite a long way. His father Henry II had been a man of impressive and commanding presence and Ela– a child at the time of his death—had felt reverence for him, but never affection. Still a child, she'd been a ward of King Richard, known as The Lionheart, who had given her in marriage to her husband William. For that she bore him eternal affection. King John, her husband's brother, had been a thorn in her side for much of her marriage. His court traveled constantly, drawing her husband from her side and sinking him into an atmosphere of considerable debauchery. Young Henry III, by contrast, had so far proven himself pious and thoughtful and—

despite an understandable obsession with regaining the territory his father lost in France—moderate in his actions.

"Countess Ela, a pleasure to see you." Henry extended his hand and she approached him.

"The pleasure is all mine." He took her hands in his and kissed them. Ela was surprised at the warmth of his affection but pleased also. She hoped she hadn't brought a serpent into his brightly painted paradise.

"Such strange and fascinating tidings from Salisbury—a man who rose from the dead and can heal the sick, and a dragon unearthed from the very ground."

"We are privileged to witness such awesome mysteries," said Ela with a brave smile. "God be praised."

Bishop Robert de Bingham scraped and groveled and flattered the king with obsequious comments. Ela could tell that he'd never met him before, whereas the former bishop, Richard Poore, had been one of the king's closest advisors.

John Bird, arrayed in even more magnificent finery than before, was now introduced to the king as "our God-given healer." The bishop went on to explain how he'd healed Ela's whole family of a deadly fever and restored them all to full health. Ela could hardly argue, because everything he said was true, at least on the face of it.

"Tell me, please, how you were raised from the dead," asked King Henry, who seemed both awed and thrilled by John Bird's presence in his palace.

"Why, Your Grace, I hardly know," said Bird. His hands flapped around as they tended to do when he was nervous. "I opened my eyes and found myself lying in the great circle of stones. There was a knife in my back and I'd been robbed of my possessions. The Lord chose to heal my wounds and quicken my body with life again, that I might do his work here on earth."

"God be praised," said Henry. "And how did you discover that you had the power to heal?"

"Again, my lord, I cannot fully explain it. The Lord moved me to lay my hands on the sick. And by His Grace they were healed."

"How marvelous," said Henry, now looking at the bishop. "I wonder if perhaps any special collections or donations have been raised from such activity?"

Everyone froze. Ela could almost hear the bishop's heart beating beneath his embroidered silk vestments. Was King Henry's interest in John Bird financial rather than spiritual?

"Why, my lord, we've hardly paid attention to such things," stammered the bishop. "Some small offerings may have been scattered at his feet, but nothing formal."

Ela wanted to laugh. She wondered how much the bishop had seized, though she did at least believe he was putting the money toward the cathedral or the running of the palace, rather than into his own coffers. Again, he wasn't Bishop Richard Poore.

"Well," said Henry, clapping his hands together. "That seems to me to be rather a waste. I wonder if there might be some benefit to creating a sort of healing shrine, like the one at the tomb of Thomas Becket in Canterbury, where pilgrims might come from across Europe to pay homage and to be healed here in Salisbury."

The bishop blinked. "We are indeed in need of funds to complete the final works of the cathedral," he said, with a tinge of anxiety in his voice.

"And such tithes as would be due to the crown could support the important work I intend to do in restoring English rule in our former lands in France. Every day those lands remain in the hands of the child King Louis is a torment to me. I speak for all of us, I'm sure, when I observe that it would be God's work to restore these lands to the crown of England."

Ela could hardly believe her ears. King Henry intended to milk John Bird for profits to support his military campaigns? She was grateful that she'd had a lifetime to learn command of her features. Otherwise, she surely would have burst out laughing. Or crying. Were all men such greedy gryphons that they must figure out how to snatch profits from every situation?

The discussion turned to the merits of a pilgrimage destination, and the features it might require. A comfortable dormitory of sorts, a hospital, to house pilgrims and to tend to the ailments that brought them to seek the aid of John Bird and his healing gifts. Perhaps they could sell small bottles of blessed holy water? Pilgrimage badges, made of cast or stamped metal and perhaps ornamented with colorful ribbon, could be sold so that the pilgrims might go abroad and tell others of the wonders to be seen in Salisbury.

Ela watched in astonishment as this mercenary discussion continued between Bishop de Bingham and the king. She studied Bird's face but found it impassive and unreadable, until at last they deigned to ask his opinion of all their grand plans.

He wanted to know where the hospital for hosting the pilgrims would be built and whether there might be a house for him built at the same time. And if he might have a full staff at the house to tend to his needs. Ela could hardly believe her ears.

The bishop made a strong case that the entire new complex should be built as near as possible to the cathedral, where pilgrims would surely want to pray and enjoy services and—of course—take theサcrament at mass.

Servants brought refreshments of spiced wine poured into engraved goblets. Then they passed around silver platters laden with sweet pastries and honeyed nutmeats. The bishop ate and drank with considerable enthusiasm, though Ela noticed that John Bird seemed more restrained in his consumption. Perhaps he wanted to be sure to keep his wits about him.

They discussed the wondrous creature whose bones were still emerging from the bank of the River Avon. The bishop excitedly told the king that Bird had foreseen the discovery by dreaming of a dragon, and had described his dream before a jury. Ela herself had no explanation for that strange turn of events.

By the time they'd finished their cups of wine Ela felt that the foundation trenches of the new hospital and Bird's lavish new palace were as good as dug. She didn't dare say a single word in opposition. There was nothing to be gained by stepping in front of a runaway horse as it bolted through the streets of Salisbury.

Her only hope lay in finding and revealing the truth about John Bird before anything worse happened.

CHAPTER 18

"Our investigations must be subtle and thorough," said Ela to Bill. They sat in chairs by the fire in the privacy of her solar, late at night. "There can be no room for doubt or discussion. Now that the king looks to Bird as the golden goose that will lay the funds for his imagined military triumphs, the stakes are higher than ever."

Bill seemed amused rather than worried by today's turn of events. "Your concern is well-founded, no doubt. But I hardly think you need worry that we're in danger of being ousted from this castle in favor of John Bird."

"Stranger things have happened, dear Bill. I've seen reversals of fortune so sharp they would snap a man's neck—if the hangman's noose didn't do it for him."

"True, my lady. But the king is your family. He's already shown affection for your children and I feel sure he intends their fortunes to rise along with his own."

"God willing, dear Bill. But I wish to ride to Wiggiford Mill myself and interview those who had dealings with the man who stayed there. I wish to determine for myself if it is indeed John Bird before I risk bringing another man to Salisbury or presenting him to John Bird in front of a jury."

"My sword and steed stand ready to accompany you. When do we ride?"

"Tomorrow at first light."

∾

ELA TOOK a good-sized entourage with her for the journey to Wiggiford Mill, including the guards who'd previously gone there and spoken with the late Piers Marsh's wife and son.

The white sky of the bright, clear winter's day illuminated the landscape. The ground was cold enough to be firm underfoot, and the frosty morning dew made the hills sparkle as they rode away from Salisbury. They alternated walking and trotting, with the occasional canter uphill, to keep their horses breathing easy as they covered the relatively long distance to the remote village.

They could hear the bells for Nones ringing in a nearby village as they rode into the hamlet of Wiggiford Mill. The mill itself rose out of the hedgerows to one side of the road. Around it hunkered a collection of straggling thatched cottages. Chickens flapped and clucked to the side of the road and a tethered goat looked up in surprise from the wall of one of the houses.

As expected, the residents soon emerged from their houses at the sound of clattering hooves and jingling harnesses.

"Where is the inn?" asked Bill. They'd decided to start with the innkeeper's son and take their investigations from there.

A woman in a blue headwrap pointed down the road to where they could just make out a high roof surrounded by oaks. "They've good rooms aplenty, so you won't have trouble finding a bed!" she exclaimed, obviously taking them for travelers. "Beset by tragedy though, so do have a care."

"What do you mean?" said Ela.

"Murdered he was! The innkeeper himself and then his brother. Some say there's a curse on them."

"Who would put a curse on them?"

"Oh, there was this terrible man who stayed there for some weeks. Made a friend of everyone in the village at first. Said he was a scribe and could help them write their wills and he wouldn't charge them a penny. But when he found out what people had he started trying to get it from them by trickery and foul means. Telling false fortunes promising riches, and getting them drunk then taking their money and treasures. One morning he was gone and the innkeeper was found dead. His brother said the man never paid him a penny for all the nights he slept under his roof and all the good meals his wife cooked for him."

"His brother came to Salisbury to report the crime."

"And wound up dead from the news I heard!"

Ela didn't want to spread the news that a suspected killer was wandering abroad in Salisbury and had just shared sweetmeats with the king, so she kept that news to herself. "I'm here to gather any information that might lead us to find the killer. I'd like to speak to Piers Marsh's son and wife. Can you lead me to them?"

~

THE INNKEEPER'S WIFE, Agnes Marsh, was a large woman with chapped red hands and a worried expression. Her white apron and her kerchief shone brightly as fresh snow. "I told him to be careful! That Daniel Witchett was cunning as a snake. Worked his way right into the middle of us and then struck! They say he stole Widow Lester's silver cups that her grandfather brought from London."

"Would you be able to identify Witchett, even if he were dressed differently?"

"Of course, I would! His face won't leave my mind. Haunts my nights, it does."

"Will you come to Salisbury with me for that purpose, if needed?"

"Do you have him in prison? I don't want him to kill me as well." She spoke quite seriously.

Ela hesitated. "I promise to keep you safe. You shall be under guard at every moment."

Her brow creased. "It sounds like I'd be a prisoner. I don't want that."

A boy of about eighteen, who'd been listening from the doorway, came forward. "I'll come to Salisbury and point him out. I'm not afraid."

"You're the innkeeper's son?"

"I am."

"This is my only son, Alwin," said his mother. "I don't like him leaving me here all alone without a man's protection. There's just a kitchen maid and a potboy left now my husband and his brother are gone."

"I quite understand," said Ela. "I wish I could bring John Bird here for you to identify, but I'm afraid that's impossible. He's a very cunning and resourceful villain, as you know."

"You do have him locked up, though?" Widow Marsh peered at her suspiciously.

Ela inhaled a shallow breath. She couldn't lie to this good woman. "I confess that we don't. He's managed to ingratiate himself with the bishop and made a very comfortable place for himself in Salisbury. I risk my reputation by even accusing him of wrongdoing."

The widow Marsh blinked. "Is he robbing the people of Salisbury blind?"

"He's doing his best, though he's running into the problem that the church has found a good use for his earnings." She didn't mention that the king himself intended to do the same. "So he's under the watchful eye of the bishop and all the brothers of Salisbury Cathedral—for now. But I'm fearful that he'll evade their hospitality and I suspect he has money or treasure buried somewhere in the area that he'll use to fund his escape."

"I'd bet my right hand that Widow Lester's cups are buried there."

"Quite possibly." If he didn't sell them to someone already, which was perhaps more likely. "So you can see that the need to identify him as a murderer and formally accuse him is quite urgent."

"I do." The widow sighed. "But I didn't see him kill my husband. And from what I understand, no one saw him kill poor Hugo, either. What will happen if he simply denies it and says we're all mad?"

This was a good question and Ela did not have a good answer for it. "I'm gathering evidence that will convince a jury of his guilt. Your testimony that he attempted to trick the people of Wiggiford Mill and that your husband was found dead on the morning he left should prove convincing on top of all the evidence we already have."

"I suppose we could lock up the inn and send the kitchen girl and the lad home to their parents. Then Alwin and I could both come. But what if he tries to kill us?"

"I'll provide lodgings in my castle to ensure your safety."

∾

THAT NIGHT, the innkeeper's wife and son slept in a room high up in the castle, with guards stationed at the door and on the ground outside. Unless Bird could somehow transform himself into a bird, there would be no way for him to enter the room and harm them.

The next morning, Ela sent for a jury and dispatched a messenger and guards to the bishop's palace to bring Bird back to face Agnes and Alwin Marsh.

The messenger and guards returned empty-handed.

Contrite and flustered, the young messenger bowed low. "My lady, I said that his presence was not just requested but urgently required by the High Sheriff of Wiltshire."

"What did Bird say?"

"I wasn't even able to see John Bird. The bishop's men said he was in seclusion—in prayer they said—and that he wouldn't be available."

Fury surged in Ela. "I shall send guards to arrest him. And I shall accompany them to make sure the deed is done. Call John Dacus to come as well. I wish to have my co-sheriff with me when I bring the weight of all the authority of Wiltshire to bear down upon Robert de Bingham."

As the bells for Nones sounded, Ela rode up outside the bishop's palace with Bill and John Dacus and a veritable army of more than twenty guards. She'd been tempted to request an entire unit of the king's garrison, since they were stationed in and around her castle, but had no wish to alarm the whole town of Salisbury.

They gathered outside the main door to the bishop's palace, and a guard approached and knocked on the door.

A dark-robed brother came out and muttered the same excuses. Ela rode right up to him so the steam from her horse's breath almost clouded his face. "I demand to speak with the bishop."

The monk muttered something and closed the door. Ela

heard him shoot the bolt behind it. She turned to Bill, astonished. Would they have to lay siege to the bishop's palace? In her current mood, she was ready to lead the charge.

But then the bolt slid back, the door opened, and the bishop—dressed in an embroidered robe and hat—emerged. "My dear lady, I believe our brother has explained that, as a man of deep piety, John Bird cannot be disturbed in his holy contemplations."

"I don't give a fig for his holy contemplations," said Ela, unable to conceal her anger at this further delay. "I believe him to be a triple murderer. I have witnesses at my castle who can confirm whether or not he's the man who killed their husband and his brother."

The bishop's face paled and his mouth hung open for a moment before he replied. "Impossible. John Bird is a man of God. As you know, there are plans afoot to create a shrine here in Salisbury that will draw pilgrims from all over the world. Even as far as Rome! These hateful accusations bring to mind the cruel taunts of the authorities against our dear savior! Let us not forget that he was accused of crimes and even sentenced and hung by the Roman authorities in their ignorance. Thank Heaven that times are different now and that, as the representative of God's Holy Church here in Salisbury, I can protect God's emissary that he sent to bring joy and peace and healing to us here on earth."

Now Ela found herself stunned into silence. This man saw her as Pontius Pilate and King Herod rolled into one? Worse yet, King Henry had been drawn in by the promise of riches and glory that this evil man had conjured with his lies.

"John Bird healed you! You've seen his holy miracles with your own eyes and felt them in your heart. Can you deny it?"

Ela did find it difficult to explain how John Bird had managed to heal even one person, but she thought it entirely possible that his powers—if they existed—came from a far darker force than God.

"If John Bird is innocent, these good people will gaze on him and say that they don't know him. They'll confirm that he's not the man who stayed at their inn and left their husband and father lying in a pool of blood on the floor of his inn's dining room."

"Do you think I would let John Bird be falsely accused of trumped-up crimes?" asked Bishop de Bingham, with unaccustomed fervor. "God has charged me with keeping him safe that the world might know him. My duty to God comes before my duty to the sheriff of Wiltshire." His voice shook a little as he said that last part. She wasn't sure he trembled with fervor for the Holy Spirit or terror at the havoc that the men of the king's garrison might wreak upon his shiny new palace and its occupants.

Ela had no intention of unleashing fury and violence here in Salisbury, no matter how much her blood boiled at this affront. "Bishop de Bingham, we have not known each other very long, but I believe my reputation speaks for me. Have you ever known me to be anything but a pious representative of God's work here on earth?"

His hesitation was troubling. "Your good works are well known, my lady. But your obsession with undermining the reputation of a true miracle worker is deeply troubling." He paused again, and his eyes narrowed slightly. "And, if I may speak frankly, there are many who feel that you might better serve humanity and the nature of your gentler sex by taking your place in a cloister. As many wealthy widows choose to."

Ela struggled to keep her expression neutral. Her horse shifted underneath her, likely disturbed by the tension in her muscles. "Your opinion of my purpose here on earth is neither welcome nor appropriate to your station. The king has appointed me as High Sheriff of Wiltshire, along with

John Dacus as my co-sheriff—she indicated Dacus, who sat mounted close behind her—and I am here to do my duty to protect the people of Wiltshire—and of all England—from a murderer in their midst. If you insist on trying to stop me I will be forced to arrest you."

Bishop de Bingham crossed himself. "Heaven forbid, my lady. I shall write to the king for his advice in this situation. Do you agree to wait until I hear back from him?"

"I shall write to him myself at once. Since he is barely a stone's throw away across the fields, I shall expect an answer by this afternoon and action will be taken before sundown today."

She turned and rode away, creating some commotion among the guards and horses who'd crowded up behind her.

How dare he? Had the bishop also been possessed by the devil himself? The king would surely side with her in wanting a suspected murderer to at least face his accusers. If John Bird were innocent, he would soon be free to go about his business. Only if he was found guilty would he be imprisoned and tried and knocked from his throne of impending sainthood.

∞

BACK AT THE PALACE, Ela composed a hasty letter to the king, being sure to mention their family association and her record of bringing evil men to justice. She wanted to take it to Clarendon herself, but John Dacus convinced her that it might be better if he went because then he could make a strong case without the possibility of her being personally affronted by a refusal.

Soon Dacus returned with the news that the king had departed Clarendon for Westminster, and that a messenger had been sent onward with her letter. Ela sat on her dais, dealing with the usual stream of petitioners. Agnes and Alwin Marsh sat at another table on one side of the hall, obviously uncomfortable in the busy, public environment. Ela dismounted from her dais, led Dacus aside, and beckoned Bill Talbot to follow. She led them into the armory and motioned for Bill to close the door.

"This gives Bird another chance to escape."

"We have men outside the bishop's palace, stationed in the street outside his window."

"John Bird is cunning as a fox and might disguise himself again and slip past the bishop's men and my guards. It's only a matter of time before he does."

"Not if he enjoys being feted like royalty," said Bill Talbot. "He seems to have adapted well to life in the bishop's palace. And now he can look forward to having a shrine built around him where people will bow down at his feet all day long."

"I suspect any man but a true saint would soon rankle under such restriction," said Ela. "We must find a way to draw him in front of a jury before he grows weary of being a living saint and seeing all his riches being snatched away by others. Does he still appear in the marketplace?"

"Nearly every afternoon," said John Dacus. "At least for an hour or so. Men and women from miles away wait there all day."

"Inside my castle walls?" She wondered why she hadn't noticed the presence of strangers so close to her home.

"No, my lady. He now sits to greet his audience in the marketplace in New Salisbury, near the bishop's palace."

Of course. The bishop wouldn't want to give her a chance to dip her fingers into his revenues. "Then we must go to him and bring the jurors with us. And we must do it in such a way that we aren't detected until Alwin and Agnes Marsh have had a chance to identify him. At what hour does Bird usually greet the public?"

"I shall send a messenger to wait until he emerges, then come straight to us."

"In the meantime, assemble a jury of at least three here in my hall. We must make a plan to surprise him."

∾

FORTUNATELY, the three faithful jurors who'd come to the hall to meet with Bird that morning, and been sent away disappointed, all agreed to come back at once. Two of them, Thomas Pryce and Matthew Hart, were of advanced years but determined in their pursuit of justice. The third, Will Dyer—in fact a cooper and not a dyer at all—was young but known for being bold and insistent in his questioning, and was an ideal juror to have as a witness.

They gathered in the armory as Ela didn't want townspeople or garrison soldiers to overhear her plan to cast aspersions and hopefully even imprison the beloved "miracle man" in their midst.

Agnes Marsh seemed very anxious and agitated. "What if the crowd turns on us?"

Ela hadn't considered this possibility and the prospect of it did alarm her slightly now that she pondered it. "We shall bring a strong force of guards with us, both to secure John Bird in custody and to protect us all from any naysayers." She tried to sound confident enough to reassure them.

Alwin Marsh, young and gangly in a tunic that might once have been his father's, had a steely look in his eyes. "My heart aches to see him face justice. When do we leave for the marketplace?"

"We await word that John Bird is set up on his throne and surrounded by petitioners. We want him hemmed in by the crowd as well as our guards. It wouldn't do for him to learn of our approach and vanish back into the bishop's palace. Short of breaching the walls and risking excommunication by the pope, I can't reach him in there.

Thomas Pryce, whose eyes glimmered with enthusiasm for the undertaking, tittered with laughter at the prospect of them breaching the walls of the palace. Then he cleared his throat and straightened his face. "Should we be armed?"

"Oh, dear me, no. Sir William Talbot and Sir John Dacus will bear arms, as will the guards. All you must bring are your eyes and your keen memory so you can recount the details at the assizes—God willing."

"How will they not learn of our arrival when there's only one road from the castle into the town?" asked Bill. "Should we ride across the countryside and approach from a different direction?"

"We shall travel in a wagon." Ela looked at Dacus. "A wagon disguised as a farmer's cart loaded high with…" she struggled to think of what a farmer's cart might bear into town in the dead of winter. "Faggots of wood." She turned to Bill. "Please arrange for such a cart to be procured and loaded. We should have wood enough in the castle stores to effect the illusion. And they must leave room for us to travel inside it."

Bill exited the armory to find the cart.

"Let the rest of us wait in here, where no one can get a whiff of our intentions. I don't want word getting back to either the bishop or his men, let alone John Bird himself."

CHAPTER 19

⌒

Bill Talbot pulled Ela aside. "My lady, surely you cannot intend to ride on a loaded wagon along with the jurors?" They stood in a vaulted passage between the armory and the courtyard where the wagon awaited them.

He made a good point. The dignity of her office demanded prudence. "I shall walk behind it." The walk was barely two miles and a wagon loaded with wood and jurors could hardly travel above walking speed. If she wore a plain cloak, likely no one would recognize her.

"Then I shall walk with you. But may I prevail upon you to ride? Then at least there is an easier escape to be made if it's required."

Ela stared at him. "You think the bishop's men may set upon us?"

He made an odd movement with his lips. "Or the townspeople. John Bird has made himself very popular with them."

"I trust that they would still respect the authority of their sheriff. And perhaps I flatter myself to think I have also won a place in their affections."

Bill's momentary hesitation chastened her. "Of course, my lady. The people of Salisbury appreciate all you and your family have done and continue to do for them. But in the heat of the moment, when passions are running high…."

She swallowed her pride. "I trust your judgment, Bill. We shall ride together, but in borrowed cloaks and plain tack that disguise our identity. No one will glance twice at hoods pulled over our heads against this February chill."

Bill looked relieved. "A clever idea, my lady. I have two such cloaks myself in my chambers. I shall send a servant to fetch them at once."

ONCE BIRD WAS OBSERVED to be out in public, a messenger conveyed the news. Horses already stood saddled—not Ela's distinctive and well-known Freya, but two mild-mannered bay palfreys. Ela—in a blue wool cloak with no fur trim or ornamentation—and Bill in a gray one, mounted while the jurors and Dacus climbed into the wagon amid the faggots of wood. Blankets cushioned the floor of the wagon to minimize the discomfort for the two older jurors.

Agnes and Alwin Marsh climbed in last, that they might be the first to jump out. The idea was to draw as close as possible to where John Bird sat to greet his admirers, then quickly make the identification before he could vanish or be whisked away by the bishop.

The journey to Salisbury passed quickly despite the chill air of the February afternoon. Ela and Bill made sure that no one passed them on the road—Bill commanded any travelers and riders to stay behind them—so that word of their arrival might not reach the town before they did.

The messenger had told them exactly where to find Bird, and they pulled up the wagon right at the edge of the crowd of people surrounding him. Immediately a few people left the crowd, interested in the price and portability of their load of wood.

"Make all haste!" hissed Ela from deep within her hood.

Alwin Marsh climbed down first and turned to offer a hand to his mother. Unsteady on her feet after the cramped ride, Agnes took a moment to find her bearings. Ela and Bill had dismounted and followed close behind them into the crowd.

"Is it him?" whispered Ela, heart pounding. Bird sat on a sort of throne—a chair raised on a makeshift dais—amidst the crowd.

Agnes Marsh peered at him and blinked. And frowned. "He doesn't look the same."

John Bird wore a velvet robe and a fur-trimmed cap more suited to a noble than a man of prayer. "He doesn't look anything like the scrawny man who arrived here just weeks ago," said Ela. "Try to picture him without his rich raiment."

"I must get closer. My eyes aren't as clear as they used to be." She grabbed hold of her son's sleeve and pulled him closer. Ela took hold of his son's other arm so that she didn't get left behind in the crowd. Bird sat in the chair, wafting his arms around as if conjuring and muttering inaudible words under his breath.

Then he looked up and his eyes fixed right on Ela. She saw recognition dawn in them. She'd pushed her hood back enough to get a clear view of the scene and it revealed her face. She saw his gaze jump from her to Alwin Marsh, and then to Agnes. His muttering stilled.

They may not recognize him in his finery, but he recognizes them.

Ela decided to seize the moment before John Bird somehow snatched it away from her. "John Bird, I bring before you two suffering souls who've lost those nearest and dearest to them. Their hearts ache for relief. Can you heal their pain?"

Panic flashed across Bird's face before he got it back under control. "Prayers to the Lord our God are the surest way to relief, my lady," he said in an uncharacteristically low voice. Was he trying to disguise his identity by changing his voice?

"Is it him?" Ela whispered again, right into Agnes's ear. They'd agreed that if Agnes did recognize Bird that she'd shout it out and the jurors would come forward to witness the scene, then Ela would command the guards to seize Bird.

"I can't be sure, my lady."

John Bird stood up, clearly ready to turn and head for the shelter of the Bishop's palace.

"Call out his name—the one you knew him by," urged Ela. She wanted to provoke a reaction that might help to confirm his identity.

Agnes hesitated, looking nervously about the crowd. But her son yelled, "Daniel Witchett!" at the top of his lungs. People in the crowd turned to stare at Alwin. Bird's face blanched and he jumped down from his dais.

"Grab him!" cried Ela to her guards. She turned to the son. "Is this Daniel Witchett?"

"He looks so different," said the son. "And sounds different too, but if it's not him, why did the sound of that name startle him so?"

Two guards had seized John Bird and each one held an arm. He resisted for a moment before realizing the futility of the gesture. "Unhand me! Send for the bishop and tell him I am being abused by agents of the Devil!"

A murmur rose in the crowd, and Ela felt eyes turn toward her.

"Your countess has been against me from the moment I arrived here!" he cried. "Accusing me of all manner of things when all I've done is try to share the healing gift God bestowed upon me when he raised me from the dead."

"It's true!" shouted someone from the crowd.

"God sent me among you, and your countess is jealous that I am more loved and appreciated by her people than she is."

A hum of approval rose from the crowd. "Blessed by God, he is!" called a woman. Ela looked around to see who it was, but everyone's lips seemed to be moving.

"And now they seek to take me into custody as they did with Jesus Christ, our Lord and Savior, who died on the cross for our sins! Will you crucify me too?" He spat the words directly at Ela.

"It's him. I know it is," said Alwin. "The way his eyes narrow when he gets angry. He looked like that when he cursed at Pa for wanting his bill paid."

Ela saw the bishop emerge from the front door of his palace, which lay only a few yards away.

"Your Grace," called Ela, hoping she could summon him as an ally. "I bring Alwin Marsh from Wiggiford Mill. He has identified John Bird as a man who—under another name—stayed in his family's inn and is accused of killing his father, the innkeeper. His uncle, Hugo Marsh, came here to warn me and to see if Bird was the man who killed his brother—and who was found murdered in his bed."

The bishop looked this way and that as if trying to consider options. His men, including several burly lay brothers, had marched up to Ela's guards and looked ready to wrest Bird away from them.

"John Bird is here under my protection," said the bishop, his voice rising. "I demand that you release him into my care."

"As High Sheriff of Wiltshire, I insist that John Bird

appear before a jury of his peers to face his accusers," replied Ela, as calmly as she could.

The crowd booed, and she even heard a jeer from the back of it.

"Silence!" shouted Bill Talbot, who'd grown increasingly agitated. "Or you'll sit in the jail yourselves."

The crowd settled somewhat, though the looks on their faces showed they were anything but placated.

"My lady, perhaps he could face an ecclesiastical court—" began the bishop.

"No, Your Grace. I must insist on an appearance before the court of the county. If the jurors find any reason to doubt that he is guilty, he shall be freed." She prayed that the jurors would use their common sense and not be swayed by John Bird's undeniable charisma. "You may attend yourself, Your Grace, and see that he is treated fairly. We will convey him to the castle at once. I have three members of the jury of the hundred here with me to make sure that all proceedings are conducted in front of reliable witnesses. And I call on any jurors present in the crowd to make themselves known and to come forward to serve."

It was a risk calling on people who had come to the marketplace of their own free will to gaze upon John Bird, but she wanted as many jurors as possible to listen to the evidence against him. "Guards, please transport John Bird to the castle at once. You may use this wagon of wood to convey him but take great care that he does not escape."

～

IT TOOK some time before Bird arrived back at the castle. Ela's gut stayed clenched the entire time for fear that he should escape. A man so cunning and resourceful and ruthless was quite capable of killing a guard with that guard's own weapon and stealing his clothes. Bill Talbot himself kept his eyes on Bird for the entire journey, along with four guards, all instructed to keep their fingers wrapped around the hilt of their swords.

Back at the castle, Ela took the precaution of chaining Bird to a heavy wooden chair in the center of the tables set up for the jury.

"Our dear Savior bore his indignities and betrayals with grace," cried Bird at one point. "May the Lord grant me mercy as I follow in his footsteps."

While a common criminal might have been smacked across the face for such an insolent outburst, Ela instructed the guards to show restraint. The pope and the king had both taken an interest in the fate of John Bird and it wouldn't do to make him a martyr.

The news of Bird's arrest traveled swiftly throughout the town, both around the cathedral and inside the castle walls. Several more jurors arrived and crowded around the tables in the hall. The bishop came and brought what seemed like fifty men—priests, tonsured monks and lay brothers—from the monastic community around the cathedral.

Ela didn't remember a time when she'd seen the hall more crowded, except perhaps for the feast after her husband's funeral five years earlier. It was also hard to recall an occasion when she'd felt under more pressure. If she didn't handle this trial carefully, Bird could walk away from here a free man and she'd have lost her last chance to find justice for his victims.

And she might even find herself in the chair—accused of heresy or apostasy—if she couldn't prove that she was pursuing Bird because he was a criminal, not because he was a holy man.

~

At last, the hall settled enough that John Dacus stood and called the proceedings to order. Ela knew that she could turn the reins over to him and have him bear the risk of censure if accusing Bird might backfire. But she wouldn't forgive herself if Dacus mishandled the questioning and left an opening for Bird to escape through.

Dacus was a good man and took his duties seriously, but did not have a particularly incisive mind and was inclined to take people at face value. John Bird made his living from preying on such folk. Ela was blessed—or cursed—with a natural suspicion about people's motives. Perhaps her mother had nurtured it in her during her youth, when she hid her away in Normandy to keep her safe from older male relatives who'd have liked to get their hands on her inheritance.

So, Ela took charge of the questioning. "We are here today because the man who has become known to us as John Bird is accused of two murders, possibly three. These two people," she pointed at Agnes and Alwin Marsh," have come here today to confirm that John Bird is the same man as Daniel Witchett, who stayed at their family's inn in Wiggiford Mill. Daniel Witchett left his bill unpaid and Hugo Marsh, their husband and father, dead."

A man in a dark gray tunic, trimmed with black, raised his hand. Ela didn't recognize him. "Who are you?"

"My name is Warin Fitz Peter and I am a man of the law."

"Who sent you here?" asked Ela.

"Word of John Bird's arrest has reached the king. His Majesty sent me here to oversee the proceedings and ensure that all is handled according to the letter of the law."

Ela's heart almost stopped. *The king had sent a lawyer? For what purpose?* "Why did you raise your hand?"

"I have a question, My lady. Did anyone see this mysterious Daniel Witchett kill the innkeeper?"

Ela looked at Agnes and Alwin Marsh. She was fairly sure of the answer to this question. "Alwin Marsh, could you answer this question for Master Fitz Peter?"

Alwin shook his head.

"You cannot answer my question, boy?" asked Fitz Peter imperiously.

"No, I mean that I did not see the murder happen. I heard them argue over Witchett's unpaid bill. In the morning, Daniel Witchett was gone and my father lay in a pool of his own blood, having been stabbed in the chest with a knife." The boy sounded surprisingly self-assured.

"So, you did not see the murder with your own eyes, but merely made an assumption."

"Yes," said Alwin Marsh aloud.

Ela's heart sank. She knew where this was going. She determined to seize control of the proceedings before Warin could do so. "On the day that the person known to us as John Bird arrived in Salisbury, a man was found, dead, in the center of the circle of stones on the nearby plain. The corpse was discovered by none other than myself and Sir William Talbot. I believe that —rather than rising from the dead by some Heaven-sent miracle—that body was hidden away in a pigsty by John Bird, who then claimed to be the dead man risen back to life."

A murmur spread throughout the hall. Ela hadn't wanted to depart so quickly from the murder of Hugo Marsh, but she wanted to remind them all of the very mysterious—nay, suspicious—circumstances under which John Bird arrived in Salisbury.

Fitz Peter raised his hand again. Ela, trying to tamp down her irritation, turned to him. "Master Fitz Peter?"

"You may call me Sir Warin," he pronounced with a rather apologetic expression. "Was a body ever found in a pigsty, my lady?"

"Indeed it was," said Ela. "And I shall call upon the coroner Giles Haughton to recall all of the grisly details for your information."

Haughton described the fragmentary findings left by the ravenous appetites of the pigs. He also revealed that the remains had been identified as one Wulf Huntley, a man known to have swindled several local people out of their money in exchange for a promised cow that was never delivered.

"I suspect that any man killing such a villain was doing the people of Wiltshire a favor," said Fitz Peter, with an amused expression.

"I prefer for justice to be meted out in a court of law," said Ela grimly. "And I leave such a weighty responsibility as taking a man's life to the traveling justice at the assizes."

"Ah, yes. I have been a traveling justice myself, though not in these parts," Fitz Peter said, as if he found the whole idea rather amusing.

Ela's heart sank even further. Had he been sent here to assist in the quest for justice? Or to undermine their entire enterprise and ensure that Bird might continue to lay his golden eggs to fund the king's military campaigns? "Do you have further questions?"

"Did anyone see John Bird in the company—dead or alive —of this Wulf Huntley, the swindler?"

Ela spoke through tight lips. "They did not."

"So, the idea that John Bird killed this Wulf Huntley is yet another supposition, with no actual proof or evidence?" He asked as if genuinely curious. Ela knew instinctively that his only curiosity was in how quickly he could bury her accusations in a manure-heap of doubt.

"We believe that John Bird encountered Wulf Huntley on his way back home after successfully swindling another victim. Bird robbed Huntley and killed him and disposed of the body."

"And then ran into the middle of the circle of stones and played dead?" Fitz Peter looked amused as if she was telling a marvelous and entertaining tale.

Anger simmered in Ela's gut at his dismissive attitude. "Sir William and I believe that we encountered the very dead body of Wulf Huntley in the circle of stones early that morning. He had a deep stab wound and his clothes were soaked with blood. Naturally, my first concern was to summon the coroner and call a jury. Since Sir William could not leave me, both of us had to ride back to Salisbury. Unfortunately, this required us to leave the body unattended."

"It would behoove you to ride with more guards, my lady," said Fitz Peter with a serious expression.

"I usually do. This was a simple, early morning pleasure ride and I did not expect to come upon a corpse. The stone circle is a few miles from Salisbury, so fetching witnesses took some time. When we returned with members of the jury, the body was gone. Later that same day, John Bird wandered into town, wearing the same blood-drenched clothes. He claimed to have been stabbed but the coroner examined Bird's back and there was barely a scratch on it. He certainly didn't bear the deep wound witnessed by Sir William and myself on the body we saw earlier that day."

"You think that John Bird stabbed himself in the back to pretend to be the supposedly dead man you saw?" Fitz Peter looked as if he wanted to burst out laughing.

Ela took affront at his mocking manner. "Perhaps the coroner should speak on the matter."

Giles Haughton described the examination of Bird that he'd performed in the mortuary on the day he was found. How the wound on his back wasn't consistent with the kind of deep, bleeding stab wound that would have soaked the clothes he was wearing with blood. He also suggested that this might mean the clothes he came to town in were soaked with someone else's blood.

The lawyer seemed to find this even more amusing. "For what purpose would he dress in someone else's blood-soaked garments?"

Ela suddenly felt very tired. "To convince the townspeople that he was a murder victim and not a murderer."

"If he'd just murdered a man, then why didn't he leave at once? Surely that's what a typical villain would do."

"Not if his clothes were splattered with blood from the killing," said Ela.

Warin Fitz Peter looked at the jury as if defying them to believe such nonsense. "What do you all make of this rather preposterous tale?"

CHAPTER 20

Ela felt Bill stiffen beside her. Fitz Peter was now acting as if he was the sheriff and in charge of the proceedings. Bill, as her closest ally and staunch defender, wanted to remind them that she was in charge. Much as she would have loved for Bill to scold him and perhaps even order his arrest, she laid her fingers on Bill's arm to stop him.

Fitz Peter had been sent by the king, to do the king's bidding, which was—at least from what she'd seen so far—to convince the court that Bird was innocent of all wrongdoing. If she tried too hard to stop him from asking questions or delving into the strange events of that day, she might help him win the jury to his side. She couldn't ignore the fact that Bird was a man of great cunning and had won nearly all the townspeople—including the jurors—to his side in his first appearance in her hall.

Thomas Pryce described how Bird had convinced them all that he was dazed, having narrowly escaped death by the grace of God. He observed that they had no good reason to disbelieve him, especially when he soon proved himself to have a strange ability to heal the sick, including those who had been ill for years.

Ela's heart sank further. She'd hoped the jurors were on her side, but now she could see at least Pryce getting sucked back into the myth of the erstwhile Saint of Salisbury.

"John Bird, do you indeed have powers to heal the sick?" asked Fitz Peter, again as if he were in charge.

John Bird fidgeted in his chair. He probably would have gestured with his hands if they weren't strapped to the wood. "For reasons unknown to me, the Good Lord does seem to have granted me the power to heal. Ask any man gathered here today if that isn't true. Why, I healed the countess and her whole family from a deadly fever even after she'd tried her best to hunt me down like a common criminal."

"You healed the countess?" Fitz Peter seemed amazed. He made a theatrical gesture toward Ela, then back to Bird. "Countess Ela of Salisbury?"

Bird nodded. "Ask her yourself."

"Did John Bird indeed cure you of a malady, my lady?" He appeared genuinely curious.

Ela drew in a steadying breath. "I suffered from a fever, as did several other members of my household. At their urging, I agreed to let Bird try to heal us. We did indeed recover, though I cannot be sure whether it was just the natural course of the illness as the body healed itself."

"But you also cannot be sure that you were not cured by the healing power of God as transmitted through the blessed hands of John Bird?"

Ela found her anger getting the better of her. "Sir, have you forgotten that we are here today to examine whether John Bird has committed not one, not two, but three murders? It appears that this gathering has turned into a celebration of his arrival in Salisbury, not the careful inquisition it's intended to be." Her voice had more of an edge than she'd intended.

Silence throbbed in the usually bustling hall as all activity and conversation ceased. Ela felt as if she were a choirboy who'd spoken up out of turn, rather than the castellan of this very castle and High Sheriff of all Wiltshire.

Warin Fitz Peter seemed to look around him and take the measure of the hall. "I apologize, my lady, if my zeal for the truth has led to me speaking out of turn. As you know, the king sent me to assist with these proceedings."

"I do not recall the king ever sending a lawyer to observe our jury. Why does he take such a keen interest in this case?" She knew the answer already but wanted to hear what he would utter in front of the jury.

"The king was very taken with John Bird during their meeting and wishes to make sure that he's given the benefit of the doubt. As you know, the very Son of God suffered at the hands of the law because sometimes the laws and courts of men are not equipped to deal with those whose powers come from a far greater and more powerful source."

"Sir Warin, I promise you that I have no desire to play Pontius Pilate and crucify an innocent man. I want to know who killed Wulf Huntley, the innkeeper Piers Marsh and now his brother Hugo Marsh. Does it not seem strange beyond coincidence that John Bird—or Daniel Witchett as he was formerly known—was present in the place and time when each man was killed? And what good reason would a man have for changing his name? Such a change is rarely made for reasons other than deception for criminal purposes." She paused to let that sink in. "It would suggest that perhaps he's used many names throughout his life, and perpetrated a string of deceptions and frauds right across England."

The lawyer rose to his feet. "My lady, such speculation is

entirely unfounded! We can only judge a man based on the evidence and witness testimony we have at hand. Otherwise, any of us could come to court full of tall tales and lock up our enemies based solely on hearsay."

Ela chastised herself for letting her emotions run away with her. "What you say is true and, as sheriff, I cleave closely to the precepts of the law. I am simply suggesting that the man before us may possess a level of cunning that we have not seen before in Salisbury and should be investigated thoroughly."

"Once again, my lady, you introduce ideas based on imagination rather than reality." He smiled at her as if indulging a simpleton. Ela felt hot anger flare in her chest. How dare he? "John Bird's ability to heal the sick—by God's grace—is undisputed, even by you, is it not?"

"I can't explain it, that is true."

"Can you explain the Mysteries of the Faith?" He made a sweeping gesture as if those mysteries might swirl in the very air of her great hall. "Can you explain how our dear Lord rose from the dead on the third day after his crucifixion?" He paused for a moment as if giving her a chance to explain the Resurrection. "My lady, these events are beyond our comprehension, and with good reason. We are but mere mortals and not charged with understanding every aspect of the great and mystifying works of Our Lord here on earth."

Now he'd pitted her against God.

Ela knew she trod on dangerous ground if she risked butting her head against both the king's lawyer and the bishop. She cleared her throat. "Perhaps we should ask the jury to question John Bird and learn what we can about his motives." She tried to sound calm and was relieved that she managed to speak without her voice shaking. Her fury at being spoken to thus—in her own hall—was only tempered by the knowledge that no man, and certainly no woman, could take up battle against both the king and the church and win.

She'd been so focused on the audacity of Warin Fitz Peter and on Bird himself, who sat more calmly in his chair than she would have anticipated, that she hadn't paid much attention to the jury. Now she watched as they shifted awkwardly in their seats, none of them wanting to be the first to risk drawing the ire of a lawyer sent by the king.

She glanced at Agnes and Alwin Marsh, who both looked worried, as well they might.

"Might I ask the jurors some questions, that I might further familiarize myself with the case?" asked Fitz Peter of Ela.

She could hardly say no. "Please do," she said curtly.

"Sirs, when you came to the marketplace to arrest John Bird, what was your understanding of the situation?"

Again, they all fidgeted. Then Peter Howard spoke up. "The plan was to bring these two people—" He gestured at Agnes and Alwin Marsh. "Into the presence of John Bird that they might decide if he was the man who'd stayed at their inn."

"Is this what the others among you, who surprised him near the cathedral, understood?" The other two jurors who'd come in the cart nodded and muttered assent.

"We were told that Bird might be the man who'd killed Hugo Marsh, the innkeeper's brother, in his room at the Bull and Bear," added Thomas Pryce.

"So, at the time that you all climbed out of a wagon loaded with wood, and surprised John Bird as he was holding an audience, you did not have any actual proof even that he was that same man, let alone that he had committed any crime?"

The jurors mumbled agreement. Hugh Clifford now

glanced at Ela sideways, as if perhaps he was now thinking she'd tricked him into something.

She cleared her throat. "We had asked the bishop to bring John Bird to the hall to face Agnes and Alvin Marsh in front of the jury. The bishop refused, which is the only reason we were forced to surprise him."

The bishop, who sat near the king's lawyer, shifted in his chair.

Ela didn't want the bishop resting too comfortably in the lawyer's shadow. "Bishop de Bingham, might I ask why you refused to allow John Bird to meet his accusers in front of a jury as the law commands?"

The bishop straightened in his chair. "My lady, the church has accepted that John Bird is a miracle worker sent by God to show his mercy here on earth. We find the continued suspicion of him by the secular authorities to be both unwarranted and unholy."

Ela could no longer contain herself. "So even if he were to stab a man in front of all of us you'd excuse it as the work of a saint and utterly forgivable?"

"My lady!" The lawyer now rose to his feet. "If we were all to witness such a godless act with our own eyes there would be no excuses and no doubt that could protect the prisoner from a charge of murder. My purpose here is to demonstrate to all of you that such a thing has not happened. John Bird, by any name, has not been seen or heard to murder a man either here in Salisbury or anywhere else. And thus I must insist that he be immediately released into the custody of the bishop."

All arguments to the contrary proved futile. Ela had Alwin Marsh swear on the Bible that John Bird was the same man as Daniel Witchett who had stayed at their inn in Wiggiford Mill. When questioned, John Bird didn't even deny it. He claimed that he'd disputed his bill, thinking it overly high, but had paid it before he left.

Ela described the "man of the cloth" seen entering Salisbury castle on the night of Hugo Marsh's murder and the "drunken woman" who'd been ejected from the castle before dawn. But Fitz Peter scoffed at her suspicions as mere theories, pointing out that no one had seen Bird departing from or returning to the bishop's palace, so there was no proof that he'd ever left it.

Ultimately Ela had little choice but to release Bird back into the custody of the bishop, as Fitz Peter insisted. However, before she did, she managed to bait a trap that she hoped he would fall into.

CHAPTER 21

"Who is the surprise eyewitness you intend to present to the jury tomorrow?" asked Bill. He and Ela sat near the fire in the hall after dinner. It was the first quiet moment they'd had to talk since that afternoon's jury had dispersed.

"There isn't one," admitted Ela.

"Then why did you say there would be?"

"I want Bird sweating, thinking he's about to be caught. I also mentioned that the traveling justice for the assizes arrives next week. Bird looked far too comfortable in my hall today, with the king's lawyer defending his interests."

"I can't understand why the king would want to defend a murderer," said Bill. "It makes no sense to me."

"King Henry needs money for his plan to reconquer the lands his father lost in France."

"Can't he just borrow it from the Jews as usual?"

"Why borrow what must be paid back when he can mint money of his own with a profitable pilgrimage site? I must say, I'm surprised that young King Henry is as prone to avarice as his forefathers. I had thought him more pious and humble."

Bill laughed. "A humble king? That would be something to see. And probably not much use to the people of England if young King Louis of France decided to invade England as his father did."

"God forbid." Ela crossed herself at the awful thought. The elder Louis's invasion had pitted her husband William against his brother King John, creating a rift that lasted the rest of John's lifetime. It had also created lasting enmity between William and Hubert de Burgh—who had remained loyal to John and henceforth considered William a traitor to the crown. Thus, perhaps Louis's war of conquest sowed the bitter seeds whose harvest had been her husband's death by poison at the hand of Hubert de Burgh.

"Are you hoping that fear of a damning witness will flush Bird out of his burrow at the bishop's palace?"

"That is exactly my intention. Bird doesn't know who this witness is, so there's no one for him to kill and silence. I hope that he'll attempt to flee. My guards will follow anyone who leaves the bishop's palace by any route—be it a door or an upper window or a chimney—and follow them no matter where they go."

"I suppose any attempt to flee Salisbury would confirm his guilt."

"Yes, and betray the bishop's generosity and the king's hopes. He already knows that any money raised by his efforts will be spirited away from him. I can't imagine that a cunning criminal wants to sit still and be fleeced for the rest of his natural life."

"Do you trust the guards not to miss his escape?"

"I chose the best men I could find. Each one came hand-picked and highly recommended." asked Ela. She had been let down by guards before. They were mortal men, after all, and some of them were lazy or corruptible. "I can hardly stand outside the bishop's palace all night myself."

"You can't, but I can."

"Bill, please don't put yourself in harm's way. John Bird is a very dangerous man. No doubt he already sees you as the enemy since you're my right hand."

"I may be older than I used to be, but I'm still a trained knight and can defend myself if the occasion calls for it." Bill looked positively enthusiastic at the prospect. "It would give me great pleasure to find myself in a situation where I'm called upon to run my sword through the bowels of John Bird."

"Don't say such a thing!" She didn't want Bill to get the idea that she hoped he'd be Bird's executioner. "It's my duty as sheriff to bring him to trial, not to send him to meet his final judgment in the hereafter. The last thing I need is for the king and the bishop to accuse you of murdering our local saint. You are far more important to me even than the exciting prospect of seeing John Bird dangling from the end of a rope."

Bill's expression grew strange. "I'm touched. Truly I am. I shall prove myself worthy of your trust as well as your affection. And I shall bring a man with me to report any news to you at once."

"I've told John Dacus to make sure that the guards don't stop Bird and arrest him if he should manage to escape. I want them to stay at a distance and follow him wherever he goes."

∼

ELA PACED IMPATIENTLY in her solar after dinner. What if Bird didn't try to escape? She'd be forced to lie tomorrow that her promised witness was absent. Even the jury would be sure to press her on his or her identity and she'd have to either confess the fabrication or wade further into a morass of lies. She knew that she could bring one of the residents of Wiggiford Mill who Bird had cheated in some way during his presence there, but Fitz Peter had already made it clear that anything short of an eyewitness to murder would be irrelevant at this point.

If I were Bird, I'd want to kill me. She knew this was also a possibility. He'd already gained entry to her castle under false pretenses and found his way into the upper floor of a busy inn. If Bird were determined, he might find a way to shin up the wall to her second-floor chambers.

With that thought, Ela walked to the window and opened it. The bitter cold February night air stung her face. She quickly closed the window and locked it, thanking God and Elsie for the warm fire in her chamber.

After some time in prayer, she returned to the hall, impatient for news. She'd told Bill to report to her even if nothing happened.

"Why are you up so late, Mama?" asked Stephen, now bent over the final battle in a chess game with his brother Richard.

"I could ask you the same thing," she replied. "Do you not have lessons and training early in the morning?"

"Bill told us that we could sleep in late tomorrow and begin our lessons after Nones."

"Ah, lucky you." She knew Bill wouldn't have told them the details of his assignment or they'd have begged to come along. And, in truth, they were both almost at the age where they'd be useful rather than a hindrance.

Still, the fewer people knew about her hopes for this evening, the better. Then she'd look less foolish tomorrow morning when it transpired that Bird had slept soundly in his bed at the bishop's palace.

A SURFEIT OF MIRACLES

~

ELA COULDN'T STAY up in the hall, pretending to amuse herself with her children or to pet her dogs, until all hours. Shortly after midnight she attended Lauds and then retired to her solar.

"Why don't you want to undress, my lady?" asked Elsie. The girl rubbed her sleepy eyes. "Are you expecting company tonight?"

Ela didn't even want to say that she was expecting Bill to report back to her. Elsie might ask questions. While the girl was kind and diligent in her work she wasn't sharp-witted enough to avoid being drawn into gossip.

"I shall attend Matins services in the night, my dear. I prefer to remain dressed. Don't trouble yourself to rise with me. I shall go to the chapel alone." She attempted a reassuring smile. She didn't even intend to go to Matins, where her presence would no doubt be quite a surprise for Father Thomas and the attendants. Another small white lie. Perhaps she should go to the service, after all?

"Go to bed, Elsie. You look so tired."

"Let me tuck you in, my lady, and bank your fire."

"There's no need, I promise you. I miss my husband fiercely tonight and wish to seek comfort at my prie-dieu." She felt a stab of guilt that she'd used her late husband as an excuse—though she was sure William would understand. "I'll see you in the morning."

Elsie slept in a small chamber near hers, where she listened for Ela's every move so she could leap out of bed and assist her. Ela hoped that Elsie would sleep through Bill's report after such a late night.

"If you're sure, my lady." Elsie frowned. "What's that noise?" She moved to the door.

Sure enough, there was a commotion of some kind rising

from outside the castle. Footsteps and shouts in the courtyard woke the horses in the stables, who called out in alarm.

Ela grabbed her wrap. "Let me go see what's amiss."

"I'll come with you, my lady," said Elsie, stifling a yawn.

"There's no need. The guards will attend me."

∽

Ela summoned the guard who kept watch at the end of her hallway to escort her downstairs to find out what was causing the stir of activity in the courtyard. She entered the hall from a door near the fireplace, where staff and soldiers now slept near the fire. Some of them sat up as she strode past.

The great door at the other end of the hall opened at that moment and a group of men burst in. The tallest one threw off a dark cloak, and Ela was relieved to see Bill Talbot striding toward her.

"We got him," he said, voice bristling with excitement. "Caught red-handed with the knife and a cloak with money sewn into the lining." Bill unfurled a dark bundle, which revealed itself to be a gray cloak. On inspection, Ela could feel coins tucked into the hem. The knife, rolled inside the cloak, still bore a dark crust of dried blood on its rusting blade.

"Where is he?"

"I told them to put him in the dungeon. It's no hour to call a jury." Bill examined the knife.

"While that would be normal procedure, the extreme cunning of John Bird makes me wary. What if he convinces the jailer that—if he doesn't want to be remembered in the same breath as Pontius Pilate—he should let him go?"

Bill seemed to contemplate this possibility for a moment.

A SURFEIT OF MIRACLES

"I shall sit at the entrance to the dungeon until morning to ensure that he cannot escape."

"Nonsense. I need you fresh in the morning when we call a jury and…" She crossed herself, "finally saddle John Bird with the guilt of at least one of the murders I'm sure he's committed. You must rest in your bed, not at the trap door to the jail. I shall speak to the jailer myself to ensure his loyalty. In the meantime, secure the cloak and knife by keeping them in your custody. It wouldn't surprise me if someone sent by the bishop or even the king tried to make them disappear before morning."

"I shall defend them with my sword if need be." Bill patted the hilt of his trusty weapon. "And in the meantime, I shall accompany you to the jail while you speak with the jailer."

~

ELA COULD BARELY SLEEP that night. She'd learned to her cost that every man—except Bill Talbot—had his price and could only be trusted up to a point. She wouldn't forgive herself if John Bird gave her the slip and escaped punishment for his crimes. Or, worse yet, if he managed to crawl back beneath the wings of the bishop and the crown and hide from her there.

"Summon a jury. As many men as you can muster." She issued orders as soon as she descended to the hall. It was still well before dawn. "And fetch Ida Huntley from the D'Auverleys manor, where she's employed as a wet nurse to their babe. I believe that the cloak we found may belong to her dead husband."

Ela had convinced Alwin and Agnes Marsh to stay another night in Salisbury. She was glad to greet them that morning with the news that John Bird had been found retrieving a buried knife that was likely the one that killed Agnes's husband and Alwin's father.

"I'd know Daniel Witchett's knife anywhere. He used to sit at the table in our inn, honing it on a whetstone before meals like he might need to cut someone's throat before paring his apple," said Alwin Marsh.

"Sir William Talbot has the knife safely in his custody and you shall see it along with the jury."

Where was Bill? Ela looked up anxiously each time someone entered from the door that led in from the castle chambers. Several jurors had arrived and partook of the simple breakfast of freshly baked bread with butter and honey that Elsie offered them in recompense for dragging them from their beds or their chores so early in the morning.

At last, she grew impatient and hurried up the stairs to Bill's chamber, where she knocked on the door. No answer. The guard who kept watch at the end of the hallway cleared his throat. "He's not there, my lady. He was summoned to meet with the bishop."

"The bishop?" Panic flashed through her. "Where?"

"I'm not sure, my lady."

How do I know nothing about this? She tried the door of Bill's room, wanting to see if the knife and cloak were still inside. But the door was locked.

Ela hurried back downstairs and spoke to Jake, the apprentice porter. "Is the bishop here in my castle?"

"Yes, my lady. I believe he went straight to the chapel for Tierce," said Jake.

"Why was I not informed of his arrival?"

"Well, he told me not to bother you. That he had business only with Sir William Talbot."

Anger flashed hot inside her. Did the bishop think he could navigate around her in her castle and jurisdiction?

"Would you like me to send for him?" The porter now looked worried. "If I may disturb a holy man at prayer…"

"I shall find him myself," said Ela, making no effort to hide the steel in her voice. "And in future, if anyone of importance arrives at the castle, please announce them to me whether they wish it or not."

It would be impractical for the porter to announce every arrival since the castle teemed with people coming and going. She didn't want to be alerted to the appearance of every wine merchant or stone mason who had business there. But she didn't want important nobles or clerics having conversations beneath her roof that she was not privy to or even aware of.

Ela strode along the colonnaded hallway toward the chapel. Candles guttered in the predawn darkness as she hurried past them.

"My lady, is anything amiss?" She turned to see Elsie running up behind her.

"Elsie, have you seen Bill Talbot this morning?"

"No, my lady." Elsie frowned. "Should I have?"

"Come with me to the chapel."

Ela opened the chapel door without her usual temerity at the prospect of interrupting a service in progress or disturbing someone at prayer. In the gloom—the chapel was lit only by two amber lanterns and the candles on the altar—she could see the backs of two men.

"Sir William, is that you?" she called out.

They both swung around, obviously shocked by the interruption. Ela recognized the bishop standing next to him.

"My lady," said Bill. "The bishop invited me to pray with him."

"I can see that." Father Thomas, who was reciting a psalm from the pulpit, now ground to a halt, staring at them. "And you thought this was more important than attending the jury in my hall this morning?" She couldn't hide her sense of betrayal. Bill opened his mouth, but she didn't give him time to reply. "Where are the cloak and the knife that are of such utmost importance for the trial this morning?"

"I have them here with me, my lady. I wouldn't let them out of my sight."

Ela's chest swelled with relief that at least he hadn't abandoned that duty.

"My lady, will you join us in prayer," said the bishop, looking from the priest—still standing in stunned silence—to Ela. "For the success of our earthly endeavors."

Ela drew in a steadying breath. She hated the delay. It allowed time for word to reach the king and for him to send back his lawyer to obfuscate the proceedings and perhaps even plead for Bird's innocence. Still, she could hardly say that she put the laws of man before their duty to praise God. If God wanted John Bird to walk free then no doubt his will would be done, whether she rushed back to the hall, or not.

∼

Finally, the Tierce service ended. Ela led the way to the hall, with Bill and the bishop behind her. Thankfully, John Dacus had taken charge of matters and the jurors were already seated around the tables, ready to begin questioning John Bird. Agnes and Alwin Marsh sat at another table nearby. So far, there was no sign of Warin Fitz Peter, the lawyer. Perhaps Bird being caught with a bloody weapon in his hand had scared off even his staunchest defenders.

But where was Bird? Panic flashed through Ela as she searched the room for him.

"John Bird is still in the dungeon, my lady," said John Dacus. "I thought it best to wait until you were here to summon him."

"Sensible," replied Ela. "Summon him now and make sure he's under close control at all times."

"I shall attend him myself," said Bill, rising from his seat next to Ela. "And I shall leave the knife and cloak here on the table in plain view of all the jury."

The bishop seated himself off to one side of the jurors, but not too near the Marshes. Ida Huntley arrived and was also seated nearby.

Ela felt a wave of relief when Bird entered, with a guard holding each arm. He'd dressed in borrowed rags to effect his escape from Salisbury, and—stripped of his rich vestments—he looked unkempt and disreputable, which suited her purpose well.

"Please chain him to the chair." The guards obliged while Ela prayed that today's trial would take an entirely different course than yesterday's.

Bill described waiting outside the bishop's palace, hidden in the shadows until he saw Bird's window open. Bird then crawled around the side of the roof and descended on the darkest, most windowless side of the building.

Bill then told how he and a guard had followed Bird through the town on foot at a safe distance. He said they'd lost him a few times as they tracked him across the countryside by moonlight, but had known that he likely headed in the direction of the stone circle. They'd managed to stay on his trail and find him again as he approached the circle across an open field, and then again when they saw the glint of the knife blade in the winter moonlight.

A short chase ensued and they'd captured him, then returned to find the objects he'd dug up from among the roots of a hawthorn bush. Bill described how Bird had tried several times to escape on the way back from the castle. They'd finally bound his hands and feet and sent for a donkey cart to carry him back to town.

Bird's expression didn't change during this entire account. His usual flinching and twitching manner seemed to have deserted him.

When Bill had finished describing the events of the early hours of that morning, Ela addressed the jury. "I believe this is the knife that Sir William and I saw sticking out of the back of the body we found in the stone circle on that early morning more than a month ago. I believe that we gazed at the dead body of Wulf Huntley. Huntley, now known to be a swindler with tales of a marvelous cow for sale, was returning from plying his crooked trade. Ida Huntley, would you please come up before the jury?"

Ida Huntley looked like she'd rather hide under the table, but she rose and nervously approached the table of jurors. Ela noticed that she wore a gray cloak of very similar material and construction as the one now on the table in front of her.

"Mistress Huntley, is this your husband's cloak?" Ela indicated the cloak on the table. Ida Huntley approached the table and took the gray fabric between her thumb and finger. Then she examined the hem, where she knew he hid his coins.

"It is my lady," she said quietly. "I've never seen such a cloak on anyone else."

"You mean a cloak made to have coins hidden in its hem?"

Ida Huntley nodded.

"Did you make it for him?"

"I did, my lady." Her voice trembled as she spoke. She likely knew that she could be prosecuted for helping him in his criminal activities by making a garment designed to hide his ill-gotten gains.

But Ela didn't want any distractions to draw the jury's attention from her main quarry. "You may go back to your seat." She turned to look at Bird. "I believe that Huntley met his match in John Bird—formerly known as Daniel Witchett, who happened to be passing through Salisbury late that night as Huntley returned from his day's work. Perhaps Huntley tried to sell Bird an imaginary cow. Perhaps he even tried to rob him? Whatever transpired, Huntley soon lay dead, killed with Bird's knife. A knife identified as such by Alwin Marsh, who saw him use it regularly when he stayed in his family's inn."

She invited Marsh forward to examine the knife and confirm in front of the jury that it was Bird's knife. Marsh said that indeed it was, and that he recognized the tooling on the handle as well as the shape of the blade. He also shot a look at Bird of such utter hatred that Ela wasn't sure she'd ever seen the like. Ela wanted to make sure the jury was aware of his pain and fury. "So you believe that this man, known here in Salisbury as John Bird, has left your mother a widow, and you fatherless, before slaying your uncle in the upper rooms of the Bull and Bear?"

Alwin Marsh nodded, with gritted teeth. "Yes. He's the one."

Ela looked at the jury. "Alwin Marsh and his mother are relying on you, the jury, to take note of all these details so that they may gain justice for their family. Even the most timely and severe justice cannot heal the gaping wound left by a lost life, but it can provide some succor for the family members left behind."

The justice at the assizes would ultimately determine whether John Bird received justice. All she could do was try to get the jury on her side.

CHAPTER 22

Ela had learned that, while a particular traveling justice was assigned to each circuit, they were liable to be substituted at the last moment for a variety of reasons. Thus Ela was surprised, but not deeply shocked, to find that the judge assigned to try the murder cases in Salisbury that February was none other than Warin Fitz Peter.

True, her heart sank at the news, but she tried to bear it bravely. Bill was less sanguine. "It's an outrage! The king hired him to defend Bird's interests at the jury trial less than a week ago. How can he be considered an impartial judge in the case?"

"I suspect that's the point. He isn't impartial. The king has an interest—a stake, if you will—in a specific outcome. I can hardly go to battle with the king."

"Your husband did!"

"My husband went to war with his brother and their relationship did not survive. But, of the two, my husband was the more loved and had the support of the barons. This present king is young but popular. I can gain nothing from pitting myself against him except perhaps to blight the hopes and aspirations of my children. This king is much the same age as my brood and may be on the throne of England for their entire lives."

"So you must please him even if it means letting a murderer smirk and strut along the streets of Salisbury?" Bill's hand kept reflexively touching the hilt of his sword, which he wore even though it was barely mid-morning and they were standing near the fire in her hall.

A considerable commotion in the hall—a meal to welcome the traveling justice and his entourage—allowed them to speak unheard. Fitz Peter himself had not yet arrived, but news of his role as the judge had preceded him.

Servants and law clerks and various functionaries and messengers milled around, helping themselves to roast pigeon and quails' eggs and pastries made with dried apricots. Servants refilled cups with wine and ale and plates and platters clanked against the wood tables. Even the dogs were on edge and barked at each new stranger who entered.

"I shall do what I can to see that justice is served."

~

"I DO HOPE that this all turns out to be a grave misunderstanding," said the bishop, who had cornered Ela before the proceedings began. He had the decency to speak in a low voice. "A trial—literally and figuratively—that our miracle worker must go through as part of his spiritual journey before he can resume God's work of healing the sick."

"Bishop de Bingham," said Ela curtly. "Bird was found having just dug up a murder weapon and a stolen cloak. You were at the jury trial where this was revealed."

"Our dear Lord's enemies gathered around him with falsehoods and mischief." He didn't dare look her in the eye but looked somewhere just over her shoulder to where the jurors were gathering around the tables again.

"Are you accusing Sir William Talbot of planting false evidence?" She heard her voice rise. "Because I can assure you that Sir William is a man of deep faith and an unbending moral code."

"He is a man of great loyalty," murmured the bishop. This time his gaze did meet hers, and she felt his accusation like a slap.

"You think he would lie out of a sense of duty to me?" She didn't attempt to hide her shock. "Why would I be so intent on seeing John Bird hang that I would concoct stories about him?"

The bishop hesitated and Ela thought she'd finally made him see sense. "I wish I knew, my lady. But from his first arrival in Salisbury, you've harbored hostility against him. Even after he healed you and your family, you seethe with misgivings and mistrust of a man who's done nothing but heal the sick."

"And murder three men in cold blood!" exclaimed Ela. She turned to see if her outburst had attracted attention. "How can you not see his guilt? Are you so blinded to the promise of crowds of pilgrims buying gilt badges and making offerings at the cathedral that you'd see a triple murderer go free?"

The bishop made the sign of the cross in front of her. "God be with you, my child, and grant you peace." Then he turned away.

Ela felt like she could spit nails. How were they all so blind? Was the love of money enough to make men welcome a murderer into their midst?

Since the last trial, a little less than a week ago, she'd insisted on keeping John Bird under heavy watch in her underground dungeon. The bishop had protested and somehow managed to rouse a letter from the king, asking that Bird might be given an appropriate chamber.

Ela had refused. She'd claimed her right—as High Sheriff of Wiltshire and castellan of Salisbury—to keep Bird under lock and key until the assizes, which, by good fortune, were almost upon them.

She knew she'd taken a risk by holding her ground, but she felt sure that the courtroom could be persuaded to see through the mist of holiness that John Bird had thrown up around himself here in Salisbury and see him for the scheming and violent criminal that he was.

Surely even Warin Fitz Peter wouldn't let him go if the entire room and all the jurors were against him.

༺

ELA DECIDED to open the proceedings. Such an action was perfectly normal since the traveling justice had usually just arrived in the area and often knew little or nothing of the case and its circumstances. Even though that wasn't true in this case, she intended to set the tone for the trial.

She'd been making some inquiries. "I'd like the judge and jury and everyone else in the room—" she looked directly at the bishop, "—to observe that not one of the people who was supposedly healed by Bird can still claim that good fortune. Lizzie Trout's limp came back, as I saw her hobbling at the market two days ago. Thomas Thicke, who did briefly regain his powers of speech, has since been struck down by another apoplectic fit and lies on his deathbed at this moment. All the other healings—my own included—can be attributed to the body's natural defense against disease and the course of nature. Despite a lot of talk and many public appearances, during which he collected a great many coins, John Bird has not demonstrated healing powers that would distinguish him from any other man in Salisbury."

A murmur rose in the hall. Warin Fitz Peter cleared his throat. "Are you finished, my lady?"

"Not yet," said Ela firmly. "John Bird, however, is distinguished by the fact that he stands accused of three violent murders. Each murder happened in a similar manner: The killer attacked the victim with a knife, stabbed him with great force, and left him for dead. Though Sir William Talbot and I both saw the bleeding, freshly dead body of Wulf Huntley amid the stones on Salisbury Plain, that body was then dragged to a pigsty and fed to pigs, to destroy all evidence. John Bird—the man seated before you—then assumed his blood-soaked clothing and presented himself to the people of Salisbury as a man lately risen from the dead. Like his purported healings and his stories of his sick mother, this tale of resurrection was an utter fiction born of a diseased and criminal mind. John Bird is a cunning and ruthless villain, and, by all that is holy, I pray that he meets judgment here on earth as well as in Heaven."

With that, she nodded to Warin Fitz Peter and took her seat between Bill Talbot and John Dacus. A glance at the bishop's face showed that her arrows had hit their target. The bishop kept taking sideways glances at Bird. Bird himself sat, chin high, stiff and straight in his chair as if he was impervious to the vagaries of earthly justice. But the third time the bishop shot a suspicious look at him, he started to twitch and writhe in his chair as if ants crawled up his hose.

Fitz Peter addressed the jury and asked each man to

describe his experience with and knowledge of John Bird. There were twelve jurors present and their accounts varied. Most described the surprise and wonder they'd felt at learning that a man had been resurrected from the dead and sent to Salisbury to heal the sick. Some of them still seemed convinced of his powers. But several said they'd lately begun to doubt him and that they thought it possible that he was the murderer of at least one of the three victims.

Fitz Peter's ebullient confidence persisted through the first round of questioning. "Does it not seem odd to you that not one person witnessed any of these three murders?"

"No," said Will Dyer, one of the younger and more outspoken jurors. "In the time I've been a juror, I'd say that murder is rarely, if ever, committed in front of witnesses. It's a crime perpetrated in private and often in the dark of night. As jurors, we find ourselves tasked with reconstructing the crime from footprints and remembered words and from cross-questioning the suspect." He looked at Bird.

"Yes, of course, the suspect must be questioned," said Fitz Peter, as if he'd been just about to do that. "John Bird, could you describe your purpose here in Salisbury?"

"I was passing through the area when I was set upon and left for dead." He looked at Ela. "Then, by the grace of God, I was raised up and—"

Bill Talbot rose to his feet. "I've heard enough lies from this execrable excuse for a man. As has the entire jury. He's collected a fortune from the gullible residents of Salisbury and most of the surrounding towns and villages based on these fictions. Rather than hear him spin another tale of utter nonsense, I'd like to hear him answer to each of the individual murder charges."

Ela blinked. She didn't remember Bill Talbot jumping up to interrupt a legal proceeding, in all the years she'd known him. And he'd been at many trials when her husband was sheriff, long before she took on the role herself.

Fitz Peter's arrogant countenance sagged somewhat. "But of course. All in good time, Sir William." He walked over to Bird. "Do you deny that you stayed at the inn belonging to the Marsh family in Wiggiford Mill?"

Bill sat down slowly and fixed his gaze on Bird.

"No." Bird's voice sounded hoarse. He hadn't been able to exercise his silver tongue down in the castle dungeon.

"Do you deny that you failed to pay your bill and had an argument with Piers Marsh when he demanded that you pay it?"

"We never had any such argument," he said smugly.

"Yes, he did!" Alwin Marsh cried out from his seat. "I heard them argue late into the night. My mother heard it, too." Agnes Marsh nodded in agreement.

"And did you hear a violent altercation such as blows raining down or furniture crashing?" asked Fitz Peter of Alwin Marsh.

Marsh paused and looked at Bird. "No. Suddenly the argument stopped. Likely because that was the moment Bird stabbed my father and killed him." His voice shook. "Unfortunately, I took the silence as a good sign and didn't go downstairs and find his body until morning."

"Did you hear your father cry out? Or try to resist?"

"No." Alwin Marsh stared straight at Fitz Peter. "My father was stabbed in the back as he stood over the ale keg. I found him crumpled on the floor in front of it. Bird must have taken him by surprise."

Bird didn't even blink.

"What do you have to say to this accusation, Master Bird?" asked Fitz Peter.

"Someone else must have stabbed him." Bird looked right at Fitz Peter. "Maybe his son wanted to inherit his business?"

Alwin Marsh cried out and had to be restrained by a guard as he lunged toward Bird. Who smirked very slightly in response.

"And why was this crime not reported to the sheriff?" asked Fitz Peter.

"It was," said Agnes Marsh. "But in Hampshire, not Wiltshire, since we live right on the border between the two. Andover in Hampshire is closer, so we reported the death there. We told them all about Daniel Witchett, but since he was nowhere to be found, they could do nothing to help us."

"Which is why my uncle hurried to Salisbury once he heard a man was boasting that he could heal the sick," said Alwin Marsh, who now sat chained to his chair. "For Witchett had claimed similar when he was among us."

Ela spoke up. "And after Hugo Marsh described the circumstances surrounding his brother's death to me, I made arrangements with the bishop for him to meet with Bird the following morning. Hugo Marsh was murdered during the night. Although Bird supposedly never left his upstairs bedroom at the bishop's palace, we now believe he disguised himself as a cleric, both escaping the palace and coming into the castle after hours, and as a drunken woman when he was leaving the castle. He wanted to silence the man who could identify him as Daniel Witchett and the likely murder of innkeeper Piers Marsh, so he took Hugo Marsh's life in cold blood in the upstairs room of the Bull and Bear."

"How did he gain entrance to the Bull and Bear?" asked Fitz Peter. "I've been there myself and it's a busy inn. Even after the doors are closed, I'd assume that the innkeeper and his wife and servants sleep on the premises."

"This is true," said juror Stephen Hale. "We believe Bird entered from the outside. The windows on the second floor of the Bull and Bear aren't made of glass but of oiled cloth and could be breached easily and silently from the outside.

The exterior of the Bull and Bear is timbered and there is plenty of purchase for footholds that would allow a nimble man to scale the building, traveling either up or down. Since we know that John Bird was able to leave his second-floor bedroom at the bishop's palace and escape to go fetch the knife and stolen cloak, we know he is capable of climbing up or down a building."

Fitz Peter looked at Bird. "What do you say to these accusations?"

"That they are the product of someone's imagination. I've never done such a thing." He spoke calmly, showing no sign of emotion.

Bill rose to his feet again. "The man shows no passion! He doesn't even have any natural human emotion. He doesn't even show fear for his own fate. I've met men like this on the battlefield and they can kill in cold blood without compunction or remorse. Any normal man would at least be disturbed by these deaths or fearful that his neck will soon snap in a noose."

Ela watched Bird's face as he spoke. Bird shifted in his chair slightly, and if his arms weren't chained she suspected they'd have made some kind of gesture, but his facial expression didn't change.

Fitz Peter appeared to ponder this observation. "John Bird, why do you seem so unperturbed by these accusations of murder?"

"The Lord my God is my only judge and he shall decide my fate." Ela saw the slightest hint of a smirk tug at the edge of his lips.

"Can you not see he's playing a game with you?" asked Bill Talbot of Fitz Peter. "He's probably been playing this same game under different names up and down the country. As a man of middling height and unremarkable features—combined with an utter lack of feeling, a talent for swindling, and no fear of ruthless violence—he's likely wreaked a reign of terror for years without being caught. If you let him go, he'll continue it unchecked, whether here in Salisbury, or elsewhere under an assumed name."

Fitz Peter cleared his throat. "You seem to have an almost prophetic ability to see the future, if such a thing is to be believed, Sir William."

Bill shot him a look that would have buckled another man's knees. "I'm well aware that John Bird's supposed healing gifts have conjured the specter of Salisbury as a pilgrimage site and center of healing to rival Santiago de Compostela—with the attendant profits for all concerned. But John Bird, or Daniel Witchett, made his intentions clear when he crept out of the bishop's palace—for at least the second time—and went to find his old knife and the money he stole so that he could effect his escape from Salisbury and start a new life elsewhere. Can you deny it?"

Bill's normally calm and easy demeanor had grown flushed and intense as he spoke.

The jurors shifted in their seats, and even Fitz Peter now looked uneasy. "Let me take a poll of the jury," he said. Ela could hear an undercurrent of doubt in his voice. "How many of you think that the man you know as John Bird committed all three of these murders?"

Ela wanted to interject. If a juror had doubts about even one of the murders, he'd have to keep his hand in his lap. She raised her hand, and Bill raised his, even though—quite strictly—they weren't jurors. She looked at the twelve men gathered around the tables in her hall. Two or three of them raised their hands right away. The others looked around—at Bird, or Fitz Peter, or Ela and Bill, or each other. One by one, each one lifted his hand until all twelve men held their hands raised into the air.

Fitz Peter regarded them in silence for a moment. "As the

traveling justice at this assizes, I find myself swayed by the unanimous opinion of the jury, and the compelling testimony given by the sheriff and Sir William. I thus pronounce the defendant, John Bird, guilty of murder. I sentence him to die by the sword and Sir William Talbot shall wield it."

CHAPTER 23

"Is Fitz Peter playing some kind of a trick?" Ela sat up late that night with Bill. The hall was so quiet they could hear the fire crackling. She kept her voice low. The game of chess they were supposedly playing had sat unchanged on the board for some time now. "Why would he choose you to behead Bird? And why beheading instead of the more customary hanging?"

These questions had puzzled Ela all day. Now that they were finally alone—Richard and Steven had just been sent up to bed—she could finally voice them.

" Fitz Peter was hired by the king to protect Bird," said Bill gruffly. He stared at his surviving black knight on the board, now boxed into a tight corner. "He's being careful to deflect the blame for Bird's demise from himself."

"If he was so intent on protecting Bird, why didn't he declare him innocent?" asked Ela. "Or send him to London to await a trial in the White Tower? That's what the justices usually do in a high-profile case where they're either unable to decide guilt or the stakes are too high for their taste."

"I suspect that our forceful condemnation of Bird, reinforced by the unanimous opinion of the jury, didn't leave him that option."

"I think him cowardly to try to shift responsibility to you," said Ela. "I don't like it. Why should you kill the man? Fitz Peter has no right to command you. You're not in his service. I can prevent it. I shall insist that the executioner carries out the deed."

"There's no need." Bill lifted his chin. "I'm a knight of the realm. It won't be the first time I've killed a man, as you know. I've killed strangers on the battlefield who were likely innocent of anything but loyalty to their lord. I feel no compunction about dispatching a triple murderer to meet his maker."

"You're brave and true, Bill, of that there is no doubt. But what if the church makes a fuss? Or if the king is angry about his new revenue stream being dammed up?"

"Then I shall tell them what I told Fitz Peter. Justice must be done, and I don't shrink from doing it. I shall sharpen my sword so the act is quick and merciful."

∽

Sir William Talbot wielded his sword shortly after dawn the next morning. Ela insisted that the execution take place within the inner walls of the castle, as she didn't want a crowd gathering that might cause a disturbance. Bird had gained such a following that a mob might become unpredictable as the time for his death drew near.

Despite the close quarters and early hour, at least fifty people gathered to watch Bird die—soldiers and servants from the castle and clerics from the nearby cathedral. The bishop himself gave Bird last rites. Ela couldn't tell if he was convinced of Bird's guilt or if he thought that a travesty was being committed. His face gave nothing away.

Bill's sword, not as long as her husband's, but still impressive, flashed in the cold February sun as he raised it above his head. Bird was restrained, on his knees, in some old wooden stocks that had been erected for this purpose. Ela closed her eyes as the sword came down and did its duty.

The body was whisked away to the castle mortuary where Ela ordered that it be stitched immediately into a winding sheet and buried in unmarked ground. She had no intention of John Bird's body becoming a source of relics.

∽

News of Bird's death spread throughout Wiltshire over the following days. Ela waited expectantly for word from the king, expressing displeasure or otherwise, but none came. The bishop came to her hall and told her that he believed he'd been wrong about Bird. That he'd been misled and swept away on a tide of prayerful hope that John Bird was indeed a miracle sent by God. That Bird had ultimately escaped and dug up a murder weapon proved his criminal nature, in Roger de Bingham's eyes. Furthermore, a young priest at the cathedral whose room was on the same floor as Bird's had admitted to misplacing a cassock and thus unwittingly providing Bird with his disguise to enter the castle walls and murder the innkeeper's brother.

"I'm sorry I doubted you for so long, my lady. If I'd listened to you sooner, Hugo Marsh might be alive today."

Ela accepted his apology graciously. "As a man of God, it's your calling to see the best in all men. As sheriff, it's my duty to see the worst. At least he can do no more harm. And I'm glad his criminal nature was revealed before all Salisbury became a pilgrimage site in his honor."

De Bingham sighed. "What a beautiful vision that was. Can you imagine pilgrims from all over England—all of

Europe even—converging here in Salisbury for prayer and healing? I'm sad it will not come to pass."

"Salisbury Cathedral is a magnificent destination in its own right. Why should men and women not come here just to gaze on its wonders? I see no reason not to cast the pilgrim badges and pour the special offering candles you spoke of. Salisbury is a holier place without John Bird in it than it was with him."

"When the dust from this misfortune settles, perhaps I shall write to the pope in the hope that our dear St. Osmund may again be considered for sainthood, hopefully this time with better results. Then we truly would have our own beloved saint here, to hold in reverence."

"If Salisbury is to have our own saint it will happen in God's time, and not a moment before," said Ela.

"You are right, of course, my lady."

THE END

AUTHOR'S NOTE

This book takes place in 1231, three years after the previous story in the series (*Palace of Thorns*). Ela first served as sheriff in 1227, after going to great pains and expense to secure the role of sheriff and shrievalty of her castle from King Henry III. Apparently, she then fell ill and was unable to perform her duties in the interim. Rather than speculate in detail about her illness, I decided to fast forward to when she retook the role of sheriff in 1231.

In this story, I mention several books of British history that Ela might have read, including Geoffrey of Monmouth's *Historia Regum Britanniae*. Written in the 1100's, this book really does suggest that Uther Pendragon sailed to Ireland—at the behest of King Vortigern—with a force of fifteen thousand men to retrieve a stone circle called The Giant's Ring from a place called Mons Killaurus. They were reportedly able to move the stones only with assistance from the wizard Merlin, who transported them to Salisbury plain, where they remain to this day, known as Stonehenge. Examination of the stones suggests that some are from the Preseli Hills in

AUTHOR'S NOTE

west Wales, an area that might have been considered to be part of Irish territory at the time. This outlandish and confusing legend from nearly 1000 years ago shows that people back then were just as intrigued and bemused—and mystified—by the history of the massive stone circle as we are.

Similarly, I have often wondered where the many British legends about dragons came from. After all, St. George, the patron saint of England, is famous for slaying a dragon. I can only imagine what ancient people thought when they stumbled across dinosaur bones. Most British dinosaur finds are from the Middle Jurassic and Cretaceous periods, known for their giant sauropods (like *Diplodocus*) and therapods (including *Tyrannosaurus Rex*). These finds seem an obvious source for dragon myths. Enormous dinosaur bones probably also spawned the British legends involving humanoid giants, such as Jack and the Beanstalk.

The character of John Bird is not a historical figure, but I'd imagine that the questions he raised cropped up regularly when someone claimed to have seen or experienced a miracle. I learned from *Sainthood in the Later Middle Ages* by André Vauchez that the Vatican formalized the process of canonizing a saint during Ela's lifetime. Previously the process was rather informal and saints often arose from local cults. In this era, there was a new emphasis on detailed witness testimony, followed by a series of reviews by secret consistorial councils. The pope himself was the final arbiter of sainthood. Although miracles (often posthumous) were the hallmarks of a saint, a candidate's virtue was also important. Pope Innocent III had observed that not all supernatural happenings were holy. Thomas Becket (murdered inside Canterbury Cathedral in 1170) had been canonized only three years after

AUTHOR'S NOTE

his death, and his tomb was a popular pilgrimage site during Ela's time. During his term as Bishop of Salisbury, Richard Poore had proposed that Bishop Osmund of Salisbury be considered for sainthood. Despite records of the deposition of twenty-nine witnesses about nineteen miracles that occurred at Osmund's tomb, the application was rejected. Bishop Osmund did finally become a saint in 1457, more than three hundred and fifty years after his death in 1099, and sick pilgrims visited his Salisbury shrine in hope of healing. Less than one hundred years after its creation, this shrine was destroyed in Henry VIII's reign as part of the Reformation. Today a raised slab from Bishop Osmund's tomb is on display in Salisbury Cathedral.

If you have questions or comments, please get in touch at jglewis@stoneheartpress.com.

AUTHOR BIOGRAPHY

J. G. Lewis grew up in a Regency-era house in London, England. She spent her childhood visiting nearby museums and riding ponies in Hyde Park. She came to the U.S. to study semiotics at Brown University and stayed for the sunshine and a career as a museum curator in New York City. Over the years she published quite a few novels, two of which hit the *USA Today* list. She didn't delve into historical fiction until she discovered genealogy and the impressive cast of potential characters in her family history. Once she realized how many fascinating historical figures are all but forgotten, she decided to breathe life into them again by creating stories for them to inhabit. J. G. Lewis currently lives in Florida with her dogs and horses.

For more information visit www.stoneheartpress.com.

COPYRIGHT 2022 BY J. G. LEWIS

All Rights Reserved.
Published 2022 by Stoneheart Press
2709 N Hayden Island Drive
Suite 853852
Portland, Oregon, 97217,
USA

Without limiting the rights under copyright above, no part of this publication may be reproduced, stored in or introduced into a retrieval system, or transmitted in any form or by any means (electronic, mechanical, photocopying, recording or otherwise), without prior written permission of the copyright owner and publisher of this book.

The scanning, uploading and distribution of this book via the Internet or via any other means without the permission of the publisher is illegal and punishable by law. Please purchase only authorized electronic editions and do not participate in or encourage electronic piracy of copyrightable materials. Your support of the author's rights is appreciated.

COPYRIGHT 2022 BY J. G. LEWIS

Cover image includes: detail from Codex Manesse, ca. 1300, Heidelberg University Library; decorative detail from Beatus of Liébana, Fecundus Codex of 1047, Biblioteca Nacional de España; detail with Longespée coat of arms from Matthew Parris, *Historia Anglorum,* ca. 1250, British Museum.